W9-BMZ-814

Beeperless Remote

a romantic comedy

A Guy, Some Girls and His Answering Machine

by

Van Whitfield

PINES ONE PUBLICATIONS

LOS ANGELES

Published by Pines One Publications
3870 Crenshaw Blvd., Suite 931
Los Angeles, CA 90008
(213) 290-1182

Jacket and text design by Laurie Williams/A Street Called Straight
Jacket illustration by Steve Johnson/Lou Fancher

Publisher's Cataloging-in-Publication Data

Whitfield, Van
  Beeperless Remote: a guy, some girls and his answering
machine
 /Van Whitfield - 2nd ed.
    p. cm.
    ISBN 1-890194-16-6
    Preassigned LCCN 97-66025
    1. Afro-American—Washington (D.C.)—Fiction. I. Title.

PS3573.H58B44 1997   813'.54
                                            QBI97-30182

10 9 8 7 6 5 4 3 2 1

"A 6 is the one perfect woman that God put on earth for every man. Most guys blow it when it comes to keeping their 6. 6s are usually dumped to make room for a babe who's a total disaster. I don't know if I've met my 6, or if I ever will. I do know this. If she calls and leaves a message, I'll hurry to call her back. As soon as *SportsCenter* goes off."

—Shawn Wayne

Universal Mottos of the **6** Different Types of Women

 1s "I just got out of a really bad realationship."

 2s "I'm not interested in a relationship, I just have friends."

 3s "What is it you said you do for a living?"

 4s "Men are dogs."

 5s "My biological clock is ticking—I need a husband."

 6s "I'm single, I'm available, and *Yes*, I'm interested."

1st Message

"YOU HAVE NO NEW MESSAGES."

MESSAGE SENT ON
MAY 25TH AT 11:13 P.M.

 I can't believe it. I just can't believe it.

But, I hope you'll believe it.

This absolutely cannot be happening to me. All of this over a stupid answering machine. A dumb machine with an even dumber feature.

It all started with my Beeperless Remote. My buddy Donnie sold it to me on a sunny Tuesday afternoon.

"Yo cuz," he said, rolling a toothpick around his mouth, "you need 'dis Shawn. 'Dis got that beeperless remote joint."

"Why do I *need* this Donnie?" I asked, inspecting the box. "And what the heck is a beeperless remote anyway."

"You can git messages from anywhere with beeperless remote," he said, smiling. "Say you out wit a honey and another little hottie calls you."

"Yeah."

"Well you can check yo messages, and din' use da' cell-phone dat I sold you and holla back at the little hottie."

"And what about the honey that I'm already with?" I asked.

"You ain't got to call her 'cause you'z already wit her," he said, laughing.

Damn. Why did I fall for that? Why did I have to check that last message? Why did she even have to leave it? This won't work. I had just turned things around. My life was looking as good as Halle Berry in a red-leather mini-skirt *with* matching pumps.

Now this—.

A nice guy like me *finally* meets a nice girl and some other woman throws me a Doc Gooden style curve. A year ago this wouldn't have happened. It couldn't have happened. But I had to have "Da' bomb answering machine wit dat beeperless remote joint," as Donnie put it, and this is where it gets me.

Until recently, I couldn't have paid a babe to call me. My super-automated-does-it-all-get-my-messages-from-any-where-so-I-can-hurry-to-call-back-answering-machine seemingly changed that. Now I have women calling who I'm not trying to talk to. My situation is too complicated, so I'll try to keep this simple.

I'm in trouble—.

Donnie is my partner. We grew up together and he has sold me lots of high-tech toys. Donnie was amazing because he could get anything. Tickets to any game or event. Clothes. Shoes. Housewares. I don't know how he got them and quite frankly, I don't care. He told me that he hadn't robbed anybody and that with me, he was evening the score; you know the old *"White guys do this for each other all the time"* crap. Anyway, he hooked me up and it didn't break me because I usually paid exactly what I had in my pocket. That worked for him because he needed cash. Crack addicts often have that problem. I'm not crazy about the fact that he probably used my hard-earned money to fund his habit, but Donnie had deals and everyone knows I'm a deal type of guy. Besides, he always assured me that the money was for food or his mom and not drugs.

Women thought Donnie was a stud. Despite his habit, he worked out and stayed in incredible shape. His dark supple skin rippled with muscles that had muscles. Until last December, long, tattered dreadlocks fell to the side of his head and over his eyes. Eye contact wasn't his thing anyway, so that was a plus for him. He's one of those guys who looked down when he talked and his deep, husky voice delivered his words at a steady, deliberate pace.

Though I knew he used drugs for years, I'd never actually seen him getting high. He once tried to be a dealer, but turned out to be both his best and worst customer. As a customer, he was always available to himself. He just never figured out exactly how to pay for the drugs so he could remain in business. He was a mess. In the past three years, I've picked him up from the county jail nearly a dozen times.

When he wasn't locked-up, Donnie sold me stuff like a ten-disc CD changer for my ride, a cool portable cellular phone, a space-age pager that actually stored words, and an awesome thirty-five inch TV with junk on it I still don't understand. The CD changer ran me $10 (a dollar a disc seemed fair to me), and I got the phone for $12.50 (he threw in the pager with it; I'd just bailed him out of jail). He got me on the TV though. That set me back $17.

My "wonderful" answering machine ran me $6.86. I remember the cost because I'd just broken a ten dollar bill at McDonald's. I got a double-cheeseburger extra value meal, which always costs $3.14. Had I super-sized it, like the lady at the window asked, I wouldn't have had the $6.86 and Donnie wouldn't have sold me that stupid answering machine. But I wasn't about to super-size an extra value meal, because if you super-size it, where's the value?

Drama—.

That's what Kelly would call this. Kelly works with me and is by far, my closest friend. She warned me that something like this would happen. The first thing she'd say is that I got suckered in by the wrong woman because I fell for all the wrong things. This fits her agenda because she constantly tells me that cute looks and tight bodies aren't everything. It's easy for Ms. Kelly Paulette Lancaster to say that. Kelly sports a stylish Halle Berry-like haircut. She also has a cute little nose which she'll turn up at anyone and anything at the drop of a hat. Her inviting almond-shaped jet-black eyes are the highlight of her face. She has a sassy Pepsodent smile and beautiful bronze skin that's so smooth it looks like it was painted on with a Duron spray-right air compressor. Kelly's cute and she knows it. She's from New York, so her words always sound a little different. Her hands are in constant motion when she speaks. *Watching* her talk is an adventure unto itself.

Kelly is as sharp and precise as the Chicago Bulls' triangle offense during the playoffs. Despite the fact that she's always crying broke, I know she'd be good wife material for the right guy. Kelly can't keep money because she wears nothing but brightly colored suits and shoes by trendy overpriced designers. She favors Donna Karan, Escada, and Tahari. I once witnessed her blow an entire paycheck at a store called Cache. She called it a boutique. I called it a store. We rarely see things the same, which actually fuels our friendship.

Kelly also likes gold and leather as much as Dennis Rodman loves tattoos and body piercing. She insists I would be a good catch if I just took her advice (which she offers plenty of). She once even told me I had potential, which was a plus. Women were attracted to men whom they thought they could work with, she said. She even told me that my innocence and the fact that I was *so* naive about *so* many things didn't hurt.

"Lots of women fall for that 'he's so helpless, he needs me' nonsense," she said. "You need all the help you can get Shawn," she added, laughing. "So you'll be especially attractive to some poor twit."

Kelly also said I needed to "expand my universe" if I wanted someone special in my life. When she asked me what I wanted in a woman, her point was made.

"I'm not exactly sure what I want," I cautiously replied. "But I know I want a babe with cable."

"A babe with cable?" she asked puzzled. "Why does she have to have cable, and why must you call women babes?"

"I call babes babes because they're babes," I casually replied. "And I want a babe with cable because I couldn't imagine dating a honey who didn't have ESPN."

"ESPN!" she exclaimed. "What the hell is that?"

"It's the only channel that counts," I answered smiling. "It's all sports all the time." "Make me understand what having cable and ESPN have to do with meeting a decent woman," she snapped while shaking her head and finger in unison.

"It has everything to do with it," I told her. "Because *SportsCenter* comes on ESPN, and I don't know anybody who doesn't watch *SportsCenter.*"

Kelly, of course, knows I hardly know a soul, so I imagine it made sense that I didn't know anyone who wasn't into *SportsCenter*. Her frown told me she didn't care for my answer, but it was cool. She didn't even know what *SportsCenter* was, so like most women, she didn't have a clue as to how important it was to most men. I like Kelly a lot, and I'm glad she cares about me. She seems to have made improving me her personal crusade, but I could never date her. She doesn't have cable. And a babe without cable is like the Bulls without Jordan. She's missing the point.

What am I going to do?

I thought everything was straight. I'd found the woman of my dreams and was ready to give it my all. But how can I commit with this hanging over my head? I'd finally beaten the odds that are so stacked against single guys in the Washington D.C. metropolitan area. Kelly says that women in D.C. don't stand a chance. "There are so many attractive, intelligent, high-caliber single women in D.C. that it's not funny," she said, forcefully. "The competition is deep."

Kelly may be right, but she always talks about women who are waiting to exhale. Guys aren't *waiting* to do anything. Like me, there are many sincere guys searching for their true soul-mates. Donnie once even told me there were five babes to every one guy in the Washington metropolitan area. He may be right too, but the way I see it, guys are the ones who get hosed because nobody ever said those five babes had to be decent. They just have to be babes. I know this because the women I meet invariably fall into one of six categories.

The first one is the classic, "I'm just getting out of a bad relationship" babe. Guys know to run from these women. They're known as 1s, and to them, every guy is just an extension of the no-good man who just hurt them.

The second type of woman, a 2, is not really interested in relationships, but she doesn't mind dating (especially when the guy is treating). They're easy to spot. Their favorite line is, "I'm not really interested in having a boyfriend, but I do have friends." 2s live for the weekend and love to hang out with their "friends" in cafes, clubs and malls. It's hard to get to know a 2 because 2s are not necessarily interested in getting known.

A 3 is a chick who's impossible to get with. She's so fine that she's just plain too good for anyone who doesn't have a major bankroll or significant power. 3s have radar and they can smell money and success a mile away which is why I never meet 3s. I believe in saving my money. I'm a book-keeper for a small auditing and accounting firm, so I don't even register on their screens.

Kelly's a 4. And just like all 4s, she meets a guy, likes him, and immediately looks for reasons to trash him. His biggest fault is that he's a man in the first place. 4s have a simple (yet universal) motto. Men are dogs. Kelly admits she's neurotic (whatever that is). She believes truly decent men are impossible to find. "They don't exist," she says. That's how 4s are. Nobody's good enough, no matter what.

5s are women who have a singular agenda. Marriage. Most guys actually blow it when they dump 5s because 5s aren't always as pressed about commitment as they seem. They just want a husband, a house, and a good benefits package. 5s can be cool, because marriage can be cool, but 5s often blow it because they usually start working the "marry me or else" line too early in the game. Most guys can round up another babe overnight (if they don't already have one in limbo). So "marry me or else" usually ends up as "or else." This makes most 5s a 1.

I never wanted a 1,2,3,4, or 5. I wanted a 6 and I thought I'd found mine. A 6 is the one perfect woman who God put on earth for every guy. Nearly every man has dated a 6 in his lifetime, but they've foolishly allowed the one 6 that God grants them to slip right through their hands. 1s through 5s can become 6s overnight when they meet the right man. But just like men, most women blow off the guy of their dreams to be with a guy who's a nightmare.

Now I'm stuck in a nightmare—.

When Donnie sold me the answering machine I was happy. I promised myself that I'd always check my messages in case my 6 called. *"I'll give that beeperless remote thing a run for its money,"* I thought.

Now I wish I hadn't.

Hopefully, *you* can make some sense of this. I would prefer not to, but I've got to deal with this mess. And maybe I will.

As soon as *SportsCenter goes* off.

2nd Message

"I'M REALLY INTERESTED, I REALLY LOOK FORWARD TO MEETING YOU."

MESSAGE SENT ON MAY 30TH AT 11:32 A.M.

It's official! I have the worst luck with blind dates in the history of modern man (probably prehistoric man as well). Today is Memorial Day. In my mind, it's one of the coolest holidays around. I dig it because you get a constant flow of free food, and there's actually a chance to meet happening females at the right cookouts. Me, I wasn't invited to any cookouts, so I settled for a blind date. I've been on two blind dates in the past three months and on both, I was painfully reminded why they were called blind dates. The only way I would have asked those two "very sweet ladies of impeccable character" out on a date, was if I had actually been blind. My choices were pretty limited, so the thought of another blind date didn't bother me like I figured it would. I even chuckled as I thought about the babes Ray Charles had probably been set up with over the years. Tanya, a good friend I used to work with, told me she'd given my number to a relative who she felt met my "rigid qualifications." I decided to check my messages in case she called.

"Hi Shawn, this is Danielle," she said in a voice perfect for answering machines. "My cousin Tanya told me about you, and I'm interested, I really look forward to meeting you."

That did it. The right voice, the right words. I was ready to get together when the message ended. There was no need to wait. She sounded so alive. She had to be a 6. Her voice sounded familiar, but I chalked it up to wishful thinking. Perhaps the long absence of any voice I cared for made me want to believe I'd heard this voice before, and perhaps I was wrong. In any event I liked it. I was more than ready to meet this latest prospect. I know Tanya (and everyone else for that matter) thinks that I'm picky. I don't see it that way. Dating in the '90s is expensive. And since I usually get stuck with the bill, I prefer to be out with someone who I don't necessarily mind wasting my money on. Danielle sounded smooth and I'm into smooth, so I've already decided that if she has a pulse and isn't married, engaged or otherwise "involved," I'll put everything else aside and make a real go of it.

I called her from the gym and suggested we get together after my workout. I was totally disgusted with myself for being in the gym in the first place. Who the hell works out on Memorial Day? She went for it though. She even suggested a quaint Mexican restaurant. I didn't dare tell her the only Mexican food I cared for was Doritos. Women get put off if they think you don't like international foods. I dig french fries, I like french toast and I'll even down a Belgium waffle every now and then. But on the whole, I don't do foreign foods.

I needed a quick out. I thought about it. "Let's hit Jasper's over in Greenbelt," I said. She agreed. We decided to meet at 2:30 in the afternoon.

"I'll be in a candy-apple red 300," she confidently stated.

"Cool," I responded, trying to hide my excitement.

A Nissan 300 ZX. $30,000 worth of prime automobile.

Donnie says 300s are the ultimate babe mobiles. Chicks who drive red sport-cars are definitely hot. I imagined us tooling her 300 down an open road oblivious to everything. We'd be half reclined with the sound system blaring, wondering how we got so lucky to find one another. I imagined she had some sassy vanity plates inscribed with something like 2 CUTE or CATCHME. That's definitely sexy. I hoped it wasn't a stick because I hate sticks and I find women who drive sticks to be particularly unappealing. Kelly told me it's some quasi-macho trip. She said sticks are cheaper than automatic transmissions. They afford the driver greater control. That may be true.

But who wants a cheap chick who's trying to be in charge anyway?

Besides, a real 6 would have to drive an automatic.

I was ready for this date. Freshly pumped from my workout, two-day-old haircut, and a gray Polo tank top that fit. I actually did three extra sets of curls to ensure the arms were just right. I'd packed a pair of soft cotton, baggy black cuffed shorts and my black and gray Nike walking sandals. I was so psyched, that I looked around for a ref to come out and toss up a jump ball. I wanted this game to start. I wasn't about to foul out. Danielle. I dug the name and I liked the voice. Tanya had convinced me that Miss Danielle was all of it. This was on time.

If my Timex is right, it's 2:30 on this balmy yet bright afternoon. Positioning myself in front of Jasper's has evolved into a minor dilemma. I have to look my best when she pulls up. "If a woman is generous enough to give you a first look, make it a good look," is what Kelly once told me. *Do I wait at the top of the stairs so she can peep at the loaded pecs and arms? Do I lean against the wall outside the door?* I knew that wouldn't work because leaning is only cool when you're driving. I was tired from my workout. Unfortunately, lying down wasn't an option. I'm hopelessly flat-footed, so I wasn't about to stand. I looked around, staked out an inviting white stone ledge and decided to sit and wait for the sweetie with the Z mobile. So I sit and think. *Wow. Am I the man or what?* I'm chillin' (as Donnie would put it), waiting for Danielle with the sexy 6-like voice to pull up in her sweet red Z, and if she's half as tight as Tanya says she is, I'm gonna be on it like a horny housewife would be on Denzel.

I'm getting nervous. My Timex says she's about fifteen minutes late. Getting stood up is like twisting your knee. It bothers you for an instant, but you get over it pretty quick. Getting stood up on a blind date is like blowing your knee out. It doesn't just bother you, it hurts. Being passed up by somebody who needs a blind date in the first place totally sucks. *Another* fifteen minutes passed. I figured a half hour was long enough to have waited. She wasn't showing up and I was going home so I could really miss all the cookouts I wasn't invited to.

I lowered my head in shame and slowly walked towards the parking lot. As I opened the door to my ride, a loud horn caught my attention. I looked up and saw a hand waving. It was Danielle. She actually showed up. My chance at my 6 was back on track.

She pulled up beside me, carefully parked and rolled her window down. "Didn't we do this ten years ago?" she asked as she reclined lazily behind the wheel of the nineteen eighty-something, obviously used 300 Z. When I realized who she was, I froze like a cheap 7-Eleven popsicle. The driver was one of the truly worst experiences in my very limited lifetime of dating. *Danielle.* Now the name stuck. I'd heard the voice before. I should have trusted my instincts. *Danielle.* The only woman I'd ever met who was a 3 before she could count to three. She liked me because she thought I was the man. If I were a gambler, I'd bet the house she was into using guys before she learned how to play jacks in kindergarten.

She popped out of the car.

"Is that you Danielle?" I asked.

"Of course it's me," she answered smiling. "Who did you expect?"

"I guess I expected you."

"Well you got me."

"You've put on some weight."

"So have you."

"Yeah, but at least mine is in the right places."

"It's good to see you too Shawn," she said flatly.

We weren't getting off to the best of starts. But, that shouldn't have surprised me. We didn't exactly end up on the best of terms when we dated ten years ago.

We walked toward the front door. Thankfully we were seated within seconds, because there's no way I wanted to be seen with her. Because of the holiday, the restaurant was pretty empty which made the sound system appear especially loud. I forced a weak smile toward her and she responded in kind. At that moment, I wished I had followed my instincts. I should have left when she was fifteen minutes late. I couldn't think of anything decent to say. I just wanted to be out of there.

I looked across the table and commented on her hair and told her how good it was to see her. I hated to lie. It wasn't good to see her, but I had to say something. We exchanged the usual BS: "It's a small world...How've you been?" I felt helpless. I wanted to leave but that wasn't really an option. Tanya was a decent friend and she hooked this up, so I had to treat her at least halfway decent. I didn't care how she had been. But, I did believe the world was truly small if I was going to be forced to spend even a little time with this incredible excuse for a woman.

I met Danielle when I was playing college hoops. I'd just broken up with Dawn. Dawn was the one woman I never fully recovered from. She was special. We broke up ten years ago, and I still think about her. I've often wondered what could have happened between us. Every guy has one of those women. Dawn was pretty average but she was sensible and incredibly smart. She didn't stand for my crap. She hated basketball and had a real disdain for jocks. She worked hard for her grades. I got good grades because I had a jump shot. People came to see me play. The school made money and graduating was the payoff. Dawn hated it. She called it the "pampered jock syndrome". I told her we weren't pampered. With our bodies, we paid the price so journalism students like her could write dumb articles that nobody cared about. Because of the revenue generated by sports, there was money to fund her scholarship. She didn't like it, but she knew it was true. In spite of her feelings about athletics and jocks, we managed to get along pretty well. She eventually dropped me and Danielle was waiting in the wings.

Danielle was cute, phat, and sufficiently bright. She liked sports and she didn't have a boyfriend. Even back then, I was into women who weren't tied down to other men. Danielle had a mischievous air about her. I found that attractive. She was laid back, yet appeared to be very interested, which I liked as well. She'd call at the right times, say the right things, and would come to my games and just wait for me. She was as sweet as she was fine (which Donnie says is still a rare combination). I knew we were on our way to a relationship. She fit the role I'd made for her, and I fit hers.

Or so I thought.

As I recall, Danielle got sick one day. Her sister and I had to rush her to the hospital. The scene was as wild as Richard Pryor's 1976 comedy hit classic LP, *"That Nigga's Crazy!"* Danielle had a flair for theatrics. She made just enough noise to get some attention, without getting us ushered off to paperwork land. Her sister, Chrissy, who was as beautiful as a Magic Johnson behind-the-back-no-look-pass, handed me Danielle's purse. She told me to call their mother. "You'll find the number in Danielle's phone book," she said panicked.

I was never one to look in a female's purse, but we were talking major medical emergency. I forced myself, gave it a peek and found the number behind her learner's permit. *Learner's permit!* I gasped. *What the hell is this?* Like Trix cereal, learner's permits were for kids. With the body she was toting, there was no way that Danielle was a teenager. Though I didn't want to, I had to check the permit out. I immediately felt as guilty as I felt relieved. Everything looked legit. *Oh no! Look at the birth date,* I was stunned. It read 12/24/70. It was nineteen eighty-three. This made sweet little Danielle (with the sweet little body), a not-so-sweet thirteen years old.

Unfortunately, I was nineteen years old, and I just knew Danielle was "my woman." Naturally, I was crushed when I discovered her signature on a Girl Scout oath card. It was neatly folded inside a Toys 'R' Us gift certificate.

"I swear your honor, I never touched her. Besides, she looked twenty-two, and she told me she was graduating next semester," I said as I imagined myself being sentenced to serve time under the jail. I never believed it when other men ran that line, but I knew it was possible after that.

When she was released, she asked me why I didn't come see her in the hospital. I told her someone told me she was basically jail bait and that I was in for nothing but trouble if we continued to see each other. In her most convincing voice, Danielle told me since we weren't "doing it," staying together shouldn't be a problem.

"I was in seventh grade when you were just in the first," I remarked.

She smiled and smoothly answered, "I was never in first grade—they skipped me from kindergarten to second."

That was the essence of Danielle. Always prepared to make shineola out of shit.

I marveled at how good Danielle actually looked as Anita Baker's soulful *Watch Your Step* flowed through the black JBL speakers that hung from the ceiling. Ironically, the music fit the occasion. The plush green carpeting, shiny oak tables, and soft-pink cloth napkins provided a sobering setting for what had turned out to be a not-so-blind date. She had put on some weight, but it was cool. She was too skinny ten years ago anyway. I guess she was just right for a thirteen-year-old. She was as tight at twenty-three as she was at thirteen. Our six-year age difference suddenly didn't seem so bad.

She had perfect deep brown, almond-shaped eyes, with just a touch of make-up. She told me her Mary Kay cosmetics lady, Angela, kept her looking good. Angie's constant attention made it easy for Danielle to lie about her age. Some things never change. She's still lying about her age, but now she *wants* to be young. Her jeans seemed to stretch just enough to accommodate her ample, yet shapely caboose. She wore a tight cream-colored tube top to accentuate her tiny pert breasts. Over it was a blue blouse that appeared to be silk, but was actually low-grade rayon. Typical Danielle. As phony as Eva Gabor on *Green Acres.*

Danielle was detail oriented and she knew how to wear make-up. Her shiny black hair was pulled back into a fancy fat bun. Even back in '83, Danielle always had her nails done. They were now painted with what appeared to be the works of an angry, despondent Q-tip swab, but they were neat and well shaped. A session with a Lee Nail Press-On video wouldn't have hurt though. There was a distracting piece of mandarin orange lipstick stuck on one front tooth, but it was clear she paid regular trips to the dentist. I'd like to say she smelled sweet but she didn't. She had that heavy lotion smell. The kind of smell you dig as a youngster, but ultimately find annoying as a man.

She had requested to be seated in the smoking section, so it didn't surprise me when she pulled out a beat-up Newport. She took long, painful drags, which of course ended up being blown right into my face. I hated smoking and I long ago vowed that I'd never date a dragon lady. I knew kissing a smoker was as bad as playing defense against a guy who hadn't discovered soap and water. That wasn't in my game plan.

The waiter slid over and did his thing. "Drinks before

lunch?" he asked, smiling. I ordered a Sprite and she, of course, ordered a glass of zinfandel. "I like a nice light wine with lunch," she said. I'm thinking, *if it's so light, why is it going to cost me four-fifty a pop?* As the waiter opened the menus and placed her drink on a tiny green napkin, I decided to navigate the waters. I was hoping to come up with a catch. Even though she was a smoker, she was a woman first. I was pressed for a babe, and I wasn't about to blow this chance. Besides, she could always quit.

"I told Tanya I'm looking for a lady who's serious, and who's not about games," I said. "So the fact that you're here says to me you're serious."

"I wouldn't put it like that," she stated. "I'm actually into my family, and spend most of my energy keeping up with them."

Her parents had divorced. Her father had remarried and her mom was tying the knot in October. She had two kids, Tess and June. Her sister, Chrissy, suffered from a low salt count. Chrissy was still "quite beautiful," she said. Low salt count? I always thought that too much salt was the problem. But then again, things were always different with Danielle.

"I was living with a guy who wanted to change me," she continued. "So I put him out." She told me she still felt for him, but she was going to let Chrissy move in to make sure she kept up with her medication. "So as you see," she concluded, "I don't have much time for a relationship."

She's not even a 3 anymore, I thought disappointed. *She's a 2. She was just looking for a date.*

I was ready to say, why the hell are you here then? Before I could utter a word, she says, "I figured there could be only one Shawn Wayne who lived on Townsend Lane in Bladensburg, so I called."

I stared blankly as she continued.

"I knew it was you as soon as your machine picked up," she told me. "I'm surprised you didn't pick up on my voice."

So am I, I thought, frustrated. *How could I forget that name and that voice?*

"I figured I'd come see what you were up to, and besides, I knew I'd be in for a nice time," she said. "You always knew how to treat a woman."

How would you know? I angrily thought. *You were still a kid when we dated before.*

"Well, we can always be friends," she said smiling. "And you can always call me. I'd love to talk," she added with the sincerity of a sand salesman at Daytona Beach.

She said she'd heard Donnie had run into trouble with the law. *Run into trouble,* I thought, concerned. *It was more like a crash.* I told her he was cool, but I hadn't heard from him in a while. She said she'd heard about my "fantastic" job. She actually had the nerve to ask if we were hiring.

"Not right now," I said, flatly.

"Well, we're friends," she casually stated. "So keep me in mind."

Keep her in mind. I was going out of my mind. At this point I truly wanted to play the beeper game on her. Donnie hipped me to it when he sold me the pager. I'd never used it, but it's an easy move. Turn your beeper off and back on quickly so that it makes some noise. Check the number and reach for the phone. "It's an emergency. Sorry hon, got's to go. I'll be in touch." You save money and save face. You don't have to feed the babe and when you leave, it's totally legit.

Besides, you're friends, and you'll keep her in mind.

Unfortunately, I met her through Tanya and I'd been pressing Tanya for over a year. If I didn't treat her cousin right I knew I was dead for future prospects. *Go through with it,* I reasoned. *Just set the stage. Order an appetizer and she'll follow suit. You can keep this as a $15 fiasco.*

The waiter came back and it initially looked pretty good. I asked for barbecued shrimp which were three for $4.99. She ordered buffalo wings. When she asked for the lobster and filet mignon, I nearly choked.

"Could you bring my wings out first?" she asked while lighting up another cigarette. She ignored my blank expression as she asked the waiter for more sauce after he brought the wings. I wasn't surprised when she didn't offer to share them, or when she ordered her second glass of "light wine," while lighting up her third cigarette. I despised hot wings as much as I hated stick shifts and cigarettes and I didn't care for women who enjoyed them. Especially her.

After she finished her feast (complete with an embarrassing belch, a third glass of zinfandel and a fifth cigarette), she suggested that we get together again.

"Real soon," was how she put it.

"I don't see why not," I said coughing.

I don't see *why,* would have been more on target.

After she ordered apple-pie (an *entire* pie to go), the waiter came back and slowly slid me the check. I guess he walked away because he didn't want to witness me suffer from sticker shock. A meaningless lunch, with an even more meaningless female (who was an obvious 2 no less) was costing me a fat $48.96!

Surprisingly, she offered to pay the tip, but before I could say "thanks," she *discovered* she'd forgotten her wallet. I didn't make a habit of reading restaurant checks, but this one was committed to memory. Besides the overall enormity of the bill, what struck me most was a $1.00 charge for two glasses of water. The ice in the water had melted during her smorgasbord so I was literally stuck with drinking watered down water to cool myself off.

My anorexic bankroll was not going to cover this bill *and* hold me to payday. Jasper's and Danielle were not going to ruin my week. Besides, I had another (and hopefully better) blind date lined up for Wednesday. I peeped through the mini-blinds and saw my ride and thought I could make it. Danielle was still sipping her "light wine" (and puffing on her *seventh* cigarette). I asked, "Do you know where the restroom is?"

She pointed toward a big green door, and I excused myself. Normally, I wouldn't leave a woman stranded like this, but after a basketball game one night, my father explained to me something that Malcolm X always said: "Extraordinary circumstances warrant extraordinary actions." I could even hear my mom saying, "Your economic state will always dictate your actions." As I made my way to the men's room, I rationalized that both Malcolm and my mother had prepared me well for exactly this type of situation.

After opening the door I looked in the mirror. I walked into a stall and wondered: *Since she did all the eating, am I legally liable for the bill? Do they really make people wash dishes when they come up short? Should I bring my next date here?*

I took out the only money I had, a $50 bill, kissed it and said aloud, "Don't worry Mr. Grant, you're not leaving me yet." After washing my hands and checking myself in the mirror, I pushed the door open and made a bee-line toward the front door. I couldn't help but notice that Danielle had left her trough. *The 'light wine' got to her bladder,* I thought. I crept through the front door and was home free.

At least I thought I was home free.

"Don't forget the check Shawn!" she said, smiling.

My heart bounced like one of those high-flying super balls that were stuffed into boxes of Captain Crunch cereal back in the seventies. I felt like a guy who misses the free throw that would have sealed a championship game. I definitely wasn't going to Disney World.

I wanted to tell her I hadn't forgotten it, but my mouth wasn't living up to its end of the deal. I prepared to run, but my legs stalled like an engine neglected of motor-oil. The sun was hitting me like George Foreman hit Joe Frazier back in '77 and I was as dazed as "Smoking Joe" was when he hit the deck and was counted out. I slowly turned my head and answered, "I'm going to my car for my wallet." That statement was as misleading as the entire date. I didn't even own a wallet.

Danielle nailed me and I'm certain she'd been through this before, because she knew exactly where to position herself. I didn't even try to save face and pretend to go to the car. I just turned around and walked toward the huge green door. A moment earlier, it had provided me a safe haven from this blind date from hell. Unfortunately, it also served as Danielle's anchor spot from which to catch me. I reached in my pocket, awakened the lint and said goodbye to the only $50 bill I'd seen in a month. I then impatiently waited for my dollar and four cents in change.

"Will you be leaving a tip sir?" the waiter anxiously asked.

"My date's getting it from her wallet," I replied, lying. "It's in her car."

I walked toward my ride which was parked next to Danielle's freshly waxed Z. She sheepishly smiled, placed her apple pie on the passenger seat, lit up *another* Newport, and waved before pulling off in a spurt. I blew $48.96 and got nothing to show for it. No future dates, no chance of a relationship, no exciting parting gifts, not even a cheap dragon lady kiss.

I stared at the sun bouncing off the hood of my ride and wondered how both Malcolm and my mother could have been so wrong at the same time. Today's date was lower than losing the final game of your career to a last place team while you sit helplessly on the bench. If it weren't so hot outside, I would have crawled back to Townsend Lane.

I heard the screech of tires and gears shifting as Danielle's candy-apple red 300 Z bolted from a stoplight. It was then that I realized the one-time 3 (who was now a solid 2) was driving a stick.

Sticks are cheap, I reminded myself. *Who wants a cheap chick anyway?*

There was still hope. Maybe Wednesday's date will drive an automatic.

Pain personified—Profile of a 1

"I just got out of a really bad realationship."

Motto of a 1

1s are 1s for a reason. They didn't start dating to become 1s and if they had a choice they definitely wouldn't be 1s. But as Shawn's mom might say, "You are what you are." Simply put, 1s are 1s. You'll find 1s at church throughout the week. They'll tell you they're celibate. But many 1s choose celibacy and the church because they need a supportive environment to help them deal with the pain. 1s also need time to develop retaliatory measures against the guy who goofed (with God's blessings of course). Some man, somewhere made a 1 a 1. And because of that man, the 1 you may be dating may not work out. To her, you are that same no good guy waiting to happen all over again.

If you shake up a can of Coca-Cola and quickly open the top, what do you get? Well guess what? The same exact thing happens when you shake a Pepsi and rush to open it. That's how 1s see men. Same product, different names, same screwed-up results. If a 1 shakes you up, she believes she'll get the same outcome as the last guy she shook up. If you must date a 1, be patient and don't push it. 1s don't stay 1s. They eventually get over the crumb that crushed them and can bloom into 6s if you have your act together. If you don't have your act together, get out of Dodge because a 1 may very well crush you.

Because they've been hurt, 1s will follow you (or have you followed). They will have their girl-friends (and other friends) report on you, and will find a way to contact your new little honey (so they can warn her about you). Most women have spent some point in their life being a 1. Watch your step if you've sent someone to "1 world." Babes tend to stick together when another sister has been dumped on. They don't like guys who have relegated a friend to the precarious life of a 1.

1s rationalize that major property damage is just a small part of the "healing process." So if you leave your new lady's place one night and find that your tires need bandages, just grin and bear it. Your past has caught up to you and your 1 has struck. And while the AAA guy snickers as he lifts your ride onto his flatbed, remember that your 1 wasn't into tearing stuff up before you burned her (and if she was she wasn't a 1—she was just plain crazy). Understand that to a 1, the healing has started. You may actually get off easy, and only have to replace some tires that probably needed replacing anyway. Don't mess with 1s if you don't mean business. They've had enough crap, and you probably can't afford new tires.

Shawn
Wayne
on **1s**

I couldn't see myself dating a 1. First of all, they're "in recovery," so they're likely to rebound more than the NBA's resident nut (and rebounding machine) Dennis Rodman. 1s are pretty pissed at guys. After they shake the guy, the cable's not too far behind. No cable, no *SportsCenter*. No *SportsCenter*, no happenings. Decisions don't always have to be hard.

3rd Message

"GIVE ME A CALL WHEN YOU GET IN."

MESSAGE SENT ON
JUNE 22ND AT 6:02 P.M.

This may be my lucky day because I'll get to teach a class. I enjoy teaching, because for about ninety minutes I feel like I'm actually running something. I'm not always overly familiar with the subject matter, but who cares? I like it anyway. I substitute when my boss, Mr. Butler, can't make it. I used to think it was a great way to meet women but I never took advantage of it. With my luck, I'd be accused of sexual harassment and end up on the evening news. I don't watch the news anyway, so I'm in no hurry to be on it. I'm sure the news is cool (because Kelly constantly says I need to watch it) and I tried to check it out, but all I saw was a bunch of young black guys who'd done something wrong. I didn't see any white guys who'd robbed, raped, or killed anybody (although I figured that some had), so I flipped over to *SportsCenter* (where black guys are usually doing cool things).

Lovely Day, the Bill Withers hit from the late seventies, played over the radio as I stood beside my bed and eased out of my Chicago Bulls boxer shorts and sleeping shirt. I always made it a point to dress nice on days I'd get to teach. Today's no different. For a moment, I imagined I'd get love at first sight treatment just because I was dressed. A mirror check quickly brought me back to my senses. Anybody who'd love me at first sight would have to be a total stiff or as desperate as me.

And anyone who's as desperate as me would end up being trouble.

Last night, I laid out my charcoal gray blended wool suit and a set of solid deep gray suspenders (Kelly always called them braces, but the thought of dental implements on shoulders didn't sit well with me). I matched it with a white satin striped shirt, and a crimson red bowtie. A Muhammad Speaks newspaper and matching bean pie were all that were missing from the outfit. My black shoes, the only ones I owned without a Nike swoosh on them, were polished and ready to go. I even cleaned the crystal on my ten-year-old, yet always reliable, Timex wristwatch.

I methodically dressed and checked myself in the mirror after brushing my teeth and hair. There was little doubt that this outfit was made to attract women. After a closer look, I concluded the suit would most likely attract women if someone else were wearing it. I'm not down on myself or anything, but my luck with women ranges from awful to horrendous on any given day. But this is a brand new day. My luck may change. My 6 may be sitting in that classroom.

As class started and I circulated my handouts, I quickly decided this was not a group I wanted to get lucky with. The classroom was typical. It was well lit and had cheap blue carpet. Worn out wooden desks and uncomfortable looking blue plastic chairs outlined the room in the shape of a big U. The blackboard at the front of the room was littered with scribbling about lunch breaks and parking lot assignments. The back window provided a welcome passage for day-dreams and other flights of fancy.

There were six women in the class. Two of them looked

to have a combined weight of about four hundred fifty pounds. One introduced herself as a drill sergeant in the Marine reserves. Two of the other three came across as typical male bashers.

"I hope you're more prepared than the other men we've had to listen to," said one.

The other quickly chimed in, "You men are so long-winded, except when you get in the bedroom."

They both looked terrible. If they prepared themselves more, their men may have at least attempted to be a little long-winded. The other woman was very attractive, plus she was quiet to boot. She was decidedly different from her other classmates. I could tell she was married, attached or something that rendered me useless, and once again, unlucky. I figured she had to be a 3 because he was major league fine.

This was a class for employees enrolled in the Council of Governments Leadership Development Institute. I was conducting a course on office politics and procedures. My own self indulgence made me believe this was an important and beneficial class. The alarming rate of discrimination and harassment complaints filed around the region convinced me otherwise. The class concluded without much fanfare and everyone participated except the attractive one. She was too cute and she probably couldn't bring herself to join the rest of us. I can't stand fine babes who think their looks make them better than everyone else, but if I looked that good I'd run the same scam, too.

I headed back up Interstate 95 to my office and actually considered dropping past my place to change clothes. This was easily my best outfit and no one at the office had seen me in it yet. Besides, the chances of meeting someone new were blown to bits when I stepped into that class. This was one of the rare occasions I didn't leave a situation upset at being single. I didn't stand a chance with the cute one and I didn't want a chance with the others.

Traffic at the Springfield, Virginia exchange was at its usual snail's pace. I rolled the windows down, popped in Pat

Metheny's new Secret Story CD, and cruised at about fifteen miles per hour until things picked back up. I was at work (still in my good-luck outfit) before I knew it. I smiled as my Timex told me it was noon. I called to check my messages and chuckled as I realized I'd made it right in time for lunch. Visa and American Express both called. What could they want? They must know that I know I haven't used my cards for nearly six months. There was a message from Mrs. Green at the training academy. I hope I didn't insult the men bashers in that class too badly. I long ago accepted that I wasn't the best instructor in the world. Still, I liked teaching classes. I knew if the right people complained, my teaching days were numbered.

I called Mrs. Green and was prepared for the worst. Surprisingly, she asked if I was dating anyone. She was well past her prime when K.C. and the Sunshine Band were still hot, so I definitely wasn't interested. Before I could respond, she stated (with impeccable diction, of course), "There is a very nice woman in the class you just taught who requested I call you."

I thought about the losers in that class. They appeared to be even more lost than me. If that's possible. I started to lie. I was prepared to say I was involved with somebody, and not just somebody, because anybody would put that group of clowns to shame.

"She is very attractive and was seated in the rear of the room," she stated properly.

"Her?" I asked surprised.

"Indeed."

"Why did she ask you to call?"

"Must you ask?!" she scoffed.

I was miffed. But thankfully, before I could totally blow it, Mrs. Green suggested we talk. She summoned her to the phone.

"Hi, I know this seems rather forward," she casually stated. "But I thought your class was great. I wanted to tell you so personally."

She could have put that on her evaluation form.

"If it's okay by you," she continued."I'd like to get together."

It's at this point that I always blow it.

Well, let me check my schedule, or let me get back to you, is what a less pressed guy would have said. "Sure, when?" was what flew out of my mouth.

"Let me check and I'll get back to you," she replied, combining both dating-correct responses to perfection. "How can I reach you?" she asked.

Anyway you want to, I imagined myself saying. Thankfully, reality kicked in and forced my phone number out of my mouth. "Take my pager number and car phone number, too," I insisted.

She interrupted, and said, "I've got to go, I'll be in touch," before I could finish.

I thought I was on cloud nine. I reasoned it was cloud 6. A total fox like her (who went out of her way to reach a lost soul like me) just had to be a 6. I was so hyped that I finished five memos, cleaned out my in box, spruced up my office (in case she ever dropped by for a visit), re-polished my black shoes, and replaced the thirty-pound container on the water cooler before I realized I didn't even know this woman's name. I thought about it. Stacey would be a good name, I imagined. No, I told myself smiling. What about Tandace? I like that name, too. Her name could have been anything. I'd even accept her with the name Danielle, as long as she didn't drive a stick.

Before I knew it, five-thirty rolled around. Not even the ninety degree heat, and the 97 percent humidity of Washington, D.C. could draw a sweat out of me. Today I was both cool and lucky at the same time.

I knew this suit was a tooky magnet, I thought as I pulled in my driveway. I couldn't wait to get in and check my messages. *You called eight times from the office, and four times from the ride,* I reminded myself. *Get a grip.* I fumbled with the lock before walking through the door. I checked my mail. Letters from both Visa and American Express. *They don't get it,* I thought chuckling. I rushed to check my messages. Visa and American Express again, I said laughing. They really don't get it. Danielle. Reminding me that we're friends, and seeing if we're hiring yet. *"Sorry miss, we've filled our quota of women who drive sticks,"* I imagined myself saying. "Call back when you get an automatic," I mumbled.

One message left.

"Hi Shawn, this is Jasmine," the perky voice stated. "We spoke earlier. I was in your class. Anyway give me a call when you get in. My number is 555-6452."

Jasmine. What a name! 6452—I knew her number would start with a 6. I'm hooked!

I'm ready to make a move but I'm not so sure I should. Kelly says you always wait at least a day to call. "You'll seem desperate if you call too early," she warned. "You need to appear like you have something or someone filling your time."

This was a dilemma I didn't care to have. I feared Kelly could be right, but how could she be? She's as bad off as me. She hasn't had a date in three months.

Jasmine said, "Call when you get in." I was definitely in, so I figured I should definitely call. I thought about Kelly's advice again. "You'll seem desperate." At that point I realized I had to call. I was both in and desperate. Two wonderful reasons to call. As if I needed any.

"Hello," said the sweet voice on the other end of the line.

"Uh, this is Shawn," I said sounding even worse than a Georgetown University foul shot looks. "May I please speak to Jasmine?"

"Don't be so formal," she casually replied. "You're speaking to me."

"Hi, uh, this is Shawn," I repeated.

"We've established that," she answered, laughing.

"You asked me to call when I got in," I remarked.

I couldn't have sounded more like a jerk had I tried.

"I'm glad you called," she interrupted. "I like a man who's attentive."

I was at a loss. I had no clue as to what to say next. Every cool line I could think of ran through my head. I could only muster up, "Why did you want me to call anyway?"

"Must you ask?" she replied, sounding very much like Mrs. Green from the training academy. "I found you attractive. My mother always told me if I see something or someone I want, to go after it," she confessed. "So that's why I called. Besides, I can't resist a man in braces."

Suddenly, dental implements on my shoulders didn't sound so bad. Jasmine liked suspenders. I may have had only one pair of shoes, but I had more suspenders than Colonel Sanders had chickens.

"If you're not busy, we can get together soon," she said, snapping me back to reality. "What do you mean when you say soon?" I asked.

"Whatever's good for you," she replied.

Good for me? I thought excited. *Right now's good for me.*

"What's good for you?" I asked.

"Anytime that's good for you," she answered.

The cloud I was on at my office had transformed into heaven. An angel, in the person of Jasmine, transported me there. I always believed whoever wove the fabric in my gray suit had a fine babe on his mind. I knew I was due for some good luck, but this was incredible. I stared down at my feet to make sure I wasn't floating. Choruses of "Happy Days Are Here Again" raced in my head. This was perfect. Even a skeptic like me could find nothing wrong with this situation.

My mom always told me good things happen to good people. I knew I was good, but this made me feel great. Jasmine, who was as fine as any 3, but who came across as an uncomplicated 6 (and who was obviously available), was interested in me. A woman who says "whatever's good for you" had to be available. I had to see if she meant it. I decided to give her a time. I wanted to see what kind of excuse she'd come up with.

"I'm tied up for most of this week," I told her in a way

that would have made even Kelly proud. "But tonight's actually pretty decent," I said, coming back to my senses.

I held my breath. I knew a flimsy excuse was coming. To my delight, she said, "Sounds good to me."

"Whadda you want to do?" I slowly asked.

"I'll let you decide," she answered.

Too much is too much. A beautiful woman wants to go out with me and says I can decide what she wants to do. What's wrong with this picture? I know, she's gay. Maybe it's Kelly. She's playing a practical joke. Maybe she had me confused with another instructor who was wearing suspenders. I don't get it. But who cares? What else would I be doing tonight anyway?

"We could go to dinner," I suggested.

"Sure," she said.

"Anyplace you have in mind?" I asked.

"I'm new to town," she replied. "But I've heard about Jasper's."

Oh no, she knows Danielle, I thought.

"Jasper's?" I gulped.

"Yeah, it's in Greenbelt," she answered, "I hear they have a great surf and turf combo."

I was in shock. There are a million places to eat in the metropolitan area and she wants to go to Jasper's.

"Jasper's is okay, but I don't know if it's nice enough for our first date," I cautiously stated.

"Well, you're the boss," she said lightheartedly. "So surprise me."

I immediately wondered what kind of sauce she liked with her Chicken McNuggets.

"What time do you want to get together?" she asked.

"About an hour," I said, brimming with confidence.

"Is casual okay?" she asked.

"It's okay with me," I answered.

The last time I felt this level of control was when I cooked a turkey dog. I was celebrating (alone, of course) on my last birthday. I turned the stove on, a flame popped up.

Turned it off, the flame stopped. Parted the bun, the turkey dog slid in. Opened my mouth, it was gone. While it wasn't an earth shattering chain of events, it was one that afforded me at least a little control and I liked it as much as I liked the turkey dog. You liked the turkey dog, I reminded myself smiling, because it was cheaper than a regular hot dog.

As I hurried to the bedroom to change, my phone rang. She's calling to cancel, I thought disappointed.

"Shawn," she softly stated.

"Yeah."

"Wouldn't you like to know where I live before you come pick me up?"

So much for control. I quickly gathered myself and replied, "Actually, I was going to call you on the way out."

"Okay," she stated, allowing me to save face. "I'll be waiting."

What should I wear?

I ripped off my clothes and jumped in the shower. I tried to dry off and hang up my good luck suit at the same time, but was having little success. Slow down and relax, I told myself. *You've been relaxing in this house for the past month, I thought. You'd better get moving so you won't be late, because late is definitely not impressive.*

Figuring out what to wear was tougher than I imagined. I wondered how to wear suspenders and still look casual. I decided to go with a pair of khaki shorts and a green, loose-fitting Ralph Lauren tee shirt which had one of those cool little horses stitched on the chest. Donnie sold it to me for three bucks. I could hear Kelly saying, "Shawn, your entire social life consists of going to and from the gym. If you get the opportunity to go out with a woman, wear something that fits. Make all that time in the gym count for something besides being strong."

She was right, but I hadn't washed clothes in three weeks. Loose was going to have to work. I brushed my hair and moustache and made sure my nails were trimmed, before splashing on a sample bottle of Cool Water cologne.

I'm glad I had that sample because as far as I'm concerned, thirty bucks is too much to pay just so you can smell good. It was time to go. I put on the walking sandals I'd just bought from Kinney's and made my way to the door.

This was the night that could change everything. Jasmine could actually be my 6. My heart raced as I eased into my ride and headed down Townsend Lane. I was so happy I couldn't help but smile. I was glad my Visa and American Express were paid up because I knew I'd need both of them to keep up with a babe like Jasmine.

4th
Message

*"SHAWN, THIS IS JENNIFER.
I'VE LEFT THREE MESSAGES."*

MESSAGE SENT ON
JUNE 22ND AT 8:47 P.M.

I called Jasmine from my ride and found she lived in Hyattsville. This put her about thirty minutes from my place. I figured I'd have to find a shortcut because I knew I'd be making a lot of trips her way. As I pulled into her development, I smiled when I located her fashionable condo. It was nestled in a cul de sac on Mt. Vernon Court. I rolled past an impressive line of Japanese superluxury coupes, which were tucked neatly in discreetly numbered parking spaces. It was clear that she had some loot. The two-story brown-stoned condos were surrounded by pleasant patches of bright green grass and each of the tiny yards featured a thickly trunked tree with spreading limbs and white blossoms. I almost blew the horn for her to come out, but I remembered my mom repeatedly telling me, "You always meet a real lady at the door." A parking space marked "VISITOR" awaited me. I pulled in and tore the little plastic bag off of the bright yellow Vanillorama tree air freshener. I knew to stuff everything that was out of place either under a floormat or beneath the sun visor because I'd been told chicks didn't dig messy rides. After a quick mirror check, I jumped out and made my way along the flower-lined sidewalk. I wondered what she'd be wearing. I hoped it was something that showed off her figure. Not that I knew what her figure was. I just figured a face as beautiful as hers had to be linked with an equally magnificent body.

I imagined she wouldn't look as good now as when I first saw her. It always works that way. When you think you can't get them, they look incredible. Once you've made contact, you realize they're not all that. *If she's interested in you, she can't be all that,* I reasoned. She opened the door and thankfully relieved me of all my doubts. She was impressive when I saw her in dress gear earlier. Now, she was get-out-the-checkbook gorgeous. Jasmine was as stunning as any 3, but the way it was going I just knew that she had to be a 6. And not just any 6. She had to be my 6. She had radiant brown skin and curly brown hair that danced off of her shoulders. Passionate deep brown eyes highlighted her face. Her lips appeared to be made perfectly for kissing. She had a sensuous inviting smile and perfectly sculptured red nails. She looked so good that I thought I'd gone to the wrong door.

"Are you okay?" she asked.

"Uh, yeah," I nervously replied, "how come?"

"Well you were just standing there staring, and you hadn't said anything," she said, "so I thought something could be wrong."

I didn't know what to say or how to act. She looked like one of those beautiful Hollywood actresses. I felt more like her co-star than like a regular guy.

"I was trying to figure out where to take you," I said. "You look absolutely too good for what I had in mind."

"Well thank you," she cheerfully responded, "You look nice, too."

She was wearing a sassy off-white linen short set with

gold accents. *She's classy,* I thought, as I stumbled past the elegant green eight-paneled door and was hit with the sweet smell of cherrywood potpourri. Classy chicks have a vision of casual that differs from us normal folks. Her hanging gold-leaf earrings gave her a quietly distinctive earthy appeal. She bore the citrusy sweet aroma of Liz Claiborne cologne. *Baby's got back,* I whispered, as she led me down the foyer pass a group of well-placed traditional oil paintings. Jasmine was well assembled. Just like one of those Hot Wheels race car tracks you got at Christmas. She had to hit the tape at an impressive 36-24-36. *She's totally tight,* I slyly thought as she walked in front of me. The top was working, and the waistline (what little there was) was just right. What struck me most was her elegantly shaped legs.

I love legs and Jasmine's were indeed perfect. Most of the guys I know are breast men. I can't relate to that. I'm a workout guy. I've struggled to get and to keep my body in decent-looking condition. I know legs can be worked on. I've watched women in the gym dramatically improve them through hard work. Breasts just sit there and bounce on the rare occasion. But what happens if a woman doesn't develop prime-time bazookas? She can firm them up a bit or have surgery (*and* the problems that come later) to enlarge them. But, that's about it. Ironically, breasts are by and large comprised of fatty tissue and nothing fat in this country (besides breasts) is considered beautiful. Most men feel that breasts are windows to a woman's sexuality. "The bigger the better," is what Donnie told me. But I knew better. I guess it didn't hurt that Jasmine looked to be sporting D-cups. My eyes sized her up like a used-car dealer who just discovered that one of the suckers who's born every minute is, in fact the customer sitting in front of him. The dealer's happy. He likes what he see. And like the dealer, I was ecstatic.

I figured we'd have to go somewhere special. Someplace where we'd be seen. She's a Hotel Washington babe if ever I've seen one. The Hotel Washington has a rooftop restaurant with an absolutely breathtaking view of the nation's capital and it's inexpensive, too. It was an intoxicant you couldn't pay for. It was generally accepted that if you can't close the deal after the Hotel Washington, the deal couldn't be closed.

"I know just where we're going," I told her.

"Actually, I was hoping that we could grab something, and come back to check out the game," she said.

I must have been pressed. How could I forget the NBA finals and Michael Jordan? Women do it to you every time. She's so tight that she remembered. I'm so pressed, I forgot all about it. She was too legit. It surprised me she was even into hoop, but it shouldn't have. I always knew a 6 would be a basketball fan.

"Okay," I quickly replied before she could change her mind. She called in an order to a carry-out around the corner. Surprisingly, she reached for her purse to foot the bill.

"Here," she said, handing me a crisp $50 bill, "this should handle it."

You haven't seen a fifty since Jasper's, I recalled.

"I've got it," I said, hoping she wouldn't take me up on my offer.

"No," she said relieving me of my concerns, "I suggested we get together, plus I need change anyway."

I hurried to the carry-out and thought something was very wrong. This was too good to be happening to me. She wanted to stay in *and* she sprung for the meal. I'd struck gold. The surprise hit by the Brand New Heavies, *Dream Come True* bounced through my sound system as I impatiently edged forward at a stoplight on Wilson Avenue. I couldn't get there fast enough. My winning entry to the Publishers' Clearinghouse sweepstakes was sitting on the couch waiting for me and I didn't want to lose it. She looks good, her body's working, she smells good, her place even smells good, and to top it off she likes hoop. I fully expected she'd be gone when I got back. To my delight, she wasn't.

She put our food on two brown wicker trays (she had two egg rolls and I a cheeseburger sub), and quietly led me to her spacious basement. We carefully sat down on a soft jet-black leather bound sofa and she turned on her forty-six-inch Mitsubishi wide-screen television *(with* Dolby pro-logic sound). I waited for someone to pop out and yell, "Smile—you're on candid camera!" *This is you,* I anxiously thought. *This can't be happening.*

But it was. Jordan was flying across the screen in stereo, and this was the perfect evening with the perfect woman I'd wished about for years.

I hoped Jasmine was the affectionate type. Nothing beats a babe who knows how to put the move on *you.* Thankfully, she was as smooth as I was awkward. Jasmine made me feel so totally at ease, that I wondered if I should try to make a move before halftime. She took my right arm, placed it over her shoulder, and slid herself close to my torso. I had to tell my heart to slow down. It was beating so hard I thought she would feel it. Jordan was on his way to thirty-five points in the first half, and we were both caught up in the excitement of his performance. I'd never been around a woman who both enjoyed and understood the game like Jasmine did. I was having a ball and everything was absolutely perfect. Until the phone rang. She answered it, shot me a quick smile, excused herself from the room and quickly headed toward the stairs. "I'll be right back," she whispered.

My Timex read 9:02 when she stepped out. At 9:20 I got up to find the bathroom but she reappeared before I could look around.

"I'm sorry about that,".she apologized. "It was business, and I had to handle it," she continued. "My husband didn't pay our MasterCard bill," she casually stated.

"That's messed up," I told her.

No, she didn't say husband, I said to myself.

"Did you say husband?" I quickly asked.

"Oh yes," she casually stated. "He's a physician up in Philly, and he sometimes forgets the bills," she casually replied. Amazingly, she didn't seem phased by the fact that she hadn't mentioned she was married.

You should have known it, I thought in anguish. *A honey like her with you. Something had to be up.*

"You didn't tell me you were married," I angrily stated.

"You didn't ask," she replied giggling.

I hadn't seen a reason to ask. I'd checked her finger earlier and saw no ring. Plus, she gave me her home number and was entertaining me in her place. *A married woman can't do this,* I thought, confused. Before I could say another word, the phone rang again. *I bet that's hubby-wubby,* I jealously thought. My Timex read 9:33 p.m. when she took off. I'd seen enough and wasn't going to be further insulted. It was her husband though. She knew she was married and she still invited me. She must be separated. I was the chosen one.

She came back after just a few minutes. This was a good sign. At least I thought it was. She smiled and casually announced, "That was my boyfriend. He's in Philly, too."

I'm crushed. This can't be happening. I'm the man *after* the other man.

"I can't get up there, so he's coming down this weekend," she said.

My mouth was wide open. I was speechless. Figuring this out was as useless as the last guy chosen during a pick-up basketball game. I just wanted to get to the door.

"I can see you're surprised," she said giggling. "Let me explain," she said sitting back down. "Like I said, my husband's a physician, and he takes very good care of me," she started. "But he's not attentive, and I need that," she told me. "He doesn't even like sports, and he stopped taking care of himself years ago," she added. "My boyfriend is the exact opposite. He's handsome, he works out, he's into sports, but he's a teacher like me, so he doesn't make a lot of money," she finally concluded.

What's a girl to do? I wondered.

I was out of my league on this one. I was angry and confused. I couldn't believe my 6 had turned out to be a no-good 2. She just wanted some company until her boyfriend came down. I was getting out of there. I was ready to make a move. She beat me to it. She cornered me, and whispered, "none of this really matters."

It doesn't? I thought puzzled.

"I called because you excited me," she said flatly. "I go after what I want, and I think I might want you," she said. "I'm not looking for a relationship, I don't want to tie you down. I just think that if we got to know each other, we could have some fun," she continued. "Is that so wrong?"

It would have been wrong if she were *my* wife. But she wasn't and this was an opportunity any man would relish. Fine babe. Badd house. Home alone. I wondered what type of fun she was talking about anyway. She smiled and edged closer to me. Before I could sort everything out, she wrapped her sultry arms around my neck, pulled my head toward her perfect lips and seductively whispered, "There's no need to ruin a perfectly good evening. Let's go upstairs."

I quietly wished she had a TV upstairs because the game was still on. She gently tugged on my arm, led me up one flight of stairs through her kitchen, and up another flight into a long hall with recessed ceiling lights. I was still trying to figure out what was going on. She opened a set of French doors, which led to a master suite that appeared to be designed with only one thing in mind. Sex. A shiny black chest of drawers sat on one side of the room and a cream-colored chaise lounge rested beside it. The other side featured the television set I had wished for, and a black Yamaha stereo with as many lights as Macy's during Christmas. My feet sunk into the ultra plush wine-colored carpet. This was like a dream. I immediately thought nobody would believe this. She walked toward the middle of the room and stepped up a platform to the huge round bed. She then turned back the burgundy satin sheets and softly asked, "Why are you just standing there?"

I stood frozen like a Good Humor Toasted Almond bar. I could hear my mom saying, "You can't trust a woman with satin sheets. Do you think she put them on just for you?"

My mom was probably right but I convinced myself it didn't really matter. I was about to strike gold. I walked toward her and clumsily tripped when I got to the step at the bed. She giggled and whispered, "Don't be so nervous, I won't do anything to you that you don't want done."

The last time I heard that was right before the dentist decided to give me a root canal without Novocain.

"I'm glad you're here Shawn," she said while lying across the bed. "My husband's a decent man, but he doesn't know how to satisfy a woman."

I would've been pretty satisfied because I knew she didn't get a spot like this from teaching.

"He sent me that $50 bill I gave you for the food," she said. "He actually believes it will last me another two weeks," she continued.

I believe it, too.

"My friend can't help me. I won't get a paycheck for at least two weeks, and I'm here all alone," she continued. "Shawn, you can help me through this rough spot, and I can take care of you at the same time."

"Take care of me?" I exclaimed. "Take care of me how?"

"Don't get excited," she quickly answered. "That's how we do things back home." I had to bite my tongue. I was ready to tell her to go back home.

"When I first saw you," she explained, "I knew you were a man of means." She then lowered her head and surprisingly started sobbing. This scene was really strange. She sounded like she was crying. There just weren't any tears.

She looked toward me and babbled, "You just seemed so nice. I thought you'd help take care of me."

I smiled. I can barely take care of myself.

"I took a job here to get away from my husband and I want to make it on my own," she sobbed. "But I need help until I get on my feet."

I wanted to say, drop dead, but wait until I'm outta here. I didn't get the chance. The phone rang.

"Honey," she happily answered. "I'm so glad you called

back. Things are going okay, but I think I made a boo-boo," she said. "Remember I told you I lost my purse," she told him convincingly. "Well someone actually found it, located my address, and brought it by. Isn't that wonderful?" she squealed. "He's here right now," she said. "Honey, I reached in to give him a little reward, but all my money was gone." She then covered the receiver, and whispered, "I think he might have taken it."

In-f-ing-credible, I said to myself. *If he falls for this, he's a bigger sucker than you.*

"You'll send it tomorrow?" she let out. "Baby, I don't know what I'd do without you," she told him. "Love you hon, let me get this guy out of here," she whispered before blowing him a kiss and hanging up.

Watch me get that guy outta here, I thought. I'd seen and heard it all. Jasmine missed her true calling. There was a reason I felt like a co-star when I first arrived. She would've won an Oscar for the performance she'd just put on.

I had to make a move. There was little doubt what it would be. Perfect time. Perfect situation. Beeper trick. I reached slowly toward my waist and nearly panicked. It wasn't there. I sat on the bed to think. I was quickly relieved when I noticed a square bulge in my pocket. I reached in, turned it off and back on quickly, waited for that wonderful chirp, and gazed at the display with deep concern.

"Do you need the phone?" she asked.

"Nah," I answered, "this looks like an emergency."

"You don't have to leave do you?"

"I don't want to, but duty calls," I said, lying. "And if I want to stay a man of means, I'd better get going." Kelly would have been proud.

She walked me toward the front door and said, "I know you'll come back."

Maybe when you move, I thought grinning. I'd seen more than enough movies that depicted exactly how to end this scene. I always marveled at how guys in movies could just turn and walk away from beautiful women, without as much as a kiss. I knew Wesley Snipes could do it because he knew he had action waiting somewhere. The only action I could look forward to was grabbing my remote, and checking out the second half of the game.

How often do you get this chance? I thought. I couldn't resist. I turned, said nothing, and walked out of the door (Kelly would have loved this, too).

"Shawn," she softly stated, "call me when you get in."

You're joking right? I thought laughing. *Don't you know only a desperate man calls when he gets in?*

I rushed home and hurried to the television. Maybe I made it in time for the only quarter that counts, the last. No such luck. I'd missed the game, and blown yet another evening. I didn't want to talk to anyone, but the blinking red light on my answering machine told me to check my messages. I pressed the play button and hoped some lost woman had called and wanted me to come find her. "Shawn, this is Jasmine. I'm glad you came by," the first message started. "Give me a call when you get in."

You're definitely in, I thought grinning. *But you're definitely not calling.*

At that moment I realized Jasmine looked like a 3 for one reason and one reason alone. She was one. I wanted her to be a 6. She wanted me to be a "man of means." Neither of us got what we wanted from the deal but I knew she soon would. A woman as fine as Jasmine will find a true man of means in no time. I don't know who I'll find. I only hope I find her soon and when I find her, I hope she's my true 6. It wouldn't hurt if she's as tight as Jasmine.

The answering machine lady kept me moving. She didn't want me to get too down on myself and my never-changing situation.

"Next message," she softly stated. "Shawn Wayne this is Jennifer Adams from American Express and this is my last call. I've left three messages. Please return the call," she pleaded. "You haven't used your card in some time, and we'd like to know how we can better serve your needs."

I need a 6. I doubt they'll help me with that.

I turned out the lights and slid beneath the sheets. I felt like crap. Despite it all, a smile came across my face. The familiar theme from *SportsCenter* played in the background and I dozed off. Things aren't totally screwed. At least I have cable.

Inside the mind of a player— Profile of a

"I'm not interested in a relationship—I just have friends."

MOTTO OF A 2

What's a 2 looking for if she's not interested in a relationship? Simple question, simple answer. Control. Some women just plain don't want a relationship which is just like some men who refuse to commit. Somehow it works if the involved parties accept it. But a true 2 is a slick 2. And a slick 2 is one who's figured how to run the same scam on men that men have run on women for years. 2s are like lightening in a thunderstorm. They move with incredible speed and they're pretty cool to look at. But when they hit, they hit hard and leave damage. 2s definitely have a control thing. They will try to control you. If you've got the time and the energy and you like the game, find yourself a 2. They love to be chased, but they love it because you'll be doing all the running.

If a guy is in a steady relationship with a babe, he knows she's usually just a phone call away. Babes are like that, and that's why men like them. They're reliable, and you can halfway trust them. But calling a 2 is usually a major exercise in extreme futility. First of all, you can't really call a 2. You have to page her or you have to reach her at work. And if you're fortunate enough to call, the relationship you'll have with her answering machine will often be more significant than the one you have with her. If she calls you, you can count on being put on hold at least three times. She'll have to take her many other "important" calls.

2s don't believe in staying home. They have to be out. They insist on doing everything with their girlfriends or with some mysterious "friend." Who exactly is that friend? "That's not your concern," is what a new 2 would tell you. But a seasoned 2 would casually recite, "Oh, just a friend," or, "I have company, I'll have to call you back." The call will probably never come but you wait anyway. You've been raised to believe women are about their word and that they don't carry men like men carry women.

Unfortunately, 2s play by their own rules, so they sometimes treat men even worse than men treat women.

Many 2s are 2s because they got tired of being 1s. They've placed themselves on what is commonly referred to as the "get-back" list. It means they're going to either *get back* at other men for the guy that screwed over them, or they're going to *get back* the lost self-esteem and wasted feelings they placed in the wrong man. They've been manipulated, they've been controlled, and they've been hurt. Now it's their turn. They'll take it with a vengeance.

Some 2s are 2s because they just like to play the field. They don't want to be tied down until "Mr. Right" makes himself known. Even more 2s are 2s because they have to be 2s. They like guys, and they like attention. They may even like sex (but their husbands or boyfriends tend to obscure that fact). Sadly enough, many a 2 is a 2 because she's actually tied to someone who may not feel tied to her. 2s aren't always trying to be 2s. They may really want a relationship. They just may not want it with you.

It's damn near impossible to figure out 2s. They'll lie and say they're telling the truth. They'll go on ski trips, but they can't ski. They go to the beach, but they don't want to swim. And they'll date you, as long as you're treating (and as long as their "friend" is unavailable). 2s are too busy, too self-absorbed, and too much of a hassle to get involved with. If you want to play games, a 2 is for you. Just watch yourself because 2s will hurt you. If a 2 says she's not looking for a relationship, she probably means it. Don't press it with a 2. You may end up a 1. Then you'll be slashing somebody's tires.

Shawn Wayne on I'm not going near a 2. If a babe tells me she's not looking for anything, that's good enough for me. I doubt 2s are into cable because they're always hanging out. They don't have time for that stuff. If they're not into cable, who needs them anyway?

5th Message

Each fall, Kelly volunteers at the Congressional Black Caucus (CBC) national conference in D.C. She constantly comes back with unbelievable stories about beautiful women in search of good men. Even though I'd heard the action's good, and that eligible men are in high demand, I skipped the opening dinner. My bankroll screamed when I tried to convince it that the $50 "donation" was an investment in our future. If they were charging $50 for one dinner, they'd have to feed me for at least a week. Kelly actually gave me an extra ticket, but I told her I probably wouldn't make it. She stayed after me though. She called several times and left a series of ominous messages. "You won't meet anyone sitting at home Shawn," she said on one. "Do you think a woman is just going to show up at your door and take you away?" she asked on another.

I wish.

The last year had been catastrophic for me. I was stood

up on New Year's Eve and spent Valentine's Day at a buddy's place. I listened to him make out with some babe while I stood guard in case his lady called or, worse yet, showed up. My co-workers, Donnie, and even Kelly, all forgot my birthday. I foolishly allowed myself to believe they thought I was celebrating with someone else. The simple truth was they just didn't give a damn. I'd dated a work-weary, alcoholic bisexual (who wanted to date one of my ex's) and spent Memorial Day with someone *I'd* dumped ten years ago. I couldn't have written a story this bad. I was ready for something better. Not just something better, anything.

Kelly convinced me the CBC conference could provide me my "something better." It appeared she was right because as I entered the Grand Hyatt hotel, I immediately noticed a lot of something betters. They were talking in groups, walking alone, sitting, standing. They were everywhere. The Grand Hyatt is in the heart of downtown D.C. and the lobby isn't really a lobby. It's a twelve-story open atrium. It has a stunning collection of exotic tropical plants. The only thing that could rival the immense beauty and opulence of this fabulous garden setting was the collection of women who literally were all over the place. Stevie Wonder could have seen how good these chicks looked. My eyes were so wide open I'm certain people thought they'd just been dilated. I had never been in the presence of collective class like I was now. The best thing about it was that I saw no other men around. I knew it was a good practice to make a move before the competition arrived, but I passed each group without uttering a word. My mouth was as wide open as my eyes. I literally couldn't force it to close to make the words come out.

This was an aggressive group which surprised me. With my luck they were all 2s. They were just looking for some fun. Many of them spoke, and several commented on my suit and tie. One even complimented me on my shoes. She wouldn't have been so impressed had she known they were my only pair. I traveled down an escalator and turned around. To my delight, I noticed two babes bending over a railing to check *me* out. This was my night. Something better was definitely in the house. Hopefully, that something better would be my 6.

I'd skipped the banquet and held out for the post-dinner party. I wasn't especially interested in parting with $25 so I could watch a bunch of highbrows dance but Kelly didn't give me a choice. The dance was for the chumps who couldn't afford the dinner, so I was in good company. I passed several salons that were stocked with those formless modern paintings that never seem to make sense. I then traveled down another escalator and spotted the line for the dance. Despite the many attractive women who were milling around, I had a brief uneventful wait. I made it to a red cloth-covered greeting table and slowly reached into the breast pocket of my jacket for my ticket. Embarrassingly, I came up with a wrinkled McDonald's napkin. I'd eaten dinner there. I couldn't believe it. I'd forgotten, or even worse, lost my ticket to this $25 dollar event. There were tight bodies and beautiful bright faces all over the place. But they weren't getting another twenty-five bucks from the kid.

I leaned toward the cute buxom hostess behind the table, smiled and said, "I'm sorry miss, but I think I've misplaced my ticket."

"That's a good one," she said between pops of her gum. "Replacements are just $25."

"That's almost as cute as you," I replied, "but I'm not paying another twenty-five bucks to get in."

"That's okay too," she casually answered. "'Cause if you don't pay it, you ain't gettin' in."

I was poised to lose my cool, and wanted to give her a real piece of my mind, but it wasn't worth it. I was the one who had screwed up. As I headed back toward the escalator, I heard a familiar voice.

"He's alright. He bought a ticket from me." It was Kelly. She saved the day. I would have gone home and fretted about the beautiful women *"I coulda' had"* before I'd have given up another $25. Kelly walked toward me. She quickly grabbed my arm and led me through a huge burgundy door. She looked around and said, "Shawn, if you can't pick up a woman in here, I'm disowning you as a friend."

I looked and saw what she meant. Women were all over the place. I didn't get out much, so I literally had to adjust my eyes. Obviously classy babes were clad in not-so-obviously-classy outfits. There were indeed some who were "dressed for success." But the overwhelming majority were dressed for the type of success I had in mind.

Kelly and I sat at a table toward the rear of the crowded ballroom. The dim lighting couldn't hide the splash of brightly colored outfits and incredibly intricate hairdos. I was in a complete daze.

"Shawn look at me," she said, as the deejay scratched in Naughty by Nature's *Hip-Hop Hooray.* "We need to work on your pick-up lines." Her hands were all over the place. It was always like that when Kelly talked. I thought she was going to take off.

"Why?" I replied concerned.

"I've seen you in action Shawn," she stated. "Remember last summer when we were walking through Hecht's and this beautiful woman stared you down even though I was with you?" she asked.

"You mean the lady with the pretty brown hair, green slacks, gold vest, ankle bracelet, and Gucci watch?"

"Yeah, that one," she smugly replied. "How do you know she had on a Gucci watch?"

"Cause that's the line I used on her."

"What line Shawn?"

"I asked her if she had the time."

"That's what I mean Shawn," she continued forcefully. "You're alone now because you couldn't pick up a woman if she dropped from the sky and landed on the floor in front of you," she explained. "That's so tired," she added. "The women in here wouldn't even fall for that."

I wasn't so sure about that. The women in here looked like they would fall for anything. My mom once told me women had a competitive edge over men. "Men like to play childish games and have a need to win even if it's short term," she told me. "Women are strategic, they develop game plans, utilize resources, and ultimately win the real battles in the game of life," she concluded. My mother's words made sense. This group's game plan was quite clear. Less means more. I could hear them getting dressed and thinking: *The less you wear, the more play you'll get.* Their strategy made sense. They were each competing with top-flight babes for the attention of the most powerful, influential black men in the country. My mom also told me power made ugly men appear to be handsome, and influence made bald men appear to have hair. I realized I essentially had no power and my influence was pretty much limited to the ladies who worked at McDonald's drive-thru windows. Needless to say, I took Kelly a little more seriously.

"Pay attention Shawn," urged Kelly. "You see three girls together, but one really grabs your attention. How do you approach her?"

My first reaction was to say that I don't approach her. "I guess I just walk up to her and ask her to dance," I answered.

"And what do you say Shawn?" she countered.

"Let's dance!"

"Let's dance?"

"Yeah, let's dance. What's wrong with that?"

"Shawn you don't tell women to dance, you ask them."

If I don't ask, they can't turn me down, I thought.

"You have zero class Shawn. None," she said, disgusted with me.

"Would you like to dance?" I said.

"No way Shawn," she quickly replied.

"No, I'm saying should I say, would you like to dance?"

"Be more relaxed," she advised smiling.

"How's this?" I asked. "Hi, I like this record, and I'd be

honored if you'd share this dance with me."

To my surprise, she just laughed. This didn't make sense. That was one of the smoothest lines I'd ever come up with.

"Shawn, that is so corny. But corny might work for you. The balance in your savings account would *really* get you over," she giggled, as her hands flew about. "Be confident, but not cocky," she said. "And Shawn," she continued. "If you really want to meet someone, whatever you do, don't be yourself."

I thought about what Kelly said as I stood and looked around the room. I needed something to get me over. Most of the guys looked like they had it going on. They were decked out in sharp tailored suits and fancy shoes with high gloss shines. They all seemed to have that, "I'm the man" air about them. Women always fall for that. They say they want someone who's honest and sincere, but they always fall for the guys with the tightest lines, the baddest rides, and the most happening jobs. My Kuppenheimer suit, resoled shoes and measly bookkeeper's salary were no match for this crowd. I figured most of these guys probably bragged about some candidate they were working for. They probably had well practiced lines that made women melt. All I had was, "Let's dance." And that wouldn't even work because I can't dance. This was major drama. Here I am. In the presence of the most beautiful collection of women I've ever seen, and I have absolutely nothing to talk about. My mind raced for a gimmick. I thought I could at least look cool by walking around with a drink, but I can't even pull that off. I don't drink. Kelly was right. If I was going to meet someone, being myself wasn't going to get it done.

The drink idea didn't seem too bad, so I decided to buy a soda. If the bartender threw in a twist or one of those cool little umbrellas, I'd at least look like I had a real drink. I waltzed through a maze of couples on the hardwood dance floor and found one of four cash bars located in the ball-room. I didn't care for cash bars. The name alone implied I'd have to spend a lot of money.

"I'd like a Sprite," I said to the moustached man behind the bar. He popped two round ice cubes into a tiny glass tumbler and methodically sprayed in the soda. He then placed it on a tiny red napkin, handed it to me and stoically stated, "That will be $2.50, sir."

"Two-fifty!" I said loudly. "I ordered a soda!"

"Our soft drinks are $2.50, sir," he told me. "Our fine liqueurs are slightly more." "Two-fifty is too much for a soda!" I exclaimed. "You didn't even fill it to the top."

The five people in line behind me started to look around the person in front of them to see what was taking so long. I didn't like admitting it. Kelly was right. I was acting in my usual frugal manner. Frugal wasn't going to work with this crowd. I couldn't be myself and hope to succeed, or to even compete. I reached into my pocket, slowly pulled out a twenty, and forced myself to hand it to him. He didn't even offer up an umbrella. The drink idea was a bust.

I turned to walk back to my table. The woman behind me reached in her tiny black suede purse. She pulled out a fifty to pay for a soda. The bartender, who must have been the twin brother of Isaac from *"The Love Boat,"* informed her he couldn't change the bill. Naturally, I seized the opportunity. I rarely carried more than $10, but tonight I knew I'd need a bankroll, so I had $60. I started to give her change, and then it hit me that I stood to gain more if I picked up her tab.

"I'll pay for the lady," I said, adding about three decibels of bass to my usually awkward voice.

"That's okay," she said. "I can get change."

"I'll put it on your tab," I said smiling.

"I think I can deal with that," she quickly replied.

The bar keep counted my change. I neatly folded a dollar bill, nodded at him and placed it in his bill-lined tip jar. I figured the tip move would impress her. I wasn't sure if it did. She just smiled and said, "Thanks," in a voice as sweet as a HoneyBaked Ham at Christmas.

We walked passed the dance floor. I knew it was time to

make a move. I had no clue as to what that move would be. I only knew it had to be smooth. It had to work. I couldn't think of anything slick. "I'm Shawn," I said.

"I'm pleased to make your acquaintance Shawn," she replied. "My name is Troi."

"As in Helen of Troy?"

"Not quite," she said giggling. "But, I have heard that before."

"Is that Ms. Troi or Mrs. Troi?" I asked, thinking about Jasmine and her sugar-daddy husband.

"Miss Troi," she said while sipping on her soda. "Definitely Miss."

I'd hit the jackpot but I didn't have a response. I always thought men were at a disadvantage when it came to proclaiming their singleness. The absence of a ring didn't get it done. Too many married men ditched their rings while they were walking out of their front doors. Unfortunately, too many women didn't care if a guy was wearing a wedding ring or not. Saying, "I'm Mr. Shawn." doesn't mean much because it doesn't specify whether I'm married or single. Being single was the farthest thing from my mind. I was in 6 land.

6s don't have availability problems. If they're interested, they say it. They don't call themselves Ms. They want you to know it's Miss. When a babe says Ms., there's room for doubt. When she says Miss, the door is wide open.

I was glad she was a Miss because Troi had a silky smooth air about her. I wasn't trying to jump the gun, but I knew she was a 6. She was so thoroughly fine she'd put any 3 to shame. A set of simple, yet elegant diamond stud earrings graced her ears. They perfectly accented the gold twist rope that hung suspended around her neck. Her sparkling green eyes were the centerpiece of a woman seemingly blessed with poise, style, and a body that made men turn their heads when they thought their ladies wouldn't catch them. Her nose, which resembled the successful part of a "before and after" ad for cosmetic surgery, sat perfectly over her

full, inviting lips. Her gleaming curly black hair fell gracefully over her shoulders, which led way to her taut shapely
back.

I let her walk in front of me so that I could get a
"panoramic view" of her championship rear end. I delight-
ed in the fact that she was wearing a simple black tea dress
that barely made it to the middle of her thighs. I liked this
dress. It showed everything, without showing anything. If
the dress wasn't lying (and I could tell that it wasn't), she
had a perfect figure. Her tiny waistline and flat tummy gave
her breasts an almost surreal appearance. She was very
petite. I knew they weren't as big as they looked. She had
wonderful shapely hips that reminded me of Jasmine.

Troi's legs rivaled Jasmine's. They were perfect. She
looked to be about five-three, and maybe one hundred fifteen pounds. Her tight, smooth thighs provided a perfect
showcase for her light, near yellow complexion. She had
lean, chiseled calves that pulsated with each step she took.
Amazingly, her knees were as light as the rest of her. That's
always a good sign. I don't think I'd want a babe who'd spent
too much time on her knees. Then again, maybe I would. I
knew I was in trouble when I noticed she was wearing the
one thing, that on the right woman, nearly paralyzes me.
An ankle bracelet.

When I was in college, my mom told me that "women
who were available" wore ankle bracelets. Over the years I
found her theory was right in many cases. I also found that
ankle bracelets, more than any other accessory, spoke
about a woman's sexuality. A lot of guys thought big hoop
earrings made a statement. That didn't work for me. It takes
big ears to hold those big earrings. I don't know anybody
who wants a chick with big ears. Ankle bracelets were sexy
and to me, sexy meant sex. I'd slept with a woman who
wore an ankle bracelet. I noticed that if that bracelet came
off, it was the last thing to come off. That was proof enough
for me. Ankle bracelets were tied to a woman's sexuality.

We sat at an empty table. I asked where she was from.

She couldn't have been from D.C. She appeared much too nice to be a local.

"I'm from Chicago," she replied smiling. "I work with Myers and Stevenson," she said. "We represent several Fortune 500 firms, and we're trying to break into political marketing," she added. "I'm in town to conduct a feasibility study and to meet with the right people to get our name around."

I liked that she talked openly about herself and it was obvious she enjoyed her job. At least she thought it was important. That was more than I could say about my job. In fact, I couldn't think of anything to say about my job. It was cool though. She hadn't bothered to ask. At this point (as is usually the case), I realized I had little to add to the conversation. I figured I'd keep her talking. I asked, "how long have you been at your firm?," but I really wanted to find out how to get invited to her hotel room. She was only going to be in town for a week, so I needed to get moving.

She told me she'd been at Myers and Stevenson for five years. "I started right before I got my master's," she said. "When I complete the framework for this political marketing piece, I'm going to finish up my doctorate."

It was clear why she was Miss Troi. She was way too busy to have a man.

We were seated at the rear of the room. The music didn't bother us too much. Unfortunately, she stopped talking about her job. I never started talking about mine. Strangely, she still hadn't asked. I could tell she was being pulled into the deejay's smooth mix. Her shoulders rocked and her fingers bounced. I knew was in trouble. I wasn't about to ask her to dance. If I was going to make a fool of myself, it was going to be on my own limited terms. She smiled at me and finished her soda. She placed it on the table and shocked me when she casually stated, "Let's dance." I was paralyzed. I searched my mind for a reasonable excuse. There was none. It was obvious she wasn't going for an excuse anyway. She grabbed my hand and moved us toward the dance floor.

Kriss Kross's frenetic *Jump Jump* was blasting from the sound system. It was the perfect song for someone like me who couldn't dance because no one on the floor was dancing. They were all jumping. I'd never seen anything like it. This could only happen to me. I finally make it to a classy event and meet a decent woman. And I end up at a human pogo-stick competition.

Troi had started jumping while I stood totally still with my mouth half-open. I was in awe of the aerial spectacle around me. Brothers were leaping and high-fiving each other over the top of their ladies' elaborate hairdos. The women went deliberately straight up and down like pistons in a sixty-five Buick. Troi yelled, "Jump Shawn, it's fun!" I didn't know what to do. Surprisingly, I looked around and saw Kelly leaping in three-inch heels. I saw a couple older than my boss, Mr. Butler, jumping joyously, but they could only get about an inch off the floor. I couldn't dance. But I could definitely jump. And jump I did. I started off slowly. Kelly was jumping higher than me. Mr. Butler was putting me to shame. I knew it was time to put it into high gear. I jumped so high and so fluidly that I could have been a body double for a kangaroo on *Mutual of Omaha's Wild Kingdom.*

Before I knew it the song ended. She reached for my hand as the deejay blended in the Ohio Players' romantic ballad, *Heaven Must Be Like This.* To my surprise we ended up in each others arms. I didn't ask her. She didn't ask me. It just happened. I hadn't slow danced since college so I knew something stupid was going to happen. I worried that I'd trip, sneeze, or do something to blow this wonderful moment. Thankfully, the song kept us moving and I soon realized if anything was going to happen, it was going to be something good. It felt like we'd gravitated to another planet or something. We couldn't have been in the Grand Hyatt. There's no way their ceiling was as high as the clouds we were in. I wasn't Albert Einstein, but I was usually aware of what was happening around me. If something else was happening, it didn't much matter. The only thing I was interested in was having Troi in my arms. I didn't know if any-one else was on the dance floor. I didn't know whether I was on beat or not. I didn't even know the song had stopped playing until Troi softly whispered, "I think we can stop Shawn. The song's over." My eyes popped open, she giggled, and we grasped hands and walked toward our table.

We sat down, clutched hands beneath the table and just looked at each other. I was hoping she'd say something because I couldn't think of anything to say. I would have even listened to her blab about her job. She stared at me, and those green eyes were sucking me in. She knew it. She smiled and asked, "What are we up to?"

"What are we up to?" I repeated. "I didn't know we were up to anything."

"I move on a fast track," she casually stated. "My free time is limited. I have to rely on my instincts when it comes to important decisions."

"Whadda you mean?" I asked puzzled. "I don't remember asking you to decide anything."

"I know that Shawn," she responded. "That's just me."

I wondered exactly what was just her.

"I meet a lot of men, but I'm usually so busy that I don't even think about them," she told me looking down at the table. "I haven't been out like this for such a long time. I for-got how good it felt to be touched by a man," she confessed. "But it's okay, because I love my work."

I couldn't believe she was going to hit me with the job piece again.

"I miss having someone special in my life. Someone to share the ups and down with. Someone to talk to and to hold onto," she added. "Do you ever feel that way Shawn?" If only she knew.

This was a moment that both Kelly and my mom had prepared me for. It was a time when I was supposed to say something deep and sensitive. Denzel Washington would know what to say. But I wasn't Denzel, so I asked, "Do you want another soda?"

She looked up at me with a straight face, but couldn't hold in her laugh.

"Shawn I just opened myself up to you. I asked you how you felt, and you ask me if I want a soda!" she blurted out. "What's wrong with you?"

"Nothing," I clumsily answered.

"What do you mean, nothing Shawn?"

"I just thought you might want something to drink to cool down," I nervously answered. "You seemed upset."

I knew I'd blown it. Her smile turned to a scowl. She was fuming and it was all my fault.

"I wasn't upset Shawn," she sighed. "Maybe it's just me. I haven't been around a man who wasn't associated with my job for so long that I don't always say what I mean," she added. She turned her chair toward me, placed her hands over mine, and calmly said, "Shawn, remember when I told you that I rely on my instincts when it comes to making important decisions?"

"Yeah," I quickly replied. "You just said it a couple of seconds ago."

"Well, I know we've just met, and that we don't know each other from Adam," she continued. "But I trust my instincts. They tell me that you're a decent guy. A little different," she added giggling, "but decent."

I wasn't about to interrupt. I didn't know what to say anyway. Besides, she'd already told me she didn't want another soda.

"You are a decent guy aren't you?" she deliberately asked. "You're not out here cheating on your girlfriend or your wife are you?"

I wanted to laugh. My mom once told me when a woman was putting the move on a man and asked him about his status, she had probably already decided what she was going to do with him. She just wanted to hear the right response. "But you make sure to tell the truth," she said.

"I don't have a girlfriend or a wife," I said. "If I did I wouldn't be here. I'd be with her."

She smiled and chimed in, "I like the sound of that." She then cautiously asked, "You are telling me the truth aren't you?"

"Definitely," I replied smiling.

She slowly stood up and said, "Shawn I've made a decision."

"About what?" I asked concerned.

"I hope I don't regret this," she sighed. She then looked at me, smiled, and softly whispered, "Let's go to my room."

6th Message

"SHAWN, I HAVEN'T HEARD FROM YOU."

MESSAGE SENT ON
OCTOBER 14TH AT 7:28 P.M.

As we left the dance and the loud music behind us, Troi said she needed to hit the ladies room.

"Cool," I told her smiling, "I'll meet you by the escalator."

I made sure she made it to the restroom, and then reached into my pocket for a quarter. It didn't make much sense but I had to call somebody. I was about to strike gold. This whole thing was happening so fast. It seemed to be going in the right direction. I didn't know if she was a 6. I wasn't even sure what was going to happen in her room. I knew what I wanted to happen. That would be cool. But I hoped it wasn't all about a quick lay. Troi seemed special. She deserved more than an Evander Holyfield-style stick and move, and quite frankly, so did I. She was totally compelling while at the same time completely uncomplicated. Just like a well-executed fast break with Magic Johnson at the point. I would have called Donnie but I hadn't heard from him for awhile. I looked at my Timex. It struck me that no one would be interested in my potential success story anyway, so I decided to check my messages. I was actually out with a *real* babe, so I figured other babes had called. It always works out that way. Nobody calls when you're at home alone every night, but go out one night, and "bam," the phone rings off the hook.

The answering machine lady totally discredited my theory. Only one message.

"Hi Shawn," it started. "I haven't heard from you. Give me a call sometime. You have the number. Take care." It was Jasmine. I wanted to call her, alright. I thought she'd like to know I was out with a woman who didn't have a husband *or* a boyfriend. One problem. I didn't have another quarter.

As Troi came out of the bathroom toward me, I noticed just how gracefully she walked. It's hard to say she walked. It was more like she was gliding. There was no wasted movement. I'd seen women who moved like her before. I always thought they were unattainable. Especially to guys like me. Troi's walk exuded quiet confidence. It wasn't one of those hard "pay attention, I'm in charge" struts. It was one that suggested poise and unpretentious strength. She could have walked just about any way she wanted. As long as she was walking toward me.

We headed toward the elevator. When it arrived, I held the door so she could step in first. My mom would have killed me if I hadn't. I could hardly believe I was on an elevator, hand in hand, with such a beautiful woman. I still wasn't 100 percent sure what was going to happen, though I knew what I *wanted* to happen. I wanted a million dollars too, but I wasn't counting on it showing up. I figured she was going to recruit me into PrimeAmerica or into some wacky pyramid scheme. I liked what was happening, but it made absolutely no sense. She didn't know a thing about me. She didn't even know my last name. She was too fine to be as pressed as I was. As a distinctive chime alerted us to each floor we passed, I desperately tried to figure everything out. What she would do. What I would do. And more important, how we could wrap it up in time to catch *SportsCenter.*

Unfortunately, I didn't get time to sort it all out (and summarily screw it all up). The elevator opened to the twelfth floor. She reached for my hand and smiled as we walked down the long majestic hallway. The hall was discreetly lit. Still there was no mistaking that the incredibly plush carpet beneath our feet was as green as the Boston Celtics' road uniforms. The walls were wrapped with an expensive looking patterned wallpaper that had green and gold highlights. Each door featured a gold-plated ornamental handle. We made it halfway down the hall and were at room 1221 before I knew it. I knew I was nervous because my knees shook as she reached into her purse and pulled out a thin plastic card. She placed it in a tiny metal slit and gently pushed the door aside. She walked in first and turned on the lights, which revealed a cavernous suite. It put Jasmine's place to shame. It had a spacious king-size bed covered with a teal blue print comforter and five throw pillows. There was contemporary flower-laden artwork adorning the walls, and a splendid round jacuzzi facing an armoire. A thirty-five inch Sony Trinitron television and matching VCR rested comfortably on the armoire shelves. Vases filled with fresh flowers sat on each night stand. I'd never seen anything like it.

I'd stayed in hotels when I played ball in college. Our bus always pulled in very late at night, and pulled out very early in the morning, so I didn't really get the chance to check the rooms out. My mom always told me to "make my bed where I laid my head." Needless to say, I always cleaned up before I left. The only time I didn't straighten up was when I stayed in a room that was highlighted by two full-size beds with different-colored sheets, a tattered towel, a leaking sink, and a commode without a seat. It also had a blurry twelve-inch black-and-white TV that ran off of quarters and a flickering lamp which was topped with a lampshade that had an advertisement for Petey's All Natural Gas and Sip.

I frowned as I thought the huge Sony in this room probably cost at least $3 an hour. I wondered if she had some quarters because I'd spent my last one when I checked my messages.

She dropped her purse on one of the nightstands, and asked me if I'd like a drink. I wasn't especially thirsty, so I passed. "I've got to get out of these," she said, while removing her shoes. She then walked in my direction, turned her back toward me and asked me to unzip her dress. I didn't know if she was making a move or not. Kelly once told me not to assume a woman wants to be intimate because she invites you to her room.

"She may just want to talk or listen to music," she advised. I'd heard enough music at the dance and I didn't want to talk anymore. She'd only run on about her job. She was testing me. She wanted to see if I was romantic. I wasn't. Screw the zipper. I was ready to pull the whole dress off, but I knew that wouldn't work. She asked me to get the zipper, and the ball was in my court. I decided to go with the slow pull.

"Shawn," she said impatiently. "What are you waiting for?"

I was ready, so I reached for her zipper. One problem. I couldn't find it. "Where's it at?" I asked.

"Where is what at?"

"The zipper," I said concerned. "I can't find the zipper."

"I don't believe this," she laughed. "Are you serious?"

I was very serious. If this was a test, I'd failed miserably.

The zipper was concealed in a tiny seam at the top of her dress. She told me where it was, and continued to giggle. "You are too much Shawn," she said. My knees shook as I pulled the zipper toward her shapely bottom. I wondered just what would happen next. I noticed a lacy black bra strap as I passed the middle of her back. As the sides of her dress spread apart, I could see her back was as perfect as I imagined. My stomach churned nervously. It was obvious I was in the midst of a Maalox moment. I nearly freaked when she stepped away and said, 'I'll be right back."

I wondered where she was going and what I should do while she was there (wherever "there was"). It didn't matter where she was going as long as she came back. Her departure gave me time to gather myself. I tried to relax. I sat on the edge of the bed and figured I should take my jacket off. I started to remove my shoes but quickly slipped them back on when I realized I could be moving too fast. I decided to move from the bed to one of the chairs at the coffee table. That way, I wouldn't look so pressed. If she came back in a gown, we were on our way. I worried she wouldn't have on a gown. The way things were going, I knew she had to. I wondered if it was going to be one of those teddies the ladies in the 900-number "come-get-me" ads wore. Either black or red would have worked, but a teal to match the room would have been too much. It didn't much matter because I'd decided whatever she had on wouldn't stay on long.

She came back in a white, floor-length, terry-cloth robe with a royal-blue monogram of GHH on the left lapel. I was disappointed. I knew her name was Troi. I wondered just who GHH was. With my luck, it was the boyfriend she forgot to tell me about when she was rattling on about her job. I didn't want to do it, but I had to ask. "Who's GHH?"

"GHH," she answered while tilting her head. "You're kidding, right?"

"No," I replied deliberately. "Is it an old boyfriend or something?"

"I'm not sure Shawn," she said smiling. "But if I had to guess, I'd say it stands for Grand Hyatt Hotel."

I was dumfounded. I felt like a complete idiot. I was falling into the typical male jealously bit over a hotel robe. I didn't even know hotel rooms had robes, and I wondered if people stole them like they ripped off towels.

She walked toward me laughing and asked, "Why do you still have that jacket on—are you cold?"

If only she knew. I hadn't been this hot since I wore a tweed blazer to my company cookout last August.

"Try it," Kelly told me. "You'll look cool. The women will

love it," she laughed.

I removed my jacket. Troi jokingly said, "You can take off your shoes if you'd like." I, of course, immediately wondered if the socks went next. My apprehension was clearly obvious, so she sat down next to me, drew closer, and slowly loosened my tie. She removed it, and flung it onto the coffee table. Before I knew it, she unfastened the top button of my shirt, and whispered, "There's another robe in the bathroom. Why don't you go put it on?"

I was nearly hyperventilating as I closed the bathroom door. I fumbled in the dark as I scrambled to find the light switch. This whole situation was as crazy as it was wonderful. I reminded myself to take my time. I was about to hit the lottery, strike gold, and win the Triple Crown all at once. I didn't want to be overly excited when I went back out. I hurried to undress. Every lame thing I'd ever thought about sex raced through my mind. I wondered what she was like when she did *it.* I wondered if she made funny noises when she did *it.* I even wondered why *it* was called *it.* I was a mess. I checked myself in the mirror. I wasn't sure if taking off my underwear would seem too forward. I smiled when I realized it would be only proper if she took them off and convinced myself that she was cool and that I was ready. I dropped to the cold tiled floor, did ten quick push-ups, and slowly exited the bathroom.

Troi was lying on the bed reading a magazine when I walked out. She turned toward me and, surprisingly, immediately broke out in laughter.

"Shawn!" she exclaimed, "I don't believe you."

I didn't know what she didn't believe, but it sure had me embarrassed.

"Shawn," she said laughing. "You still have your socks on!"

I was totally embarrassed. I knew I should have taken them off. She smiled. She then sat up, reached out to me, and asked, "Why don't you take the socks off and join me?"

I wasn't sure what to do next (even though I knew exactly what I wanted to do next). I asked her what she had in mind.

"What would you like to do?" she bashfully responded.

It, I thought, still not fully sure why it was called it.

"I don't know. You want to talk?" I replied.

"Is that what you want to do Shawn?" she asked smiling.

"Not exactly."

"Well, what exactly would you like to do?"

"It's up to you," I said, shrugging. She smiled, reached over, and placed her hands behind my neck. Then she slowly pulled my face toward hers and gently pressed her lips against mine. I wondered if it was too early to slip her the tongue.

I never found out. Troi moved quick, and I liked it. This was the perfect situation for me because all doubt had been removed. To me, it was always difficult to figure out when it was okay to make a move with a woman. My interpretation of a woman's "yes" was usually a little off from hers. I'm not the type to force myself on someone so if a lady said no, I believed she really meant no. I would stop pursuing her. I felt strongly about babes saying no, even though my mother once told me that "no" sometimes meant "not yet." Adding to my confusion was the fact that "not yet" at times meant "not now." What made it worse was that "not now" could really mean "not here," and "not here" could unfortunately lead you right back to "no—not yet!"

I wanted it simple. I wanted yes to mean positively yes, and no to mean absolutely not. I felt that women used, or worse yet, misused their ability to control these very situations. Too many women would say no, and would then, minutes later say yes, if the right form of persuasion was used. That actually wasn't too much of a problem. The dilemma usually arose when the babe said yes, and later changed her answer to no. I wouldn't like it, and I'd probably be pissed, but if a babe ran that on me, I would just stop and get out. I know leaving sounds unrealistic, but sitting in a cell like Mike Tyson did was unrealistic to me.

We embraced and I silently thanked her for putting everything out in the open where it belonged. She passionately kissed my neck and wrapped her arms around me. Then suddenly, yet slowly, she pulled away. I wondered what I'd done wrong. Troi seemed possessed. She kneeled over me with her knees at the sides of my waist and looked me in the eye. She slowly untied the belt around her robe. It didn't seem to make sense, but Public Enemy's *Don't Believe The Hype* played inside my head as she spread each lapel apart, and unveiled the most spectacular view of frontal nudity I'd ever seen in person.

I definitely believed the hype. Troi was as stacked as a plate of Log Cabin pancakes.

I'd never seen a woman with such a tight body, who wasn't being paid for her services. I tried to close my eyes. I couldn't. She leaned over, kissed me, and slowly ran her tongue across my neck. I wanted to be cool. I didn't want to lose the type of control I couldn't afford to lose. She seductively kissed my chest and worked her way down toward my waistline. I felt like I was paralyzed. I literally could not move. She then loosened the belt on my robe and took it off in one smooth swipe. Unfortunately, she started giggling as she got back to her knees.

"What's up?" I asked concerned.

"Shawn," she said laughing, "you are too funny."

I prided myself on my sense of humor. But being funny was the farthest thing from my mind right now. I figured it was the underwear. I should have taken them off. She laughed, looked down toward my feet, and blurted out, "Take off those damn socks!"

I couldn't believe it. I was too eager to get busy with her. When she'd said "take off the socks and join me" a few minutes earlier, the only thing that registered was "join me." Before I could bend over to reach my socks, she started the process. She laughed as she took each one off and threw them in the trash can saying, "I never want to see these again."

I looked at her like she'd lost her mind. Those socks ran me five bucks. I still had on my underwear and wasn't exactly sure when to remove them. Fortunately, she again took charge. She reached and slowly rolled them down my thighs and over my trembling feet. I wanted to stay cool. I literally could not believe *it* was about to happen. Unfortunately, I couldn't help but stay cool because there was a long unbearable silence. It was strange. I lay on the bed and she just stared at me. She inspected me like a USDA meat grader with an acrylic clipboard and a useless plastic hard hat. I was ready for action. I asked, "What's up-what are you looking at?"

"You," she said seductively.

"Whadda you mean me?"

"You," she repeated. "Your body is wonderful," she told me. "I just want to look at you."

What the hell was she talking about? This situation fit the pattern that had become the odyssey of my life. I work out extra hard to keep my body tight so I can attract a decent woman. I didn't do it for all those b.s. health benefits that guys I worked out with talked about. I did it solely to attract women. So now I attract a woman (who may very well be my 6), and all she wants to do is look at me? I didn't get it.

She stood up and walked around the bed. She continued to stare, and whispered, "I just love your legs."

I loved hers too. But I didn't just want to look at them. I'd never had this happen before and had no clue on how to refocus her back to the business at hand. She sat down and ran her hands over my biceps and asked, "How often do you work out?"

"About four nights a week," I proudly replied. "But why are we doing this?"

"I'm just admiring you Shawn," she answered. "And as long as I'm looking at *you,* there shouldn't be a problem."

She had me there. It shouldn't have been a problem. But it was.

Normally, it would have been flattering to have a woman

with a body as beautiful as Troi's enamored with mine, but I was embarrassed. I was stretched out on my back, in the company of a gorgeous nude woman, and I have an extraordinary erection sticking straight toward the ceiling. It felt funny having her staring at me while I'm lying there with a major league hard-on. It was like trying to catch up to a bus when you know the driver has seen you and still pulls away. He sees you, but for some reason ignores you. This is how I felt. I knew she saw it, but she seemed totally committed to ignoring it. I couldn't believe she didn't know that men didn't like women seeing their erections. They just want them to feel it.

She lay back down beside me, rolled over, and gently grabbed me in the right place, in just the right way. "I see that you're ready," she whispered.

I thanked God. She wasn't a bus driver.

She propped herself up, looked me in the eye and then smiled and said, "I've never done this before Shawn."

"Done what?"

"I've never slept with a man that I just met," she said. "Have you?"

"Not really," I told her. "I've never slept with a man at all."

We both laughed. She suddenly closed her eyes and pulled me on top of her. She slowly opened her thighs. As she pulled me toward her, I heard Louis Armstrong playing *Oh When the Saints Go Marching In,* inside my head. I reasoned that this made more sense than *Don't Believe The Hype.* I was almost in. Ready to hit the jackpot. No such luck. She backed away, looked me in the eyes and said, "Shawn, you're not wearing anything."

"Whadda you mean?" I asked surprised. "You're the one who didn't want the socks."

"No," she said. "I mean protection."

"Protection," I quickly stated. "Protection from what?"

We slowly sat up and looked at each other. This was an unusual dilemma for me. I didn't have sex that often. On the rare occasion when I did, protection wasn't an issue.

"Aren't you on the pill or something?" I asked, immediately wondering what "or something" could be.

"Yeah," she replied casually. "I'm on the pill."

"So what's the problem then?"

"This is the '90s Shawn, and there are things out there that I'm not trying to get." "That's good," I said. "Because I don't have those things, and since you don't want them, you obviously don't have them, so we're okay."

"It doesn't work exactly like that," she told me. She then grabbed my hand and looked down at the bed. "I like you Shawn, and I'm ready, but we're not doing anything without protection," she said.

I was out of luck. I didn't have a snappy response. My erection had gone south, and worse than that, I didn't have any protection.

7th Message

"PLEASE SHAWN."

MESSAGE SENT ON
OCTOBER 14TH AT 11:03 P.M.

"Are you sure?" I asked, hoping she'd change her mind about the protection.

"Absolutely," she said.

I cleverly pulled the cover over my faltering erection. "That's cool Troi, but there's only one problem," I said.

"And what might that be?"

"I don't have any on me."

"If that's the only problem," she said smiling, "then we don't have a problem at all." "Whadda you mean?"

"I have some," she confidently replied.

"Why?"

"For moments like these."

"How often do you have moments like these?" I asked squirming.

"Not very often," she giggled.

She couldn't have hit me with a better answer.

"Hand me my purse," she quickly stated.

I had an empty feeling. She was planning to sleep with

somebody. She wouldn't have been carrying rubbers if she weren't.

"I know what you're thinking Shawn," she said. "And, it's not like that. I'm not a loose woman. I wasn't looking to sleep with someone."

"I wasn't thinking that."

"Don't lie to me," she said forcefully. "I haven't been with a man in a long time," she said. "I've never even used one of these before," she added. She handed the pack of condoms to me.

I took it as a good sign that the pack was unopened. I smiled as she dropped her purse to the floor. She lay on her back, laughed and said, "I'm yours when you're ready Shawn."

She was mine alright. I tried to be extra smooth opening the "healthy 3-pack," as the label put it, but I wasn't having much success. I searched for the instructions as I peeked at Troi out of the corner of my eye. She looked gorgeous. But I knew she'd be asleep if I didn't hurry.

"Is something wrong?" she asked.

I started to tell her it was too small, but reality kicked in. I embarrassingly told her, "I can't get it open. There's no directions."

She sat up and laughed. "I don't think they come with instructions Shawn. Let me see." I gave them to her. This time, I lay on my back. She kneeled over me with her knees at my waist and ripped the pack open with her teeth. "Let's get you ready again," she whispered. That was the best thing she'd said all night. My eagerness was quite obvious. It took all of six seconds for me to "get ready." She rolled the condom over me.

"Impressive Shawn. It barely fits."

I figured it was the wrong size. I wondered if they even came in sizes.

She then softly kissed me, and said, "Wait. I've got to do something."

I didn't know what else she had to, but it gave me more

time to figure out why "it" was called "it."

She bent over, slowly removed her ankle bracelet, and dropped it to the floor.

Game, set, and match. Just like I thought. Off with the bracelet, on with the sex. Those things are magic.

She positioned herself on top of me and slowly lowered herself down. Before I knew it, I was inside. My heart raced as I wondered what to do next. I didn't know what noises to make or if I should make any at all. I wasn't trying to complicate things. I just wanted this to be good. It had to be right. I'd never slept with a woman on the first date and knew if I wanted to get to a second one, I'd better do it right.

For her part, Troi was making it more than right. She really hadn't been with a guy in a long time. She was as tight as Mr. Mooney, the money-hungry banker on *The Lucy Show,* and as hot as Popeye's chicken on a Sunday afternoon. Troi was rolling and I was in for the ride of my life. She was incredible. I knew only a 6 could pull this off. As the headboard rumbled and the bed springs squeaked beneath us, I still wondered why it was called it, and if condoms actually came in sizes. Troi didn't seem to be thinking about anything. She jumped off me and lay flat on her back with her legs opened as wide as a six-lane highway going west.

"Please Shawn," she moaned.

"Please what?" I clumsily replied.

"Please put it in," she sighed.

The rest is a blur. Not that it wasn't great, because it was. It was magnificent. But when it was over, I realized the details of what we'd done weren't nearly as important as the fact that what we'd experienced was figuratively and literally breathtaking. What was more important than that was the fact that this wonderful, fulfilling, breathtaking experience was ours alone. We made it, or better yet, allowed it to happen.

We lay there, drenched in the sweetest of sweat, and I softly said, "Thirty-eight times."

"You were incredible Shawn," she said smiling. "But I

don't think I could go thirty-eight times."

"No," I said. "The ceiling fan has gone around thirty-eight times since we finished."

She then kissed me and ran her hand across my chest. "It won't go around another thirty-eight before we start again," she whispered.

A moment with a gold digger — Profile of a

"What is it you said you do for a living?"

MOTTO OF A 3

Let's get one thing straight. Unlike the other categories of women (1 through 6), being a 3 is not (and never will be) a state of mind. Guys can coax women into being 1s, 2s, 4s, and 5s. Babes can be worked with. They can be coached into being 6s (although true 6s evolve into 6-dom). But just like gifted athletes, 3s are born. They are not made. A female can have the bomb body, a sensuous smile, and happening hair. She can have a sexy strut and all of the other important tools that make a honey a "real babe." She can even have that, "shoot your best shot, it'll never work" air about her that many babes have, and that even more men find alluring and appealing. She can look so good that spending cash and buying gifts become things you want to do, as opposed to things you have to do to keep the peace. There are lots of fine babes that can screw you up like that.

But after them, there are 3s.

3s don't have to have that sassy, playful air. You give it to them. They don't have to have common sense. You give them that as well. 3s don't even need bank, because unlike the fine babes you don't necessarily mind spending your cash on, you will gladly give it to a 3. And that's the fundamental problem with 3s. They look so f-ing good that you just want to give them stuff.

You part with cash, perfume, clothes, and all sorts of gifts. You give them so many compliments that they ultimately have a hard time believing anything you say, and you keep dishing it out anyway. You know they've heard it before (from every other stiff), but you just want a leg up on the last guy.

One problem.

If she's a true 3 (and not a pretender who'll try to fool you with hair weaves, underwire push-up bras, or complex make-up jobs), you can believe the last stiff who constantly fed her that, "You're the most beautiful babe in the history of babes" line was probably no stiff at all. He probably didn't feed her that corny overused line too often either. He didn't have to. He didn't have to because he (unlike regular stiffs like us) had a crazy bankroll or, worse yet, big-time power.

One of the worst feelings you can experience is when you and that fine honey who you think you're impressing decide to check out a game. And not just any game-let's say the seventh game of the NBA finals. You're rooting for Tommy Neckbone (who didn't even bother to graduate from Soft Pretzel State Community College) to sink the front end of a one-and-one. You want his squad to win. You have to cover your stupid bets. Suddenly, the babe squeals, "You can make it Tommy!" The other team calls a timeout to ice him, but the babe has already iced you. You know Tommy from Soft Pretzel C.C. is no superstar. You definitely know that babes don't know regular NBA guys who only make two million bucks a year.

You try to play it off and convince yourself that she just knows hoop. You check her out. You know that a babe as fine as her didn't just happen upon basketball. You fake a ten cent smile. Your neck tightens. You hate to ask, but you have to. "How did you know his name was Tommy?" She hits you with a twenty-five cent smile, sips on her soda and casually replies, "I used to date him." You knew what the deal was all along. But you're a stiff. You had to ask. Suddenly you don't care about your dumb bets. You actually want Tommy to miss that foul shot.

But Tommy once dated the 3 now sitting beside you. You *know* he's going to make it and win the game because life sucks like that.

And after he sinks the shot, she jumps for joy and screams like she won your bet (and she may as well have won it because if she hangs around long enough, you'll be giving it to her anyway). You feel like crap du jour. She thanks you for such a nice time and hurries out. You feel wasted because you know you wasted your time. It's screwed up, but don't get too down on yourself. 3s often date regular guys when jocks are stuck in their seasons or when the guys with the big bucks (and the big power) are stuck with their wives. If you get the chance to swing with a 3, do it in style. Enjoy the ride. Just make sure you're seen in public with her because other babes will think you're happening. That can make for steady action when the 3 you're hanging with decides to break camp.

3s are not always the "bimbos" everyone makes them out to be. They've figured out exactly what it takes to please the level of guys they deal with (and they give it to them big time). But don't count on them giving too much to you. You'll be too busy giving way too much to them. If you must date a 3 (or if you're lucky enough to date one), be aware that if you're not a major player with major power or influence, you'll be in for major disappointment if you think she's the "real thing." Not that 3s can't be the real thing. They can and often are for the right price. But is it a price you want (or can afford) to pay?

Shawn Wayne on 3s

Telling a guy not to date a 3 is like telling Wile E. Coyote not to chase the road runner. That dumb coyote knows he won't catch that stupid bird, but he chases it anyway. And that's the deal with 3s. You'll go after them, but you'll never get them. I bet 3s can't bear to watch *SportsCenter*. They probably dated one of the guys featured on *Plays of the Week*, and they're pissed. They know some other 3 is staking out their old claim. If they can't watch *SportsCenter*, they're lame. Who needs a lame chick anyway?

8th
Message

As Troi predicted, the ceiling fan never made it to thirty-eight revolutions before we did *it* again. And it, once again, was incredible. I was exhausted so I decided not to count ceiling fan turns anymore. I didn't want to challenge her. She might want to do *it* again, and I was in no way ready for that. To my surprise, she was fast asleep, which for some reason made me proud. I knew I must have hit it right. Otherwise, she'd have been bugging me for more.

I was always intrigued with the fact that women were always capable of going again. A guy could work his butt off and think he really gave it to her, and she's like, "Is that it? I want more." Meanwhile, he's half asleep from working so hard, and she's all over him in a mad attempt to make him "get it back up." I know guys who said they did it five or six times a night. Amazingly, I didn't know any women who'd actually slept with a guy five or six times in one night. Kelly once told me if she could get a guy to go even twice in a night, it was like striking gold. I was pretty much a "one time and out" partner, so I was surprised when Troi got me back in the groove. As I considered it, I realized a 6 would easily bring out the best in a guy. Troi had absolutely brought out my best. Only she did it twice!

My mom once told me that the "higher mental capacity" of women made them more suitable to endure the rigors of *second time sex.* "Men constantly think about sex until they get it," she told me. "And after they finish, they suffer a mental lapse, which makes them *think* they can't get another erection," she continued. "Those mental lapses have ruined more relationships than you care to know about," she said laughing. "Women don't waste a lot of time thinking about sex," she said. "But when it happens, and if it's any good at all, they make a mental adjustment that allows them to continue, while the man lies there *pretending* that he can't go again."

I laughed as I considered what she was saying.

"Women get just as tired as men," she said. "And, they can go again at the drop of a hat—if I'm wrong," she concluded, "prove it to me!"

I was dumfounded. I wanted to tell her women didn't have to get it back up. But I realized it wouldn't be too cool to say that to my mom.

I carefully slid out of Troi's arms, and tiptoed to dig my socks out of the trash can. I figured she wouldn't have tossed them had she realized they cost five bucks. I tucked them inside my shoes, and walked around the bed. I made sure she was still asleep before I ducked into the bathroom. I flipped on the light switch and stared at myself in the mirror. A smile as wide as Luther Vandross was in the '80s came over my face as I thought about what we'd just done. Even though I worked out, I didn't usually like how I looked in the mirror. But over the years, I'd noticed I looked pumped after sex. I gave myself a thorough gaze and realized why she was asleep as I watched my biceps appear to pop out of my arms. I went through a series of muscle-man poses and stood as if I were on center stage at a body-building contest. I paused as if I heard the announcer saying, *"And the new Mr. Universe is Shawn Wayne,"* when in the mirror I noticed Troi standing in the doorway. She was laughing with her hand over her mouth.

"Shawn!" she exclaimed. "Do you always do this?"

"Do I always do what?" I asked alarmed.

"Do you leave a woman you just slept with so you can pose in the mirror?" she asked while walking toward me. Before I could respond, she wrapped her arms around my waist and gently placed her head on my chest. "You were great. It's just what I needed," she said.

I didn't know whether she *needed* the hug or the sex, although I wondered why she needed either. All I knew was that it didn't matter. As long as she needed anything and I was there to provide it, it was cool with me.

She led me out of the bathroom and laid down on the bed. She then turned on that magnificent Sony television. "Anything you want to watch?" she asked.

"Yeah," I responded hoping that I could still catch *SportsCenter.* "Could you find ESPN?"

SportsCenter is the sports nut's version of the evening network news. And for one wonderful hour, ESPN, the definitive cable sports network, ensures its loyal viewers are in touch with the only news that really counts for dedicated sports fans like myself. Scores updated to the minute. Highlights galore. Plays of the Week. Locker room outbursts. Stuart Scott, Keith Oberman, Dan Patrick, and Chris Berman anchoring the broadcasts with nonstop laughs. They do it all, and they do it well. I love watching ESPN, and rarely miss SportsCenter, which airs at least six times a day. I often wonder what people did in the old days, before cable TV and descrambler boxes were invented, rescuing us from the "Punt, Pass and Kick" competition for little kids that used to run on ABC's *Wide World of Sports.*

While she channel surfed with the remote, I washed up.

I put my underwear and socks back on, and started to dress.

"What are you doing?" she asked in a surprised tone.

"Whadda you mean?"

"Why are you getting dressed?" she continued. "I know you don't think you're just going to hit it and run."

I smiled. I didn't know women said "hit it" too. What did she think I was going to do? It was 1:38 a.m. and I had to work in the morning. I was usually in the bed by 9:30 on week nights, so it was already well past my regular bedtime. She was at a conference and probably wasn't on anybody's schedule. I knew my boss didn't want to hear I wasn't on time because I finally got some, and that I had to stay up late to get it. We'd already done it twice. What did she expect?

"Shawn," she told me slowly. "Tonight was perfect."

"I thought so too," I said.

"No," she continued. "It was really perfect."

I wondered if she expected me to say that too.

"I told you earlier that I'd never done this," she said. "And I was worried about how I'd feel about it afterward." She reached for my hand and softly said, "I figured that you'd just leave when we were done, and it was okay. I was ready for that."

I figured I was going to leave too.

"But now I don't want you to leave," she told me. She stood up and walked toward the huge sliding glass door. She then turned around, looked me straight in the eye, and said, "Stay Shawn."

I don't know if it was the way she said it (because she definitely didn't ask), or if it was her standing there with her perfect naked body, and alluring green eyes. Maybe it was the fact that the adrenaline had worn off, and that I was exhausted. Something made me say, "Okay."

She walked up to me and passionately kissed my ear, before removing my robe and whispering, "Let's really make this a perfect night."

"Yeah," I replied exhausted. "Let's get some sleep."

"That's not what I meant Shawn," she told me laughing.

"That's what I was afraid of."

She then pushed me on the bed and jumped on top of me. She loudly exclaimed, "Shawn if you don't take those socks off I'll..."

She didn't finish.

I could tell she was upset. She had me again. This time she slowly removed my socks and held them up. She edged toward the balcony and slid the glass door open. She walked outside and threw my socks into the stiff night air to the ground, some twelve stories below. "You'll never get back into this room or on his feet!" she yelled laughing.

I couldn't figure out what was crazier. Her standing outside nude at two in the morning, yelling at a pair of socks, or me being upset at the fact that those socks that she'd thrown and was yelling at, cost me $5. I never found out. She ran back inside, quickly jumped in the bed, and whispered, "Make it perfect muscle man."

We both laughed and were at it again before I knew it.

Troi and I made history that night. People's definition of history is generally limited to conventional events like tragic wars and great discoveries. In spite of what my mother had told me, until now I was convinced that having sex even twice in the same night was a physical impossibility. Troi, with her wonderful touch and dogged insistence helped me make a "great discovery" of my own. It was definitely major, but I didn't anticipate making the books anytime soon.

This time she was asleep and I knew she'd stay asleep. Sometimes a guy does it right, and he knows it. He doesn't have to ask if she liked it or if it was good, because he knows she liked it and that it was good as well. It's cool to talk about sex, when there's something to talk about, but conversation was unnecessary at times like this. I just looked at her and thought about how fate sometimes plays funny games with you. I thought about the way we met and about the fact that I'd almost left the dance because I didn't want to buy another ticket. I remembered *Seven Whole Days* was playing the first time we danced and smiled as I thought about us jumping to Kriss Kross' record. Everything was so special. It was like magic. She had to be my 6.

Troi asked me to make this night perfect. I felt I did. But, I wanted to wake her and thank her for making the night perfect and totally wonderful for me. Earlier today, I was just another horny guy who was going to waste his time (and, of course, money), at a high-brow dance with a bunch of uninterested 2s. Now I was laid out in a jacuzzi suite with a big bad Sony Trinitron. This was indeed perfect. Well, almost perfect. She'd actually tossed my $5 socks. I quietly walked to the balcony and looked over the rail to see where they may have landed. The cold air forced me back inside. She might as well have thrown away a $5 bill.

I was happy I hadn't run into anyone from my job at the dance. I could wear my party suit to work without fear that someone had seen me. I made sure the suit was properly hung, and placed my shoes directly underneath it. I didn't want to be fumbling around looking for anything when I got dressed, especially if Troi was going to be awake. I thought about how Ron O'Neal got dressed as he left a babe stretched across the bed in the '70s smash flick, *Superfly*. He had some corny threads, but the way he got in them was perfect. It was as though every item just jumped into his hand and to the right part of his body in one slow, smooth motion. His date awoke and quietly sat near the headboard as if she was in awe of the man dressing in front of her. I could actually hear Curtis Mayfield singing, *"Who is the man, who would risk his neck for his brother man,"* when I realized how truly tired I was. *Why are you singing Shaft, when you're thinking about Superfly?* I wondered. When you are unable to properly identify your '70s super brothers, it's time to get some sleep.

I decided to check my messages. I figured no one had called, and I knew I wasn't calling anyone back, but it was a habit. I couldn't sleep without knowing my machine was cleared. I picked up the phone and walked toward the bathroom. "Damn," I said, as the phone fell to the floor (the cord was too short, and I just plain dropped it). I looked up. She hadn't budged, so it was cool. One message. *Who the hell could this be?* I wondered.

"You have a call from the county jail," said the woman who introduced the message.

"Yo, wake up cuz," said a familiar husky voice. "Shawn, it's Donnie. I'm coming home tomorrow. I beat my charge."

What charge? I wondered.

"Pick me up bro'. I should be down da main lobby 'bout 7:30."

I didn't even know Donnie was locked up again. It was 2:47 a.m and I had to be to work in about six hours. I didn't really want to pick Donnie up, but I knew my mom would make me suffer major attacks of guilt if I didn't. I could hear her saying, "Everybody needs somebody, and Donnie needs you." That may have been true, but he didn't need me or anyone else as much as he needed crack. I grew up with Donnie, and though our lives took us in different directions, we always remained tight. I was too tired to worry about dealing with him. I looked at Troi. Donnie's in the county lockup with some hairy-butt cell-mate, and I'm here with the second coming of a young Jane Kennedy. This makes no sense.

I liked being there with Troi. But I knew I wasn't the type who could function without a full eight hours of REM shut-eye. I jumped in the bed and smiled as Troi slid her head onto my chest. She wrapped her arms around me, sighed, and whispered, "This is perfect." The nightly encore of *SportsCenter* was playing. I left the TV on and watched highlights of the Cowboys trouncing the Redskins. I was out of it before I knew it, but it was totally cool because I was out of it for all of the right reasons.

9th Message

"THAT WAS A CUTE WOMAN YOU LEFT WITH LAST NIGHT."

Message sent on
October 15th at 7:22 a.m.

 I slept like a baby although I never really understood how that phrase evolved. Everyone I knew who had children had woeful tales about babies who kept them awake all night. I woke up at about 6:30 and turned over to find Troi lying motionless, with a naughty smile etched across her face. I wanted to kiss her but I thought about the "morning breath" ads I'd seen for Scope mouthwash. I was definitely brushing my teeth first. My mother once told me most people have both a bad and good side, and that many potentially good catches were lost because people unwittingly showed their bad sides too early in the game. She said natural functions weren't bad, as long as you didn't force them on others. She asked me, "How are you going to feel about a woman who passes gas in your presence?"

I thought about it and hurried to the bathroom. I knew morning breath could be pretty rotten. I didn't want Troi to wake up and want to talk, while my breath wasn't at its best.

I finished with my teeth, left the bathroom and stared at Troi lying gracefully across the bed. I then looked over at my neatly hung clothes as I sat on the edge of the bed and tuned the TV to BET. *Video Soul,* its most popular program, was on. Donnie Simpson, the cool green eyed vee-jay who also has a happening morning radio show, introduced a video by En Vogue, the wannabe model girlie group. They broke into a routine to their hit, *Never Gonna Get It,* which featured a poppin' bass line and guitar lick from James Brown's *The Big Payback.* They posed like they were at some glamorous on location photo shoot. I marveled at both their pipes and their legs.

I always liked the song because it made me move. And, although it was now 6:45 in the morning, this time was no different. I walked over to the mirrored closet doors, and felt I had to dance despite the fact that I had the rhythm of a broken kitchen blender. I reasoned that some songs just give you rhythm. This was one of them. The last time I could dance was during the '70s, when I was a teenager. I actually did a pretty mean Shaft. The Shaft worked for me because you didn't have to keep a beat to do it. It was like a Russian can-can with a soul brother's flair. The music was pumping and before I knew it, I was Shafting harder than Richard Roundtree himself.

Troi, whom I had inadvertently awakened, exclaimed "Shawn, I know you're not doing the Shaft!" I just nodded and kept at it. Within seconds, she joined me. We were clad in our robes, and down on the floor trying to out-Shaft, each other. It had to be a sight. The song abruptly ended and we both jumped up and tried to assume some appreciable level of dignity. Naturally, we just looked at each other and laughed. She then reached over, hugged me and asked if I was staying for breakfast. "Nah," I told her. I figured eggs in this joint probably cost at least two bucks. I'd already blown five bucks when she'd tossed my socks.

She dug in. "Well, what about tonight?" she whispered.

"What about it?"

"Are we getting together this evening?"

"Sure," I told her smiling.

I liked the way she put it. "Are we getting together?" As if I would say no. This is why I took an immediate liking to Troi. She didn't seem to play games (which was typical of 6s). Most of the women I'd been involved with were 2s. They spent a great deal of time manipulating situations. I had to always make the move. They would want to spend time together. They would just never come out and say it. Instead of a babe asking me out to a movie, she would call and talk about her boring day. She'd then hint she wanted to go to a flick, but didn't want to go alone. The stage was then set. I would feel like I had to suggest that we go together. I always fell for it. I'd also get stuck with the costs for the tickets, the parking, the gas, *and the popcorn.*

Troi didn't make me do that. If she wanted something, I could tell she'd just put it out there. And she'd probably spring for the popcorn too.

She slipped into the bathroom (and thankfully, brushed her teeth). I got dressed and once again fretted over my socks which she'd thrown over the balcony. Even though *Superfly* had prepared me, I realized I wasn't ready to get dressed in front of her, so I rushed to finish before she came back out.

She opened the door, sat on the edge of the bed and casually stated, "I've got a busy day ahead of me."

"Yeah, I do too," I said, knowing I had absolutely nothing of substance awaiting me.

She walked toward the balcony, drew back the drapes and told me last night was as beautiful as the sun now rising over the Washington Monument. The sky was captivating. It was as clear and as blue as a University of North Carolina warm-up suit. "I really look forward to this evening," she told me before walking over and pretending to straighten out my tie. She said nothing else and laid a kiss on me that made my heart jump like microwave popcorn. Right before we pulled apart, something shot through me. I understood how Ben Franklin felt when the key in his hand and the thunderstorm that followed gave birth to the phrase, "Go fly a kite."

Something happened for both of us during that kiss. The worst feeling you can have is when you feel something the other person doesn't. If you were hearing bells and the other person was hearing buzzers, there was bound to be trouble. It felt like we bonded because we looked at each other as if we both heard bells. We hugged as hard and as tight as passengers stuck on a Metrorail subway train during rush hour. The captivating scent of her perfume, which I recognized as White Linen, danced through my nostrils and I was happy she'd brushed her teeth before we kissed.

"Look babe," I confidently stated, "I've got to move out." I wrote my phone numbers (all of them!) on the GHH monogrammed stationery and told her to call me later. She said she would and asked me what time I was coming back through. I thought about Kelly. "I'll check and let you know," I said.

She walked me to the door and playfully kissed me on the check. "See you later doll," she whispered. My Timex told me it was 7:14. I had about fifteen minutes to get to Prince George's County to pick Donnie up from the jail.

My walk to the elevator was one of triumph. Much like that of Reverend Ike when he made his way to the pulpit on Sunday nights. He walked proud and strong because he knew that within minutes, he would inspire people all over the globe to dish out big bucks for a prayer cloth or a lucky coin. By his personal accounts of wealth and fame, I knew Ike was actually the lucky one, and like him, I was lucky for spending a wondrous evening with Troi.

I saw a tall guy wearing a Nike jogging suit and some cool shades walking toward me. The elevator finally made it to the twelfth floor. "Would you hold that for me brother?" he asked as I stepped in. I didn't feel like waiting, so I just stood there and hoped the doors would close before he arrived. Unfortunately, he stepped in just as the doors were closing.

"Thank you, brother," he said as he reached to shake my hand.

"No problem," I replied, wondering why he insisted on calling me his brother. I knew that I'd seen this "brother" somewhere before. After just a second, I realized he was that Jesse Jackson guy whom I'd seen on *SportsCenter* one night. He was the first preacher I'd seen who actually had the juice to get a mention on *SportsCenter.*

"Are you here for the conference friend?" he asked.

"Not really," I told him. "I don't put much stock in politics. All of those political guys and all of the guys who've appointed themselves leaders have an angle. They're all crooked," I said. "Think about it," I added. "Who told them they could lead anyway? I know I didn't."

"Well, brother," he started. "Leaders don't have to be elected, but they are selected."

I wondered what was up with the rhyme.

"If you don't like the leaders and you can't stand the strife," he smoothly continued, "get involved in the system, make a change in your life."

"Why would I want to waste my time like that?" I asked.

"Because," he replied in a serious tone. "You are somebody."

"Thanks," I said smiling. "You are somebody too. I'm glad we're both somebody. But I'm really here for the chicks." The elevator stopped at the tenth floor. We picked up another "brother" who'd been hit with an extreme case of male-pattern baldness.

We looked each other over, like guys always do when they're stuck in elevators together. The bald headed guy commented on the women at the dance. "I had a field day," he said, laughing. Jesse Jackson laughed and looked toward me. I had to say something. I wasn't about to look like a loser in front of someone like him who had been on *SportsCenter.* I smiled and said, "I met the baddest honey in the camp last night. She's from Chicago, so I've only got a week to get my thing off."

As soon as I said it, I wondered just what "my thing" was.

"We rolled-out all night," I bragged. "I don't see why Michael Jordan got married if they've got babes like her on the prowl in the Windy City."

"Well brother, you know I'm from Chicago," said Reverend Jackson."I might know your friend."

The bald guy said, "I'm sure his friend knows you."

I wondered what that was supposed to mean.

"Her name is Troi, and she works at some PR firm," I told them.

"Troi from Myers and Stevenson?" asked Reverend Jackson.

"Yeah, that's her," I replied.

"She's a beautiful sister," he said, "I think we're having lunch this afternoon."

I instantly knew what cardiac arrest felt like. I couldn't believe she had a date with him. I couldn't compete with a guy who had been on *SportsCenter.*

"She's trying to sell me on a political marketing piece," he said.

I instantly felt better. The blood flow returned to my system, and we stopped at the fourth floor. The bald guy stepped off the elevator. He blocked the door with his arm, and said, "Give me a call later. We're playing spades this afternoon."

The doors opened again at the second floor. Another guy walked on and hugged Jesse Jackson. "What's up Rev?" he asked. They chatted and laughed about a morning meeting they were having with some other guy named Bill. We arrived at the first floor and were immediately ambushed by a group of TV-camera toting reporters. As we stepped out, Reverend Jackson nodded and slapped me a high-five. The other guy gave me a '60s style black power fist. Everyone was yelling, "Reverend Jackson, Reverend Jackson!" He stopped to talk, and smoothly removed his shades as they focused their cameras toward his face.

My heart started pounding like a boyfriend's fist banging on a motel door when he suspects he's caught his lady with another man. I couldn't believe it. I'd actually been in an elevator with a real celebrity. Jesse Jackson had to be big-time. He's been on *SportsCenter.*

I jogged up G Street, and over to 11th to see if I could find my socks. I searched behind some cleverly manicured hedges and beside a car that was double-parked on 12th, across from the Metro Center subway station. I looked down at my Timex. It was already 7:28. I literally couldn't believe it. Five bucks down the drain.

I jumped in my ride and turned on the radio which was tuned to WOL. I'd been listening to their sports-talk program last night. Cathy Hughes and her sidekick, Dick Gregory (the diet guy from the Bahamas) were on the air. I didn't listen to them often. They got too deep for me. They were cool though. They talked about sports sometimes, plus they had a "down home" way about them. I'd never been to "down home," but I knew people who were from there. Cathy and Dick reminded me of them. They didn't waste a lot of time being proper, but they made a point of being right, and of making sense.

"Thanks for calling in," said Ms. Hughes. "You make sure to tell Bill Clinton he needs to drop in and talk to the WOL family when you meet with him this morning."

"Sister Cathy, I may bring him there myself," said the man she was speaking to. *That voice sounds familiar,* I thought.

"I want the family to know they need to come to this conference and get involved," he told her. "I was just on the elevator with a young man who reminded me that our leaders may not be in touch. I invite them to come down to put us in touch," he said laughing.

I couldn't believe that the same guy who I'd been on the elevator with earlier was now on the radio. I hoped he wouldn't tell Cathy, Dick and the "WOL family" I'd made it with Troi. Hell, I hoped he wouldn't tell Troi that I made it with Troi as I recalled they were meeting for lunch.

I was too excited to worry about it. I flipped on my CD changer. Disc three, track three chimed through as I thought about Troi, and put our evening into perspective. Three was looking like a pretty solid number for me. I'd had sex an unprecedented three times in the same night. Used three condoms in heroic fashion. Spent a captivating evening with a babe who looked every good as a 3 (but who came across as a happening 6), and found that disc three, which was Pat Metheny's *Secret Story,* perfectly summed up our evening (even if I had no idea what the title of track three was). This song was as beautiful and as soft as Troi was during our first dance. It spoke to me like it never had before. Kelly gave me the CD and said I needed to "get with" jazz as an art form. It was okay, but it was too complicated for my taste. I could tell though, that whoever wrote disc three, track three was thinking about someone like Troi when he wrote it. *I bet his babe had an ankle bracelet too,* I thought smiling. I pulled onto the Pennsylvania Avenue ramp, which took me into Southeast Washington. The early morning traffic jam was typical D.C. Cars. Guys hawking the early editions of the *Post* and the *Times.* And, of course, more cars.

I hit the repeat button and listened to the tune again. I had to find the title of disc three, track three. This wonderful song told the story of our encounter. Troi was the exquisite violins that governed the melody and flowed throughout the song and I was the burgeoning guitar, waiting to be strummed. I didn't know what it was called, but from now on I would call it Troi's song. Or better yet, our song.

I thought about some of my other dates and realized just how perfect last night had been. I had to part with fifty bucks to find out Danielle was a 2, and therefore, "wasn't really looking for a relationship." I'd wasted so much money on so many bad dates, that the mere thought of it made me run through a red light at the busy intersection of Pennsylvania Avenue and Silver Hill Road in Prince George's County. It made me think. The evening with Troi cost just $2.50, and she said she'd pay me back for that. I really made out. I wondered how to bring the two-fifty up, without pissing her off, when I realized she actually owed me $7.50. I couldn't forget the five bucks for the socks.

I turned on my cell phone, and called to check my messages. "Pick up Shawn," urged the caller. "That was a cute woman you left with last night, but I know you're at home,"

Not this time, I thought smiling.

"Look Shawn, if she crushed you and you don't want to pick up, that's okay, but it's me. You can pick up," said the caller. "Fine," it went on. "Just call me when you're feeling up to it—I hope you're alright."

"How sweet," I said as I pulled into the parking lot at the jail. It was Kelly. I could just see her hands flying all over the place while she left that message. But I knew her sudden concern for my well-being was actually hidden beneath a plea for a ride to work. *I'll zoom by there after I drop Donnie off,* I thought.

She'll go into shock when I tell her about last night.

10th Message

 It was nearly 8:00 when I spotted Donnie walking across the parking lot. He had a huge green duffle bag thrown over his bulging shoulders. A pair of ultra-thin navy blue prison-issue deck shoes was all that separated him from the rough black pavement beneath his feet. His eyes were glazed. His dreads were ragged. He looked worn out. It was one of the few times it was clear that prison life had taken a toll on him. I could tell he hadn't seen me, so I blew the horn. In typical Donnie fashion, he dropped the bag, and sprinted over to my ride like a long lost lover running across a field of daisies in a bad musical.

"My nigga!" he yelled as his toothpick rolled around his mouth.

I've gone from being one man's brother to being another man's nigga that fast, I thought. *Life sucks.* We hugged, which is something I didn't feel totally comfortable doing with men, and he asked, "Where the hell you been man?"

"Whadda you mean, where I been?"

"Don't fake with me nigga, where's your black ass been?"

"I don't know what you're gettin' at," I told him, "but I know where I ain't been." "Jail!" we both yelled, laughing.

We'd been through this routine at least seven times over the past three years. Donnie was a junkie, but he seemed happy with it. At least until he ran out of cash to feed his appetite for crack cocaine.

Donnie and I grew up together, played pee-wee football together and discovered girls together. We double-dated with twin sisters, and played high school football and basketball together. The only thing we didn't do together was get high. I hated the fact that my best buddy was strung out on drugs and was totally shocked when I found he was into crack. He didn't fit the profile. He kept a job and never lost too much weight. He just didn't look like a crack head. Donnie always maintained a near perfect bodybuilder physique. He was never into the violence and shooting that crack addicts seem to be into. Donnie tried to get me into drugs, but I knew they weren't for me. There were lots of reasons I never got high (including the fact that drugs are illegal and just plain no good for anybody). The main reason though, was that I thought drugs were too expensive.

I almost got killed at our neighborhood basketball court when we were sixteen. Donnie convinced me to invest in some nickel bags of weed. It was pitch black out. He told me to keep the money in my pocket until the deal was made. "I'll do the talking," he said. "You just bring the dough and have it ready." This big guy cussed him out for even bringing me around.

"This twerp looks hot," he told Donnie. "How do I know he ain't no narc?" he asked, referring to the teenage drug agents who were working across the country.

"He's cool," Donnie said.

"Yeah, I'm cool," I told him as I imagined getting so high that I'd float out of my beat-up Pro Keds sneakers.

"You sure you want five bags?" he asked Donnie.

"Yeah," he answered. "We want five nickels."

"Little man's got the cash?" asked the big guy.

"I got it bleed," I replied, realizing I meant to say blood.

"You lucky you'ze a regular," he told Donnie.

He directed Donnie to a hollowed-out tree stump and told him to take five bags. Donnie jogged to the tree and reached in. He held the bags high atop his head.

"That nigga's wild," the big guy said laughing. He then turned to me and snapped, "Where's the cheese?"

"I didn't know you smoked it with cheese," I foolishly answered.

He stood over me laughing and angrily yelled, "Where's the money, nigga?"

I was so afraid, I thought I'd need a jumbo box of Pampers.

I tried to relax. I'd brought a quarter to buy the five nickel bags. I must have looked like a turtle with his head tucked in as I raised my shoulders while extending my arm to pay him. He turned to look at Donnie (who had taken off into the woods). He then grabbed me and forcefully dragged me to the tree. "What the fuck is this?" he yelled, as he searched through the trunk. "That nigga took me for bad," he exclaimed. "He took ten bags!"

"It must have been a mistake," I nervously told him. "But it's cool, I'll cover it." I reached into my pocket and gave him another quarter.

"Nigga are you sick?" he yelled as he stared at the quarter.

"Nah, bleed," I replied, knowing I again should have said blood. "I feel fine."

Something was definitely wrong. I figured I shouldn't stay around to find out what it was.

"I'll kill your young black ass!" he yelled as I took off.

All those years of extra laps for screwing up at practice paid off as he chased me around the court.

"Slow down!" he yelled panting. "I can't kill you if you don't slow down!" I saw an opening and headed up a hill, and away from the court. I never looked back. I knew he wasn't going to catch me. A thoroughbred at the Kentucky Derby wouldn't have caught me that night. I ran home, slammed the door behind me, and closed every window in the house.

Donnie called the next morning. He wanted me to come and get a hit off "our stash." I told him I was through with drugs (without ever starting) and reminded him he owed me fifty cents for financing the deal.

"What you mean fifty cents?" he asked coughing.

"I gave him two quarters for ten nickel bags," I told him. "That comes out to fifty cents."

"A nickel bag costs five bucks Shawn!" he yelled. "He'll kill us!"

"He told me that," I said. "Donnie," I cautiously asked, "does this mean you owe me $50?"

He hung up before I could say anything else. I didn't hear from him for two weeks. It was the first time I didn't hear from him on a daily basis. It wouldn't be the last. To this day, I know if I don't hear from him, he's either binging on crack, or he's in jail. It always works out that way.

He threw his duffle bag into my ride. The sight of the jail in my rear view mirror was a sobering reminder of the toll drugs had taken on Donnie's life. We pulled onto White House Road and headed toward the sleepy little town we called home, Bladensburg. Donnie had taken so many trips to the county jail that the unlit tree-lined winding roads that dominated the ride now seemed serene. The roads were always dark because the trees blocked the sunshine. I can't recall ever seeing a jogger or anyone walking their dog on our rides from the jail. It was pretty screwed up. But I guess it was a decent spot to keep people locked up. My mind was on Troi. I couldn't imagine where Donnie's mind was. But I figured he was already working on his next high.

"So where you been cuz?" he asked.

"C'mon man, we've already done that bit," I replied.

"Serious up money," he continued. "Where you been?"

"I been home."

"Nigga, I know you ain't been home, cause I just saw your tight ass cheesin' on TV." I wondered what he was talking about.

"You been swinging with Jesse?" he asked.

I figured he must have meant Reverend Jackson. But I was surprised. I didn't know they had *SportsCenter* in jail.

"Yeah," I told him smiling. "Jesse's my man."

"My nigga," he said grinning. "I knew you was gonna hit it big one day."

"Hit it big," I said. "I hit it big last night."

"With Jesse?"

"Hell no," I fired back. "I made it with a honey I met at a dance last night."

"Let me get this straight," he interrupted. "You, Shawn, made it with a honey that you met at a dance last night?"

"Yeah."

"Was the dance free?"

"No."

"Was people dancing?"

"Yeah."

"Then why was you there?" he asked laughing.

"Cause you wasn't available," I shot back.

We laughed and high-fived as we pulled into his mom's driveway. I asked him if he was okay. He just nodded and toyed with his toothpick. He told me he was tired of jail. This was going to be his last time. He wanted a new start. Of course, this is the exact same thing he said the last seven times I'd picked him up from jail. I didn't bother pressing him about it. I didn't know whether he'd ever stop doing crack. I only knew that I wanted him to stop. All in all, Donnie was a decent guy. Like everyone else, he has his problems. But he's a good friend. When he isn't locked up or totally strung out, he's a lovable, funny, and brutally honest dude. His mother came to the door and yelled for him to come inside. He jumped out and told me to call him later.

"Be easy," I said.

He smiled and replied, "Peace out cuz."

Donnie had me worried. When he was in jail, I never worried. I knew where he was and figured he couldn't do too much damage behind bars. But at thirty-one, he was getting too old for jail. He needed to straighten up and get his act together. I knew I needed to get my act straight too. I had to pick up Kelly, and was nearly out of gas. I searched for an Amoco, but drove right past it. They actually thought they could get away with a $1.02 a gallon for self-serve regular. I'd walk first. That was outrageous. I found an old no-name station and pulled in. They had decent prices. I could deal with ninety-five cents a gallon even if I had to pump it. After filling up, I called Kelly and told her if she wasn't outside in five minutes, she'd be left. She only lived about ten minutes from Bladensburg, but I always told her to be ready in five. Kelly had a thing about time. She didn't like it. At least she didn't like being on time. She had to make an entrance everywhere. And she couldn't make an entrance if she arrived before everyone else.

To my surprise, Kelly was outside when I pulled up. I'd left her several times over the years, so she knew to be ready.

"What's up T?" I said as she opened the door to get in.

"What's up with you?" she asked. I was smiling like a husband whose wife had left him without knowing he'd just hit the lottery. "What *is* up with you?" she said looking toward me.

"Tell me," I said proudly.

"Tell you what?" she asked impatiently.

"Tell me I'm the man," I said.

"What man did you become?" she replied, bursting my bubble.

"You know that cute woman you saw me leave with?"

"Yeah."

"I did her."

"You did what to her?" she nervously asked.

"I hit it," I proudly replied.

"You hit it?" she angrily exclaimed. "That is so typical Shawn."

"What's that supposed to mean?" I asked.

"You get lucky enough to find a woman who is willing to spend an evening with you," she said exasperated, "and you have to come out to announce the details." She then rolled the window down and flatly stated, "I don't want to hear about it."

We pulled into the traffic on New York Avenue. She looked at me and asked, "What's the hold up?"

"What do you mean now?" I asked puzzled.

"When are you going to tell me what happened?" she said laughing.

I thought about my mom. She once told me the basic difference between men and women was that men treated sex like a commodity. "Men make money, and they spend it in ways that make others take notice," she told me. "They need the biggest car and the fanciest house," she continued. "The money defines them, and they want everyone to know it."

I wondered where she came up with this stuff.

"They do the same thing with sex," she said. "If they get it they have to tell, because like money, it defines them. They think that somehow they're more masculine," she told me. "Real men don't kiss and tell."

I hadn't been with a woman in nearly a year. I was definitely telling.

Traffic actually turned out to be pretty good. We were at work before I could give her all the details.

"I don't know what you did," Kelly said, "but I know you did something."

"How do you know that?"

"Because she marked you."

"Whadda you mean she marked me?"

"Lipstick, Shawn. She made sure you left with lipstick on your collar."

I wondered why she would do that.

"She wanted everyone who saw you to know that you were with someone," she said. "So she left her mark on you."

If that were true, it was cool with me.

"It's like a territory thing," she added.

Territory, I thought to myself smiling. *She could mark me anytime.*

We parked and headed for the elevator. Kelly laughed and

said, "The strangest thing happened this morning."

"What's that?" I asked.

"Well, I was ironing my blouse and I turned on Fox Morning News."

"You mean channel five?"

"Of course I mean channel five," she said. "So anyway, Lark McCarthy is talking to Jesse Jackson, and I see this guy who looks sort of like you standing right beside Jesse."

"Sort of like me?" I asked concerned. "What does sort of like me look like?"

"Well," she started. "He had that same 'I'm lost' look you have, but he was much cuter than you."

"Cuter than me?"

"Definitely," she added. "That's how I knew it wasn't you. Besides, I knew there was no way you'd be hanging with Jesse."

"What's that supposed to mean?"

"Shawn, you barely read the paper, and the only things you watch on TV are *Def Comedy Jam,* and *SportsCenter."*

"So?"

"So if someone isn't fortunate enough to get air time on those small minded, socially irrelevant programs, you don't know them."

"What are you saying, Kelly?" I asked concerned.

"I'm saying this," she said as the elevator opened and we stepped into the hallway of our tenth-floor offices. "Jesse Jackson is one of the top African-American leaders on the planet," she added before pausing. "And had he just been on that elevator with us, you wouldn't even recognize him."

She knows me too well, I thought, ashamed.

It was nearly 9:00 and I was feeling pretty good. I was seeing Troi this evening. Donnie was back home (again), and Kelly all but told me I was cute (even though she didn't realize it). As I walked into my office, I noticed a yellow Post-It note in the middle of my desk. It read: Call Troi — Very Important. A quick check of my machine at home confirmed she had called there as well. "Shawn," it started, "we

have to talk. Call me when you get this message."
We have to talk. The four dreaded words.

My mom once told me if a woman wants to see a man squirm, she needs only say, "We have to talk."

"They'd rather hear 'I'm pregnant,' or 'I caught you,' as opposed to hearing, 'We have to talk,'" she told me.

"Why's that?" I asked.

"Because," she continued. "If she says she's pregnant or she's caught him, he knows exactly what the issue is and can then concentrate on just one response."

"And?"

"Well, if she throws 'we have to talk' at him, he doesn't know what she wants, or what he did, or exactly what she knows about what he did," she added.

"I get it," I told her. "If the guy knows what's up from the jump, he can stall and work on one good lie," I said. "But if she keeps it vague, he's guessing about everything and doesn't know exactly what to lie about," I confidently stated.

"That's close," she said laughing. "But's it's really about control."

Control? I wondered.

"A woman has more control if she keeps a man guessing. She knows he'll wonder about everything and may actually tip her off to something else in order to avoid her real issue," she concluded.

All of this over four little words? I wondered what Troi wanted to talk about anyway. I thought of everything. She couldn't be pregnant. We used protection each time. She couldn't have run into my wife or girlfriend. I had neither of those. It hit me. Jesse Jackson probably called her and ratted me out. I knew it would be hard to refute anything that a preacher said, but I had to have a response. The old "it wasn't me line" wouldn't work because this isn't a movie. I paused to think. I could tell her that since he was a reverend, I was confessing. She wouldn't buy that either. I thought about telling her the truth, which was that I was both excited and happy. I just wanted someone to feel as good as I did. *She'll really like that one,* I sarcastically thought. I wasn't trying to put her business out in the open, but I figured it would look that way to her. I'd listened to men talk about what they'd done with women for years. This was the first time I'd ever bragged to people I didn't know. Ironically, it was the first time I actually had something to brag about. I knew I had to call. I was ready to face the music even if it meant my big mouth was going to make her cut me off.

I closed the door to my office, slowly sat down at my desk and hung my head as I dialed the number. I felt like Ben Johnson. He won the one hundred-meter dash at the '88 Olympics. He stood high atop the medal stand and wore the gold medal home. He probably went into shock when he got his dreaded call. I bet it was some woman who started with, "Ben, we have to talk." Ben had to forfeit his medal. He had tested positive for steroids. He, like I, knew he was guilty the moment he got the call. He tried to lie too. But when you're caught, you're caught. To me, the elevator was my medal stand and for five minutes, I felt like I'd won the gold. Like Ben, I'd experienced the pride and happiness that comes with it. I couldn't believe I was about to lose Troi, just like Ben lost his medal. Worse yet, I couldn't accept the fact that a "brother" sold me out to a woman.

She answered the phone and ripped into me.

"Shawn, was that you on the elevator with Jesse this morning?"

"There was a couple of guys on there," I said, as I wondered just what lie would work.

"I'm not talking about them Shawn, because I saw you," she said excitedly.

"Maybe it was somebody else."

"Shawn I know exactly what you were wearing, and I saw you wearing it on NewsChannel 8 this morning," she exclaimed.

"NewsChannel 8?" I asked, as I recalled that Kelly had seen me on Channel 5.

"Yes," she told me. "I even saw the lipstick I left on your

collar," she said laughing. "Look Troi," I pleaded. "I don't know what he told you, but I didn't say it like that."

"Like what?" she asked surprised.

"Like he said I said it," I nervously responded.

"Like who said you said what?"

I was confused. This was about control, just like my mother explained. Troi was baiting me to get a full-blown confession and I was ready to give it to her.

"I'm sorry Troi, I apologize, I was wrong, let me make it up to you," I begged in rapid succession.

"What are you talking about Shawn?"

"Well, you said we have to talk," I anxiously stated.

"Yeah," she interrupted. "I want to talk about this evening."

"This evening?" I asked relieved.

"Yes, Shawn," she told me. "There's a major black-tie dinner this evening."

"Black-tie?" I asked.

"Yes," she said, "It's black-tie and I absolutely cannot miss it."

"So what's the problem?"

"The problem is that I can't get a ticket."

"Why not?"

"Because the tickets were sold out months ago and even when they had tickets they were a thousand dollars."

"A thousand bucks?" I asked, surprised. "Who would pay a grand for some food?"

"I would," she answered. "If I don't make the dinner my trip is ruined."

"It's that important?"

"Shawn," she said, sighing. "This dinner means everything to me. I'd pay to wash the dishes if it meant I could get inside."

That was deep. As nice as she was, Troi didn't strike me as the type who could deal with dish-pan hands. She must have really needed to be there. I couldn't relate. It didn't sound like my kind of event. I'd never been to a black-tie anything before. But then again, I don't even own a black tie.

"I've got to figure out a way to get to that dinner," she said, concerned. "But you've got to have some real juice to get a ticket this late."

A pet rock had more juice than I did. I hated feeling so useless. Though she hadn't come out and asked if I could get her a ticket, I felt she was challenging me. Troi made sure I knew how important the dinner was. She told me that the only person who could pull off a ticket would be someone who had it going on, which pretty much eliminated me. Still, I felt I had to do something.

"The tickets are really $1,000?" I asked, concerned.

"They're a thousand apiece."

"I think I may be able to help," I said.

"And just how do you plan on helping Shawn?"

"I think I can get you a ticket."

"*You* can get a ticket?"

"Yeah," I casually stated, "It'll be a piece of cake."

"Are you serious?" she asked, excited.

"Of course I'm serious."

"You can really get a ticket?"

"Definitely."

"Can you get two?" she asked, laughing. "I need an escort."

"I could probably pull that off."

"You can get two tickets?" she asked, surprised. "Can you get them in time to make it here by 6:30?"

"I think I could swing that."

"I don't mean to seem ungrateful Shawn," she said, "but how do you plan on getting two tickets when it's near impossible for anybody else to get one."

"I'm not just anybody," I said, smiling. "Let's just say that I'm connected."

"I'm impressed," she said, "This is the biggest black-tie event in the country. If you can get two tickets, you must be connected."

I was connected alright. Donnie could plug me into just about anything. He may have just gotten out of jail, but I knew he could raise the tickets with little effort. It may cost a few bucks, but it would be worth it. A quick call confirmed I was right. Donnie said he could get the tickets and would drop them by my office when he came in town. He told me he needed $200 to close the deal.

"I don't have two-hundred bucks," I said.

"What do you have cuz?"

"I have a twenty."

"Hold up money," he said, forcefully. "You expect me to get $2000 worth of tickets for twenty bucks?"

"Not really," I cautiously stated.

"What you mean 'not really'?"

"I really need you to get 'em for ten dollars, I have to buy a tie."

"You ain't got no tie?"

"I got plenty of ties," I said, while searching for the Posts' sports section. "But I don't have a black one."

"Why you need a black one?" he asked.

"Cause the dinner is black-tie," I told him.

"You got to come correct," he said. "If it's black-tie, I guess you do need a black-tie. I can problee get 'ya one cuz."

"I can handle that," I answered.

"You sure?" he asked.

"I got it."

"I'm 'mo holla at 'ya," he said, before hanging-up. "Peace out."

I was set. Donnie was going to hook-up the tickets, which of course, would impress Troi. I was happy he was going to let me have them for $10, because I really needed the change to get a decent tie for the dinner. As I flipped through the Sport's section, I noticed a full-page ad for Kmart. They were having a clearance sale on men's separates. Lady luck was hitting me harder than a Mike Tyson uppercut. I would get the tie there and still make it to the hotel by 6:30.

11th Message

"HELLO HANDSOME."

*Message sent on
October 15th at 2:28 p.m.*

Kelly called twice to get the 4-1-1 on last night's happenings, but we couldn't talk because someone kept buzzing through on her line. To my surprise, she marched into my office and sat down. Through the steam of her coffee, she demanded I tell her what went on. Kelly was especially sharp and she was always a little more demanding when she was really dressed. She had on a simple black dress that made a u-turn at her knees and rose to her thighs. Kelly's legs were as skinny as Manute Bol was tall so they weren't much to look at for a leg guy like me. A black silk jacket with soft satin lapels covered her shoulders. It brought out the string of pearls that hung around her neck. She of course had matching black satin pumps that had a strand of tiny white pearls lining the edges. Kelly would go barefoot before wearing shoes that didn't match her outfit. She was crazy like that. A pair of perfect diamond stud earrings dominated her tiny earlobes, and she'd polished her shapely nails to a mirror-like white glaze. She was clearly overdressed for work. But so was every other single babe in the metropolitan area. When the CBC hit town, the stakes were high. Big time guys with big time power, flaunting big time money were there for the taking. Women took their approach to bagging a guy up a notch. Kelly wasn't about to lose out because she'd been out dressed and outclassed by some other babe.

"So tell me exactly what happened," she said, between sips of her coffee.

"I don't think I can tell you," I cautiously answered.

"What do you mean you can't tell me?" she asked. "You tell me everything else."

"That's because I never have anything to tell you."

"That's unfair Shawn."

"Whadda you mean it's unfair?"

"Because," she started. "If she had dumped you, or hurt your feelings, you would have told me in a heartbeat."

That's true, I thought.

"So when you actually have a little success, you can't tell me?" She then stood up, crossed her arms, and deliberately stated, "Do you think that's fair?"

"Fair?" I slowly asked. "Is it fair that I put her business out in the street?"

Her angry expression told me I'd said the wrong thing. I was surprised she'd taken it as an insult. Kelly looked me dead in the eyes and said, "What the hell do you mean in the street?"

"I didn't actually mean in the street."

"Well that's what you *actually* said," she retorted, shaking her head with each word.

"Think about what *you* said Kelly," I responded. "If I announce the details, I'm a typical man, and if I don't I'm unfair."

"Yeah," she replied unimpressed.

"Yeah what?"

"Yeah Shawn, it's unfair, so what's your point?"

"Point?" I shot back. "I don't think I have one," I said laughing.

She sighed and said, "You're not typical if you're telling a friend." She then gently closed my door, and placed her coffee mug on my desk. "Besides," she continued laughing. "Who else would you tell?"

I'm glad she wasn't on that elevator, I thought smiling.

"Well Kelly," I cautiously started. "Let me tell you this."

"Tell me what?" she said anxiously.

"Last night was very special."

She sat back down and leaned forward. She excitedly asked, "What was so special about it? Was it romantic?"

"Very," I answered.

"Well, what did you do?" she asked smiling.

I thought about it and looked toward the ceiling (as if a magical answer would appear there). I coolly stated, "We did the Shaft."

"You did the Shaft?" she yelled, confused. "What do you mean you did the Shaft?"

"We did the Shaft," I replied smiling.

"What the hell is the Shaft?" she asked. "Is it a new position or something?" she whispered, while looking around as if someone had walked in.

"Nah," I said laughing. "It's a dance from the '70s."

She then stood, crossed her arms and asked, "You mean to tell me that you get lucky enough to spend the night with an attractive woman and all you do is a dance from the seventies?"

"I didn't say that's all we did," I responded, smiling, "but we did do that. Look Kelly. *You* sound like a typical man."

She sat back down and asked, "What's that supposed to mean?"

"You want to know what I did, but you don't even know who I did it with," I told her. "You don't care about the person, you just want the juicy details of our evening. Isn't that how *typical men* do it?," I asked smiling.

"Shawn!" she fired back. "Save that eighth-grade psychology crap for somebody else. Just tell me what happened!" she said, looking as exasperated as country music legend

Johnny Cash would had he been thrown on stage at a Snoop Doggy Dog concert.

I could hear my mom feeding me that "men treating sex like a commodity" line, but Kelly was my friend, plus she was a woman. I figured it had to be okay to tell her.

"Okay Kelly," I slowly stated. "First we went to her suite."

She again smiled and leaned forward. Before I could say another word, the phone rang. "Don't answer it," she said. "Just keep going."

"Whadda you mean don't answer it?" I replied. "It may be her." I picked up the receiver and put on my best "official" voice. "This is Shawn Wayne," I robustly stated.

It was our office manager. She told me we had an 11:30 meeting. "Could you tell Kelly?" she asked sarcastically. "I can't find her, so I figure she's lost herself in your office." "No problem," I replied laughing. It was 11:25. We left. As we made our way to the conference room, I told her we'd talk at lunch.

"But I have a lunch date," she told me.

I smiled and said, "That's your loss."

Our boss was pretty liberal with leave when the CBC's annual conference was in town. I knew this year would be no different. He usually gathered us and gave us a "pep talk" about why we should support CBC. He believed it looked good for the company to have a "presence" at their events. Kelly always went, but she went for the hook-ups. She cared only about the connections she could make and the men she could meet. The "cause" and our company presence were secondary. I imagine those reasons probably got in the way.

Mr. Butler slowly walked in and quickly started the meeting. He was a pretty cool boss. He always made sure you knew where you stood in both his mind, and in the corporate structure. He was an old, bald, fat geezer, but he had a heart of solid gold. He was a constant reminder of how truly boring my life had become. I was reminded of my plight when I saw him and a beautiful woman dining at the

American Cafe in The Shops one evening. It was about three weeks ago. I liked the American Cafe. They had a tasty cream of chicken soup, even though it costs $2.75 a bowl. My date and I were sharing a soup and sandwich combo (she ate the sandwich, and I had the soup) when I noticed old man Butler sitting near the F Street window of the restaurant. We didn't get to interact much at the office, so I thought I'd actually score a few points by saying hello.

As I walked over to his table I thought of what I should say. I couldn't think of anything clever. I looked up and wondered why he and his date looked over at me and started laughing. "You must have had quite a meal," Mr. Butler said.

"Why do you say that sir?" I asked.

"Because you have that huge napkin tucked under your collar," he said, laughing.

I was embarrassed as I jerked the napkin from my collar. The top of my navy blue clip-on necktie fell to the side of my shirt. They both laughed, and Mr. Butler asked, "Don't I pay you well enough to buy real ties Wayne?"

"Not really, sir," I answered. "You don't pay me well at all."

He looked as embarrassed as I felt. He grunted, "Is there something I can help you with Wayne?"

It usually took a lot to get old man Butler riled up, but I'd done it. I couldn't help but wonder what parking lot rates were like near the unemployment office.

"I don't need any help sir," I told him. "I just dropped by to pay my respects to you and your lovely madam." I figured I'd work the wife angle. If I could look cool to her, I'd definitely look cool to him. I wasn't a breast man, but her abundant cleavage did wonders for the skimpy red minidress she was wearing. Butler's babe was fine and although it shouldn't have bothered me, I was envious that an old fart like him was married to such a fox.

I thought about my mother. She once told me that most successful men have a woman who deserves considerable credit for their success. "Many of these so-called successful businessmen have had to rely on their mates to be resourceful, supportive, and patient while they struggled," she told me. "Many women sacrificed education and their own careers to follow the dreams of their mates," she continued. "If it didn't work out, the woman often had to pick up the pieces and hold the family together," she added.

I looked at her and asked, "And what if it worked out?"

"If it did work out," she solemnly stated, "the man usually left." She sternly warned me to never do that and I promised I wouldn't.

I figured Mrs. Butler probably paid the price to get the old man to the top. "Mr. Butler always tells us we wouldn't even have jobs if it weren't for you," I said.

She reached across the table and held his hands. She smiled and whispered, "That's so sweet."

I knew I had her going. I winked at Mr. Butler, but he just shook his head and waved me off.

"Mrs. Butler," I casually stated. "The boss has always told us how lovely his wife was, but I had no idea you'd be this beautiful."

"Neither did I!" she screamed before suddenly bursting out in tears.

I handed her my napkin and asked, "Was it something I said?"

"No!" she yelled weeping. "It's something he didn't say!"

I figured he didn't tell her she was beautiful too often.

"You didn't tell me you were married!" she yelled while standing up.

He then stood up and yelled back, "You didn't ask!"

That sounds familiar, I thought as I recalled Jasmine using that exact same line on me. I knew I'd really screwed up. I edged away from the table and ducked my head. "I'm sorry you're not Mrs. Butler," I said.

She cried even louder and ran off yelling, "So am I!"

Mr. Butler looked at me like I'd squandered his last dollar on a duck running in a high stakes horse race. I forced a weak closed-mouth smile, waved, and said, "See you in the morning, sir."

You hope you see him in the morning, I thought as I hurried back to my table.

It made me think about what my mom had told me about power and influence. Butler's bankroll probably made him look like Billy Dee Williams.

I picked up my date and walked her to the bus stop where I gave her a dollar bill for a token and a transfer. I explained to her that if she got off at Union Station, she'd be only six blocks north of her condo.

She looked at me like one of us was crazy, and asked, "Is that it?"

"Not really," I casually replied. "The token was only seventy-five cents, but you can give me the quarter later." I bent over, gave her a quick peck on the cheek, and asked her if she enjoyed her sandwich.

She rolled her eyes like a pair of cocked dice. She stepped back and asked, "Are you sick?"

"Nah," I replied smiling. "I feel fine."

I was glad Mr. Butler had called the meeting. I'd finally attended a CBC event and felt I would at least be familiar with what he was talking about. I wasn't so sure he wanted his staff to go there to get laid, but if he saw Troi, he'd have been proud. He asked if anyone had been to last night's events. I eagerly raised my hand like a second-grader who knew that George Washington was the first president.

"I knew that was you," he said loudly.

"You knew who was me?" I replied puzzled.

"I was having an apple biscuit this morning," he started, "and I saw you and Jesse Jackson being interviewed on CNN."

Everybody congratulated me, and then gave me a truly undeserved round of applause.

"Did you mention the company to CNN, son?" he asked.

"No sir, not really."

"Did you talk about us to Reverend Jackson?"

"No sir," I nervously replied.

"Well what, pray tell, did you talk about son?" he asked.

"We talked about last night."

"Last night?" he asked. "What happened last night?"

"I met a nice woman at the dance."

Kelly kicked my ankle underneath the table, and I let out a big, "Oww!" I looked at her, but she just shook her head no and stared down at her notepad.

"You told *him* you met a nice woman?" Mr. Butler asked.

"Sort of," I cautiously stated. "He knew her from Chicago and wanted to know how she was doing."

Butler just shook his head and asked if anyone else made it to last night's affair. Kelly and a few others responded. He gave us the usual, "If you don't support yourself, no one else will support you" dribble. He then stood up and informed us he'd be at a big CBC dinner this evening. "We're shutting down at two this afternoon," he told us. "I expect to see everyone at a CBC event tonight."

Butler was right on time. I could hit Kmart after lunch and catch some shut eye before the dinner.

It was two before I knew it. Donnie had left the tickets with our receptionist and I hurried to Kmart where I had little trouble finding a black tie. As I headed to the register, I noticed a stand of nice clip-on ties that were two for $5.00. I inspected the ties. *Why are you still holding this if it's $6.50 and these are two for $5.00,* I thought. I didn't want to waste a lot of time. I picked a snazzy red one, and a regal looking black one. *Troi's gonna love this,* I thought as I held the tie to my neck. I smiled in the mirror and knew I'd gotten over. The way I looked at it, they were charging me less money for a tie they had to tie up. Besides, I needed one of those red power ties anyway.

I headed toward the registers. To my delight, I heard a familiar line boom over the store PA system:

"Attention Kmart Shoppers."

My ears swelled. I knew my favorite light was getting ready for some action. "We have a blue light special for the next ten minutes."

Where? I anxiously wondered.

"In our men's accessory department. We have stylish polyester clip-on neckties with our special stay-fit finish and a patented chrome-plated stay-put fastener."

I proudly looked at the ties I was ready to purchase and smiled. I didn't know they had special stay-fit finish.

"With your purchase of two of these fashionable ties at a discounted $4.00 for the pair," continued the announcer, "you will receive a free tie to add to your collection."

Three clip-ons for four bucks. This had to be a mistake. I rushed over to the stand selected a nice solid gray tie and hurried to the register (before they changed their minds).

"Thank you for shopping Kmart and for making Kmart your personal one-stop shopping spot," said the announcer as I walked toward the door.

Thank you, I whispered, as I basked in triumph over my savings.

I jumped into my ride and flipped on the CD player. Disc three, track three came on again. As I listened to it, I thought about Troi and headed home. *She's got to be a 6,* I convinced myself. I wondered if I should pick up some condoms on the way, when it struck me that it didn't make sense to pay for the pleasure of wearing one of those things. If she wants them, she can buy them.

Traffic on New York Avenue was light, so I made it home before 3:00. I checked my messages and smiled as I recognized Troi's melodic voice flow through my speaker phone. "Hello, handsome," it started. "I was just wondering if you could stop by a little early."

I wondered why she wanted me to stop by early.

"I'd like to start the evening off the same way that we finished last night," she added before seductively whispering, "Call me."

That's cool, I thought as I reached for the receiver to call her back. *But we finished last night by sleeping.*

Why would she want me to come by early for that?

12th Message

"CALL ME WHEN YOU GET THIS
MESSAGE—IT'S IMPORTANT."

*Message sent on
October 15th at 5:07 p.m.*

I was so excited about seeing Troi that I couldn't sleep. I decided to check-out my outfit. I laid my clothes across the bed to make sure everything was matching. She told me we were going to a black-tie event so I knew the red tie wouldn't work, even though it went well with my light grey double-breasted suit. I picked out a soft off-white cotton shirt I'd found at Marshall's for $6.95 and placed a red felt hankie in the breast pocket. Red makes chicks hot. I had to smell decent, so I carefully sprinkled a few leftover drops of Joop cologne across the front of my outfit.

I took my shoes into the bathroom and gave them a quick polish job. I'd bought these shoes from Donnie about three years ago for $8.00. They were an authentic pair of $295 Bloomingdale's dress shoes. According to the label glued to the sole, they were "guaranteed for a lifetime of comfort." Every time Donnie saw me with them on, he would laugh and say, "Dem' shoes is gonna walk away from you if you don't give 'em a break, cuz." He didn't know I'd had them resoled twice since he sold them to me. I didn't think three years was anywhere near the "guaranteed lifetime of comfort" the shoes came with so I wasn't about to part with them.

My mom told me that women paid special attention to the shoes a man was wearing. "You may attract attention with your eyes and your smile," she said. "But a bad pair of shoes may send that attention elsewhere." It didn't make much sense to me, but she just kept going. "Nice eyes and smiles are God given. Women know you didn't earn them," she stated. "Your shoes say something about you, and about how much effort you'll put into taking care of yourself."

It'll sink in one day, I thought. I just let her go on.

"Your shoes make a statement about where you're going, and where you've been," she added. "They don't need to be expensive, but they absolutely have to be neat," she warned. "A man who would travel in bad shoes is not giving himself or his feet fair treatment," she concluded. "And a woman knows that a man who won't be fair with himself will never be fair with her."

I smiled as I polished my shoes. Moms was on target. But I knew I'd always treat Troi right. Bad shoes or not. I took a quick shower and shaved. I was dressed and out of the door before 5:00. I took my usual route into town, but it seemed slightly different this time. I saw trees and flowers I'd never really noticed. I was capturing the very real beauty of Washington through my windshield. I passed Thomas Circle and wondered what the birds talked about as they pranced around the fountain. I hung a left onto 14th Street and caught a glimpse of the incredible feats of architecture that were commonplace throughout the city. A tiny man in grey jeans and a purple sweater was selling flowers at the corner of 14th and H streets. He wanted ten bucks. That was out of the question. I'd gone this way every day for the past seven years, but I never once really noticed how captivating a ride it was. I never appreciated the simple beauty and structure of D.C. It made me think of Troi as Tom Browne's hit groove from 1980, *Jamaica Funk,* played over the radio. I was at the Grand Hyatt in no time and luckily found an open parking space on 11th and F streets in the northwest section of town.

I was about to step out of my ride, but I decided to check my messages before I went into the hotel.

"What's up money?" said the caller. "Call me as soon as you get this message. It's important."

It was Donnie, and as far as he was concerned, any time he called it was important. I called and asked for him. Surprisingly, his mother said, "Donnie's with you."

"He's not with me," I said.

"Well he's on his way to your house then," she calmly stated.

"When did he leave?"

"About 2:00," she replied.

"It's 5:30 now Mrs. Lee," I said alarmed. "Don't you think he'd be there by now?" "There?" she asked concerned. "Where are you Shawn?"

"I'm in town."

"Well, that answers it," she said laughing.

"That answers what?"

"You're not home," she said happily. "So he's probably there waiting for you."

"I guess you're right Mrs. Lee," I replied shaking my head. "I'll talk to you soon." She could give the Redskins lessons on denial. They actually believe they'll be in the playoffs with the team they have. It won't happen.

"Shawn," Donnie's mother said. "God is going to bless you."

"I sure hope he does," I said, as my thoughts switched backed to Troi. I hope she blesses me too. We hung up and I headed into the hotel lobby and up to the twelfth floor.

I wasn't as nervous as I'd been last night and was pleasantly surprised when Troi answered the door with a towel snugly wrapped around her upper body.

"Hi," I sheepishly stated.

"Would you like to come in, or should I join you in the hall?" she said smiling.

"I think I'll come in."

She ducked behind the door and reached her hand out toward mine. I grabbed it, walked in, and nearly passed out when she threw her arms over my shoulders. She kissed me like she hadn't seen me for months. Our tongues collided like two seals trying to get the last spot on Noah's ark. I dropped my garment bag to the floor, it contained my suit for work tomorrow, and she ran her hand across my back and forcefully removed my jacket. We both looked down toward my feet, and she laughed and said, "Get rid of them Shawn." "As soon as you get rid of the towel," I smoothly replied.

She seductively whispered, "No problem," and unwrapped the towel before dropping it to the floor.

I didn't understand why Troi was being so romantic. Especially since neither of us was dressed for dinner. She pushed me to the bed and jumped on top of me. It happened so fast that we didn't use a condom. I worried for an instant, but it felt so good that my concern quickly faded. I prayed she was as safe as she seemed and figured she wouldn't pop-up pregnant. That wouldn't be her style, plus it would totally ruin her body. She made me feel like a newborn steer at a rodeo. Troi said all the right things and made all the right moves (just like I knew a 6 would do). She made me feel like we'd been together for a long time. I'd dated women for months, and they never fulfilled me like Troi did. We arrived at a thunderous simultaneous climax (the kind you only read about in books or see in the movies) and looked at each other and started laughing uncontrollably.

"What's so funny?" she said laughing.

"You," I replied trying to regain my composure.

"Me?" she asked.

"Yeah," I said grinning. "You."

"What do you mean me?" she asked while propping herself up on her elbows.

"Give it to me Shawn-work me babeee," I quickly replied. "You know what I'm talking about."

She laughed and said, "And what about you?"

"What about me?" I shot back.

"Mr. This-is-how-Ken-gives-it-to-Barbie. Mr. Daddy's-bringing-home-the-bacon-so-get-out-the-pan" she responded, laughing.

"I didn't say that," I replied embarrassed.

"You most certainly did," she said before sitting up.

She told me I was fantastic and looked up at the clock. She said she wished we had time to do "it" again, and then coolly stated, "We need to get dressed." She was right. It was 6:15. The dinner started at 6:30. Our time was limited. I took a shower while she did her nails. She showered when I finished. "I'll be dressed when you're done," I said as I walked out of the bathroom.

I was dressed in minutes. I checked myself in the mirror to make sure my tie was perfectly centered between the lapels of my suit. The only time I *knew* I was sharp was when I wore my charcoal gray wool suit (the one I was wearing when I met Jasmine). But this suit, combined with my new clip-on necktie, looked great. I smiled as I walked pass the mirror, paused, and slowly leaned back to get a better look. The tie brought the whole suit out. My shoes were gleaming and my hair was brushed just right. I knew this was going to be a wonderful evening because I felt so good and because I'd gotten such a good deal on a black tie for the dinner.

I walked into the parlor of the suite, turned on the television and I tuned to channel 37 which airs ESPN in the District. As the *SportsCenter* theme played in the background, I peeped through the french doors of the parlor. I nearly lost my breath. Troi was gently brushing her hair in the mirror. She had on a beautiful black silk dress that clung tightly to her torso and swept gracefully out over the top of her thighs. The sexy black satin pumps she wore seemed a perfect fit and a gold herringbone ankle bracelet fell softly over the sides of her right shoe. She carefully applied a dash of soft crimson lipstick to her sultry lips and gingerly powered her nose. She then delicately sprayed two precise shots of Yves Saint Laurent's Paris on her wrists before placing an exquisite gold bangle over her right hand. Troi looked as stunning as she had last night. It was obvious she knew exactly how to get the best from her clothes. *We'll be the baddest couple in the house,* I thought. I'd never been to a black-tie event before and I definitely couldn't relate to someone blowing a cool grand on a dinner, but, for once, I wasn't nervous. Troi made me feel comfortable. It appeared she really enjoyed my company. She accepted me. I felt we found something in each other that we couldn't get from ourselves. We hadn't discussed it, but something good was happening between us and we both knew it. I could read her, she could read me and we connected in simple, yet meaningful ways.

I stood up and anxiously waited for her to come out. *She's gonna love this outfit,* I proudly thought as I adjusted my tie. She grabbed her tiny black purse and headed toward the parlor. Though my stomach churned as she walked through the door, I stayed cool. I spread my arms wide open (to greet her), like Nat King Cole did when he was singing the last verse of *The Christmas Song.*

She opened the door and looked at me. She surprisingly yelled, "Shawn, it's 6:30! When are you getting dressed?"

This didn't make sense to me.

"Whadda you mean, when am I getting dressed?" I asked puzzled. "I am dressed." "Oh, no you're not," she dryly stated, standing back with her arms crossed.

"You're not making sense Troi," I replied.

"No mister man," she angrily responded. "You're the one who's not making sense." It appeared that we were at an impasse and I wondered if we were having our first argument.

She sat down and looked toward the floor. She then smiled and slowly said, "Okay Shawn, you got me, the game is over."

I wondered what game she was talking about.

She looked up at me and calmly stated, "You had me going for a second."

"Whadda you mean?"

"You actually had me believing that you were prepared to leave with what you had on."

What's she talking about? I wondered.

"You look very handsome," she said quickly. "But we're already running late. You need to change."

"Change into what?" I asked perplexed.

"Shawn, I told you this dinner was black tie."

"I know," I proudly stated as I grabbed the bottom of my tie and held it in my outstretched hands. "That's why I bought this new tie."

Her eyes tightened like the Detroit Pistons' defense during their championship "Bad Boys" days. I could tell she was steamed.

"That's it Shawn!" she yelled while heading toward the door to the hall. "If you don't change right now, I'm leaving!"

"Change into what Troi?" I yelled back. "What are you talking about?"

"What am I talking about?" she angrily replied. She walked toward me and said, "I told you we have to be there at 6:30."

"And?"

"And!" she yelled. "And you insist on standing here and playing with me instead of putting on your tux so that we can leave!"

I know she didn't say tux. Those bad boys cost at least seventy-five bucks. *Then they expect you to give them back.*

"Did you say tux?" I cautiously asked.

"Of course I said tux," she answered. "I told you it was black tie."

I immediately thought of my mom, who once told me that all people (not *just* men and not *just* women) need to ensure they communicate effectively, particularly when it comes to key events or decisions. "Men don't always communicate well," she started. "A man will tell a woman he intends on picking her up in the evening instead of saying 7:30." That made sense to me.

"That type of vagueness has killed many a relationship. The guy often thought if he wasn't specific, he could explain away anything," she insisted. "Don't leave room for misinterpretation or misunderstanding. Don't say this evening, if you mean 7:30. Make it clear." It was all falling together. "Real men say what they mean and mean what they say," she added. "You don't want Miss Jane thinking you have something with her that you don't really have."

Now it really made sense. *I wouldn't want Miss Jane thinking we had anything,* I reasoned as I thought of Mr. Drysdale's homely assistant on the *Beverly Hillbillies.*

Troi said black tie, so I naturally assumed she wanted me to wear a black tie. All she had to say was "wear a tux." I'd led a pretty sheltered life. I'm not surprised I didn't know that black tie didn't actually mean black tie. If I told her I was taking her to a basketball game, I wouldn't expect her to show-up in a dress. I'd say dress casual. I just wondered why she didn't make it simple and say formal or something like that.

She sat down and folded her hands on her lap. She then smiled at me and said, "Okay Shawn, this isn't really that big a deal." We looked at each other and laughed. She stood up, reached out for my hand, and whispered, "I'm sorry."

"*About what?* I wondered.

"I gave you such short notice, then I asked you to come by early," she said. "I didn't really give you time to go home to pick up your tux."

"No Troi," I interrupted. "You really didn't."

"I know," she answered softly. "And this is all my fault."

That lets me off the hook, I happily thought.

"I have an idea," she said excitedly. "Let's drop by your place and pick up your tux."

I laughed because before tonight, I didn't even own a black tie, and she actually thought I'd just have a tux lying around.

"What's so funny?" she asked.

"Troi," I calmly replied. "We're already late. We don't have time to go all the way to my place, and still make the dinner."

"I guess you're right," she answered, looking at her watch.

Thank God she doesn't know I live only ten minutes away, I thought grinning.

We clutched hands, turned out the lights, and walked out of the room towards the elevator. I immediately thought about my earlier ride with Jesse Jackson and his homeys. *I hope he's not there,* I thought as we entered the spacious, opulent ballroom. This spot is laid, I said to myself, smiling. I saw why they could get a thousand dollars a pop. The ceiling was as high as the nosebleed seats at a sold-out football game. The jazz ensemble, which was decked out in white tails, was playing a relaxing version of Sade's poly-rhythmic groove *Maureen.* The room was surrounded with aqua blue-patterned 3-D wallpaper that felt fuzzy when you touched it. There were chandeliers all over the place. Each huge round table was encased with a beautiful glossy silver and black table cover. The arrangement of fresh flowers placed near the center of each table was so spectacular, that I wondered how I could snatch one for Troi without getting caught.

This is too cool, I thought as I noticed all types of beautiful women, in all types of exquisite outfits parade around the room. They looked incredible, but not a one of them could touch Troi. Donnie once told me you really couldn't judge a woman until she was around a group of other fine women.

"Whenever you think a honey is all that," he said, "just imagine how she'd stack up in the swimsuit part of the Miss America pageant."

I just shook my head because I never even thought I'd be around a woman who could qualify for the overcoat competition of a beauty contest on my street.

"They got some boss honeys in them swimsuit joints," he

told me. "And if your honey can stay with them, she's all of it."

I knew Donnie was right. The one thing he had a real feel for (besides drugs) was women. He made it a point to keep me abreast of what I needed to know about the opposite sex. He told me to never pick up a woman who was driving a station wagon. That was a definite sign of multiple kids and depleted funds. He told me to check out a babe's shopping cart before hitting on a woman at the supermarket. "Too much chow means kids, a husband, or a eaten' problem," he said laughing. "And you don't want no chick wit a eaten' problem." He believed a lady who had a four-by-four or a ride with custom wheels had to have a man. Babes just didn't care about rides that much, he said. More than anything else, Donnie believed that a babe who had a car that was clean and well maintained was a babe who would be nothing but trouble. "If the rides too tight," he forcefully stated, "there's a nigga around."

Donnie didn't always make sense. But his Miss America theory was on target because Troi was definitely all of it. She was classy and it radiated off of her like the sun off of a basket of fresh Georgia peaches at a farmer's market. If the women in here were those paint-by-the-number cardboard art kits that your parents force on you as a child, she was the rare masterpiece that evolves when you go out of the lines. Women as fine as Troi were usually 3s. They of course came complete with a major attitude and a radar tuned directly to a man's wallet. Troi wasn't like that. She was as regular as sunshine on a beach, while at the same time, as spectacular as Michael Jordan on an ESPN highlight reel.

We sat down at a table reserved for VIPs directly in front of the crowded head table. I didn't recognize anyone, but Troi knew everybody, and everyone seemed to know her.

"Hi, Senator so-and-so," she smoothly stated. "Good to see you again, Representative so-and-so," she said waving. She smiled at me and said, "Shawn, I can't thank you enough for getting these tickets. This means so much to me."

I was happy that she was happy, but I felt as out of place

as a piece of ground beef stuck on a vegetarian pizza, as I sat amongst this group of tailored tux-clad bigwigs. Troi made me feel at ease though. She held my hand underneath the table and gently stroked my palm with her forefinger.

My mother once told me when a woman stroked your palm, she's sending you a message.

"A message?" I asked.

"Definitely," she said. "If she strokes your palm, it's often-times a sign that she wants a higher level of affection than you have at that moment."

That didn't require a lot of explaining.

I was happy Troi wanted "a higher level of affection," and I hoped it didn't take long to eat a thousand-dollar dinner.

I wondered what function Kelly was attending. She'd be shocked if she knew I was here. I was glad old man Butler gave us time off to attend CBC events. I now understood why it was so important to him. He gets to hang out with all of these top-shelf babes. I sipped some water from the crystal stemware in front of my tiny bread plate but sprayed it all over my lap when I looked and saw Mr. Butler walking towards our table. I was shocked, because he was with the same babe who didn't know he was married three weeks ago at the American Cafe.

"Mr. Butler," I said reaching my hand across the table. "Good to see you." I looked at his date and said, "Good to see you also, Mrs. Butler." She just smiled and winked at me.

Damn, I thought, embarrassed *How could you do that?*

Butler's babe looked great and he actually looked pretty sharp for an old fat guy. She had a beautiful long braided ponytail she didn't have three weeks ago. I couldn't believe her hair grew so fast.

Butler looked at me confused and whispered, "How did you get tickets to this?" I started to lie and tell him that I payed for them, but I figured I'd ruin any chances I had for a raise if I did that. I just nodded my head toward Troi. He pointed toward Troi and whispered, "You're with her." I just smiled and nodded back. He gave me a big thumbs up and

shook his head in approval. This was the first time I felt that
Butler and I were equals, though it bothered me that his
acceptance of me was based on the fact that I was with a
badder babe than he was.

The attentive wait staff placed heavy cotton napkins in
the laps of all the ladies. They politely asked everyone if
they wanted tea or coffee. Troi said no, but I asked, "How
much extra does it cost?"

The waiter just looked at me, smiled, and called on his
best fractured English to say, "I bring you some right away
sir." I didn't want to cause an international incident, so I just
waved him off. I figured the coffee had to run at least twenty bucks if the food was a grand. I picked up my napkin,
tucked it under my collar, and dug into the fresh salad in
front of me. I was excited. I'd never eaten food that was val-
ued at a thousand dollars. Even though Troi said the grand
was for "the access," I didn't see it. I had access to Butler
everyday, and it definitely wasn't worth a thousand bucks.

The salad left me disappointed. It closely resembled the
chef salad that I'd paid $2.98 for at McDonald's last week. I
didn't really care for salad anyway. I just like the dressing.
Nonetheless, it was disappointing. The waiters brought out
dishes covered with silver-plated domes and sat them down
in front of each of us. I imagined it would be a thick cut of
delmonico steak trimmed with some exotic seafood concoc-
tion, but I was again disappointed. The dome was removed
to reveal a paltry chicken breast, crammed with what
appeared to be Stove Top Stuffing. The gravy had the gooey
texture of Elmer's Glue-All. The vegetable medley looked
like Safeway-brand succotash. I forced myself to eat it and
realized Troi was right. The thousand dollars had to be for
the access, because the food absolutely sucked. They gave
us some terrible almost melted ice cream dish and offered
us more coffee and tea while we were dissecting our
dessert.

Everyone was still trying to figure out how to creatively
hide the ice cream, when an old guy stepped to the podium

at the head table. A hush fell over the room as the stately elder gentleman started introducing the honored guests. Troi happily smiled as he ran down the list. She squeezed my hand, leaned over and whispered, "I have meetings with most of these people this week." She sipped some water, and everything was going smooth. Unfortunately, it didn't go as smooth as I wanted it to.

"And last but not least, the Reverend Jesse L. Jackson," he said applauding.

I was ready to jet to the bathroom and would have done so had we not been seated at the front of the crowded ballroom.

"It's good to see so many of my good friends," said Reverend Jackson, "but I'm happy tonight because I see that we've made some new friends."

He paused and everyone applauded. It was obvious that he had a lot of family in the audience because people kept yelling, "Speak on it, brother." They edged him on and he kept going. He drove the audience into a frenzy. Reverend Jackson was by far the most powerful speaker I'd ever heard. It appeared everyone agreed with me. It also appeared that they were anxious for him to get to his next line. "Our message of unity and peace will not thrive!" he forcefully shouted, "if we don't get out there and keep hope alive." Everyone stood, raised a fist in solidarity and yelled back, "Keep hope alive—keep hope alive!" He pumped his fist and shouted several times over, "Keep hope alive—keep hope alive!"

Who the hell is Hope? I wondered. I knew she had to be pretty sick since they were making all this fuss over her, so I quietly wished her well as the crowd calmed down.

He looked out over the audience and said, "We have a special guest tonight." Everyone looked around to see who it was. I figured it was Jordan. He could stand to blow a grand for this lousy food.

"This morning," he slowly started, "a young man reminded me that we sometimes lose touch." Everyone applauded.

"He challenged me," he said, "and reminded me that we have to be accountable to all of our brothers and sisters."

They clapped louder and yelled, "Preach brother, preach!"

"This young man revitalized my energy, and I know he didn't give up on us because I see him here tonight." Everyone looked around, applauded and yelled, "Bring him on brother, bring him on!"

I realized I couldn't hide that awful ice cream, so I was trying to finish it off. To my surprise, he pointed toward our table and stated, "I don't know your name brother, so stand up and introduce yourself."

I looked over at Butler. He gestured for me to stand up. I pointed to myself and whispered, "Me?"

"You," he whispered back.

I hastily swallowed the rest of my ice cream, and slowly stood up. I looked over at Troi who motioned for me to remove the big napkin from my collar. I hurriedly snatched it away. To my dismay, the top of my tie fell slowly to the side of my shirt, just as it did at the American Cafe. The whole place broke out in laughter. I was pissed. The tie was supposed to have a special stay-put fastener. Mr. Butler was laughing so hard he knocked a glass of red wine into his date's lap. She shrieked and started standing up. He tried to help her and accidentally grabbed her by the back of her long braided ponytail. It didn't make sense, but as she stood there trying to wipe the wine away, Butler held her ponytail in his hand. Amazingly, she didn't know Butler had her hair.

I looked up at Jesse Jackson. He was trying to maintain an air of dignity, but he couldn't help but laugh. Troi just sat there laughing with her hand over her mouth while Butler's date was still trying to clean off her dress. Butler looked flabbergasted and just shrugged his shoulders. He handed her the ponytail. She took it without looking and just kept wiping. When she realized it was her hair, she screamed. She was so shocked, that she threw it toward Troi who was just as startled. When it landed in her hands, she instinctively tossed it back toward Butler. He leaned back, but it landed in his coffee and splattered over the front of his beautiful white shirt.

It was an absolutely incredible sight. I couldn't believe this group of highbrow, tux-wearing big shots was playing hot-potato with Butler's date's ponytail.

Troi stood up and nodded towards the door. We hurried out while everyone was still laughing. A waiting elevator shot us up to the twelfth floor. We ran to her suite where she jumped on the bed and laughed uncontrollably. I searched for the receipt to my tie.

"Shawn!" she yelled laughing.

I didn't know what to say.

She kept laughing, and again yelled, "Shawn!"

"What's up Troi?" I asked.

"Shawn," she said still laughing. "I've never had so much fun at one of these tired events in my life!"

"Neither have I," I said smiling. *You've never been to one of these tired events,* I reminded myself.

"Did you see her extension?" she asked as tears rolled down her face.

"Yeah," I laughed back. "I even saw you throw it."

"Did you see the expression on her date's face?" she cried out.

"Yeah," I replied smiling. "I've never seen him like that before."

She sat up and asked, "You know him?"

"Yeah," I calmly answered. "He's my boss."

She covered her mouth, and said, "He's your boss?"

"The one and only," I responded.

She laughed louder and balled up like a warm baby left in a cold crib.

I realized all the commotion caused by Butler and his date's hair made her forget about my tie. I figured if she forgot, everybody else forgot too.

She sat up, reached her hands toward mine, and said, "Take off that stupid tie *and* your dumb socks."

We both laughed as we raced each other to undress and I wondered how I got so lucky. I knew it was going to be sticky at work tomorrow, but I knew it would be harder on Butler than it would be on me. He had much more to lose than I did.

Troi passionately kissed me, and pulled me toward her as she lay flat on the bed. She smiled and seductively whispered, "The pan is ready Shawn."

"The pan is ready?" I asked.

"It's ready," she said smiling. "So bring home the bacon!"

Donnie's mom was right, I thought as I reached to turn out the lights. *God did bless me.*

13th
Message

MESSAGE SENT ON
OCTOBER 16TH AT 7:02 A.M.

 Troi surprised me because when I awoke, I found she'd ordered a lavish room service breakfast spread. I'd only had room service once, and that was after I'd had surgery back in college. I thought it was odd that they delivered food without asking me what I wanted. I was equally surprised when the orderly left without asking for any money. *He never showed you a menu,* I remembered thinking. *So how could he expect you to pay anyway?* This room service was different than the one I'd had at the hospital. Everything was covered in the same silver-plated domes they had at last night's dinner and red wax clung to the sides of the candles she'd placed around the room. I stumbled to the bathroom to brush my teeth, and wondered why she wanted to eat in the dark.

I quickly brushed and flossed before walking out of the bathroom. I then turned on the lights near the balcony.

"Shawn," said Troi softly. "What are you doing?"

"I'm trying to see."

"Turn off the lights, and go back to bed," she said. "You won't have to see anything." "Whadda you mean I won't have to see anything?" I asked concerned.

"You won't have to see anything," she seductively whispered. "Because I'm going to feed you."

She stood beside the bed and laid a red cloth napkin across my lap. She then placed a glowing candle on each nightstand, and whispered, "Good morning, handsome. Last night was wonderful." I dug this treatment, although I wondered why she wanted to eat in the dark.

"I hope you like the candles," she sweetly stated. "I thought they would be romantic." Eating in the dark made me feel like I was at a Boy Scout jamboree, but it was cool because I was camping out with Troi.

She took a dome off one of the plates and asked, "Are you surprised?"

I was indeed surprised. It appeared Troi had gone through a lot to pull this off. It was a wonderful gesture, and it confirmed my suspicions that she was feeling as good about me as I felt about her. I almost laughed. It didn't make sense that she sprung for breakfast and had this fancy set-up but didn't want me to see it. *Only a woman or an owl would want to eat in the dark,* I thought.

She turned on the radio, which she'd apparently preset to WDCU. WDCU is the University of the District of Columbia's professionally run student station. It features a distinctive blend of main-line standards, and community-oriented talk programs. Faunee Williams, their morning drive-time hostess, whose voice is so hot that it could melt ice in Alaska, surprised me when she smoothly stated, "My good friend from Chicago called and asked me to play a special song for a special man."

Why would someone call all the way from Chicago to a station in D.C.? I wondered. I recognized the tune and froze like a husband who'd been caught in bed with his girlfriend.

"The artist is Pat Metheny and the tune is Cathedral In A Suitcase," said Faunee. "My special friend Troi, asked me to play this for her special friend Shawn." I couldn't believe it. The song she was playing, the song Troi had requested, was our song. It was disc three, track three!

"It's a beautiful song," she said smiling. "It reminds me of you." She leaned over and kissed me. I held her tighter than I'd held anyone, or anything in my life. I wasn't about to let her go. We pulled each other closer, and lost ourselves in our song. I knew we were now connected and I prayed she was my 6. There was no way she could have known this song embodied the feelings I was developing for her. Thankfully, it appeared she was feeling the same way.

I didn't exactly understand love and how it worked, but I knew it made you feel like watered down Play-Doh. My mother told me that's how she felt when she first met my dad. "I felt like Play-Doh left in the rain," she said.

"The Play-Doh that we used in kindergarten?" I asked.

"Yes," she answered softly. "That Play-Doh."

I remembered using it to reproduce cartoons from the Sunday comics, and I'd heard love was funny, but I didn't think that's what she meant.

"When it first hit me," she started, "I got all soft and mushy, just like Play-Doh does when it gets wet."

I understood that.

"And then, just like Play-Doh," she continued, "my movements, my thoughts, and my feelings lost control to someone else."

I didn't understand that. I didn't know Play-Doh had feelings.

"Your father took control of me, just as I took control of him," she said sighing. "And we both bent and shaped ourselves and our relationship."

"Just like Play-Doh," I eagerly chimed in.

"Just like it," she said as her eyes filled with tears. "If you shape Play-Doh right, work with it, and allow the water to absorb" she told me, "it takes form and stands strong and solid."

"Just like you and Dad?"

"Just like me and your father," she said while tears ran down her face.

I held my mom nearly as tight as I was now holding Troi. My mother's words suddenly made sense. I knew my mom missed my old man, just as I would miss Troi when she left for Chicago. Our song, *Cathedral In A Suitcase,* had stopped playing for several minutes, but we held on, just as we'd done when we first slow danced to *Heaven Must Be Like This.* As we pulled apart, Troi smiled at me, and a tear rolled down her cheek. It reminded me of my mom so much that I just closed my eyes, lowered my head, and wished that she was as happy as I was at this moment.

We looked at each other and smiled. With our arms outstretched in mid-air we held hands. She sighed and whispered, "Let me feed you."

"No," I solemnly answered. "Let's feed each other." She smiled and slid beside me. We exchanged eggs like newly-weds trading wedding cake. It was the best breakfast I'd ever eaten, and I realized I would have payed ten bucks for those eggs, if it meant we could eat them together.

I understood how my mom felt when she first met my dad. I knew Troi was special and I felt special in her company. I sat on the bed and thought about all of the wonderful memories we'd developed in our two days together. I remembered my mother telling me she fell for my dad the very first time they met. *It took moms a day, and you've already had two,* I thought to myself smiling. So it must be cool.

"Are you alright?" Troi asked.

"I'm just thinking."

"Thinking?" she asked. "About what?"

"About Play-Doh."

"Play-Doh?" she asked. "Do you mean Play-Doh, Play-Doh?"

"Yeah," I deliberately answered. "Play-Doh, Play-Doh."

"I don't think I get it Shawn," she said.

"Don't worry," I softly stated. "It took me a while too."

The skinny on male bashers— Profile of a 4

> "Men are dogs."
>
> *MOTTO OF A 4*

When a babe tires of being a 1 and decides she's ready to date again, the first stop on the road to recovery is usually an ungratifying stay in 4 world. 4s believe men stink for one very basic reason. They're men. 4s have been there, done it, and seen it all when it comes to guys. That's how 4s became 4s. Much like 1s, 4s certainly didn't start dating to become 4s, but you can bet that some screwed-up guy had a hand in driving them to their unfortunate state of mind. Think of it this way. Nearly every woman has made or received one of those, "Hi, this is Milton's girlfriend," calls. Most babes can relate to the dilemma of the woman on the other end of the line. They often have revealing conversations about what you've done with both of them, and that's when 4s become a problem. Unlike 1s who will track you down (and spook the hell out of you), 4s will set you up so thoroughly that Perry Mason couldn't save you.

4s believe that dating in the '90s is war, and as the old saying goes, "All's fair in love and war."

It's important to understand that 4s believe little (if anything at all) that you tell them. They believe guys are inherently immature and selfish and that men can do little right without urging and input from some woman. Because they think so little of men, and because too many guys screw up and give them ammunition, 4s often rationalize some pretty bizarre behavior.

First off, 4s have no problem hiring private eyes to get the real scoop on you. If you call your lady one day, and she's suddenly as cold as an overpriced bag of liquor store ice, you can bet a PI has hit her with a hefty bill and some cool pictures of you hanging out at the Red Roof Inn. You, of course, told her you'd be out with the fellas. 4s know the fellas aren't swinging at the Red Roof Inn. And if they are, they're not swinging with you. They're hanging with some other babe who's not their girlfriend. It justifies why they're 4s in the first place. 4s will know more about your wallet than you ever will (trust me, they've been through it). They will have an intimate relationship with your glove compartment (if that's where you hide your numbers and other important secret information), and they will know your complete history long before you ever give it to them. When you're caught by a 4 (and if you're doing dirt they *will* catch you), you'd better confess or break camp. 4s won't stalk you like 1s. They don't trust men anyway so they figure you were no good in the first place. But they will make you take the weight for any damage (especially if they really dug you, and you drive them to 1 world).

Unfortunately, that weight often becomes a permanent part of their mindset. Even a decent guy stands little chance of prospering with a 4.

You can be the most sincere, caring, understanding, compassionate, honest man ever known to earth. It will matter little (if at all) to a 4. You could have every last one of those endearing qualities. A 4 won't believe it. She'll think the fact that you're a guy means you can't possibly be decent, and if you are at all decent, you're only being that way because you have an angle. Take a 4 flowers. She'll immediately ask, "What did you do wrong?" A woman checks *you* out as you walk through the mall. She'll ask, "Why are you all up in her face?" Mow the grass on Saturday. A 4 will try to trap you on that. "Don't think that you're hanging out with the fellas just because you mowed the grass," she'll say. You look at her like she's crazy (and she's not crazy, she's just a 4), and wonder just what her problem is. You mowed the grass on Saturday so you can catch the NFL *Game-of-the-Week* on Sunday. Sadly, 4s won't even let you watch the NFL in peace. They know you only watch it for the sexy cheerleaders.

4s are a mess. But if you remember that some guy had a hand in creating the mess they've become, you may actually be of some long-term help. Just be prepared to be ultra patient, incredibly understanding, supersensitive, and as open as a 24-hour-a-day 7-Eleven.

And if at all possible, don't mow the lawn on Saturdays. 4s don't play that.

Shawn Wayne on What's all this stuff about men being dogs? That's crap. But you can believe that a babe who thinks that guys suck isn't going to be too keen on cable. And I guarantee that ESPN isn't part of the grand scheme with 4s either. No ESPN. No *SportsCenter.* You know the rest.

14th
Message

"I WANT THE BOOK ON YOU."

MESSAGE SENT ON
OCTOBER 18TH AT 2:23 P.M.

 Neither of us wanted me to leave after we finished breakfast that morning. She once again asked me if I was coming back later. I of course responded, "Yes."

Is she crazy? I remembered thinking. *Why wouldn't I come back?*

The way I saw it, coming back wasn't even a decision. I was in the midst of the best two days of my life, and I had Troi to thank for it. Everything was going perfect. I knew I couldn't have planned it that well (Then again, I figured I'd never have to plan it that well with a 6, because things just go right when a guy's dealing with a 6). Butler shook my hand when he saw me at work the next morning, which really shouldn't have surprised me. He wanted to win my confidence so I wouldn't blab about his babe's flying hair.

Troi called regularly. She told me her meetings were going well and said she thought the political marketing plan she was devising would be successful. What I liked most was that she whispered, "I miss you" at the end of each conversation. I missed her too, but she always hung up before I could say so. We met each evening and had a series of wonderful, enchanting dates. I saw more of D.C. in four days than I'd seen in seven years. Each date was the best I'd ever been on, until the next date occurred, which totally eclipsed the previous one. We were totally immersed in each other while we were together and spent our time apart planning what we'd do when we saw one another again. She was heading back to Chicago on Sunday. On Friday, she left a curious message. "Shawn," it started, "before I leave town, I want the book on you."

I couldn't imagine what she was talking about. Nobody had written a book about me.

Troi and I had spent a great deal of time together. We engaged in complex, yet thrilling sexual encounters. We spent whopping amounts of her company's money at the very best restaurants in Washington, D.C. There was only one thing that we didn't do. We didn't talk. Our conversations were pretty much limited to, "Wasn't that fun?" and "What do we do next?" I don't think either of us was trying to avoid conversation. We were just trying to enjoy every minute we had together.

I knew conversation could be an important part of a successful relationship. My mom hipped me to it long ago.

"Sex has its place," she told me. "But nothing exceeds the ability to converse."

Talking never gave me the same pleasure that sex did, but I knew not to stop her. "When sex is over it's over," she flatly stated. "But good conversations and what you can get from them sometimes last forever."

"How's that?" I asked.

"Well," she started. "You may learn something that you never knew, which you could later use to your advantage."

I could deal with that.

"But more importantly," she continued. "Someone may learn something important about you, that may help you down the line."

Something like what? I wondered.

"You never know who knows who," she continued. "And you may make a strong impression on someone who is connected with someone else who could hire you, or help you get where you're trying to go."

I knew what she meant, but couldn't relate it to talking with Troi. I don't have a problem with sex being over when it's over, as long as it means you get to have sex. And the only place I was trying to get was closer to Troi. Those reasons, coupled with the fact that we were having so much fun, greatly contributed to our lack of conversation.

We were enjoying ourselves at the rooftop restaurant of the Hotel Washington one evening (the one I'd wanted to take Jasmine to), and Troi turned serious. It was a beautiful clear night. We clutched hands and walked over to a side restraining wall to take advantage of the magnificent aerial view the restaurant perch provided. She stood in front of me, draped my arms over her shoulders and gently rested her head on my chest. She sighed as we watched a plane appear to fly right through the lazy full moon and over the Washington Monument. We smiled as we noticed Bill and Hillary Clinton squat as they departed an Air Force One helicopter (we could see them because the Hotel Washington is so close to the White House, you could hit it with a Frisbee on a windy afternoon). *Women run everything,* I thought as we watched them enter the White House. *He's the president, and she makes him go through the back door.* I figured she didn't want him tracking up the carpet.

"What do you think they talk about in there?" she softly asked.

I'd heard Bill Clinton had a good eye for beautiful women, but I didn't think that came up too often.

"I guess they talk about stuff," I answered.

"Stuff?" she quickly replied. "What do you mean stuff?"

I didn't know what I meant, so I said, "You know, like things."

"No," she said exasperated, "I don't know. What do you mean things?"

Who cares what they talk about? I wondered. *Why is she pressing me about them anyway?* I was about to say that like every good couple, they probably discussed sports. But before I could, she turned around and said, "Shawn, I want to talk about you."

I knew I had nothing to talk about, but I thought about my mom and realized it would probably be a good idea for us to talk. Kelly would have been proud of my next line. I answered, "I'll talk about me, if you talk about you."

"I think we have a deal," she said, smiling.

We returned to our seats, held hands across the table and looked at each other in silence for about ten seconds.

I was hoping she'd start because I couldn't think of anything to say. It reminded me of when we first met and she ran on about her job. Fortunately, it was a short-lived moment. Thankfully, she talked about something besides her job. She told me she was a big Chicago Bulls fan. She'd bought expensive court side seats in Chicago Stadium, because seeing Michael Jordan up close justified the ticket prices. She was born in Chicago in 1964 (which made her 27 years old, something we'd never discussed). Her parents divorced when she was 10. "I think my dad caught my mom with our neighbor," she told me.

"Why do you think that?"

"Because he left his wife, and moved in with us a week after my dad left," she answered.

"How did you handle that?"

"I didn't," she deliberately stated. "So I moved to my father's place."

"That must have been cool," I said smiling.

"No way," she forcefully replied. "My father definitely wasn't cool."

The way I saw it, if a dad was around or was supportive, he was cool. I wasn't prepared for what she told me next.

"I quickly found out why my mother cheated on my

father," she said, looking toward the ground.

"Why was that?"

"Because when she was around, he abused her," she solemnly stated. We held hands tighter and eased closer together. "And when I was around," she whispered while lowering her head, "he abused me."

I'd never been abused and I wasn't really sure what to say. I only knew I instantly felt her pain and wanted to help if I could. I empathetically asked, "Are you okay now?" She looked up and said, "Of course Shawn, I'm always okay when I'm with you." SWV's tender groove, *Right Here (With You)*, played softly through the well-concealed speaker system. She edged toward me and I held her in my arms as she cried. I didn't know what to say or what to think. I only knew that no one, including her dad, would ever do harm to her while I was around.

She later told me her dad was a co-founder of Myers and Stevenson, the company she now worked for. "He was bought out by my uncle, who was his partner," she said. There was a tremendous sense of bitterness in her voice. "My uncle gave me a chance to keep our 'good family name' on the marquee." She talked about "surviving" years of private, all-girls boarding schools, and of being so focused that she graduated from both college and grad school with a perfect 4.0 GPA. "I studied so hard because I needed to block out my dad," she added. Her mom, a retired school teacher, was happily remarried to their neighbor (she had grown to both like and respect her stepfather). Her father was trying to fight his way back into the business. She, like I, was an only child, but she said she was close to many of her cousins. "I would stay with them on break," she said. "Because there was no way I was going home."

"How did you explain that?" I asked.

"It was easy," she told me. "He was always off on business with his girlfriend, or somebody else's wife."

I knew about her childhood, her education, and her family. But Troi was so stunning, and so seemingly perfect, that

I wondered why she didn't have a man. I knew she was into her job, but any man with good sense would learn to put up with that.

"Have you ever been in love?" I asked.

"I don't even think I know what love is," she answered, laughing. I smiled as I thought about Play-Doh. I'd have to explain it to her someday. She told me every man she'd dated had, at some point, cheated on her or lied to her. "I can't tolerate a liar," she sternly warned. She talked about how she always gave her all and trusted men until they crossed her. "They stole my money, screwed me and left, took advantage of me, and walked over me like I was a human doormat," she said with a chilling edge. "Ultimately," she continued, "I lost all respect for myself."

"What did you do?" I asked, concerned.

"I started drinking, I put on a lot of weight, and I had an affair."

"How could you have an affair?" I asked. "You weren't married were you?"

"No," she said, embarrassed. "He was."

She'd slept with one of her co-workers after she'd gotten drunk one night. It escalated into a scandalous affair. He had promised to leave his wife. When he didn't, she called her and ratted on him. The wife put him out and they hooked up. She saw his car at his wife's place two weeks later. She took all of his clothes there and torched them right in their front yard. She said watching his clothes burn to ashes liberated her.

"I saw the faces of my dad and every man who'd ever mistreated me burn away in that fire," she told me. "And after that, it was like they were gone. I've never looked back."

"What happened with your boyfriend?"

"What happened?" she said laughing. "I fired him."

"You fired him?"

"Yup," she answered smiling. "I fired him."

"Is that fair?"

"Definitely," she told me. "He was a good lay," she said bluntly. "But he was a lousy employee."

We both laughed.

"That's amazing," I said.

"Yeah," she replied. "It is pretty incredible."

She then wrapped my arms around her and asked, "You know what's more amazing Shawn?"

"What could top that?"

"You may find this hard to believe," she confessed, "but, I've never shared that with anyone."

I felt special. She had confided in me. I now understood what my mom meant about conversation. My opinion of Troi didn't change a bit. In fact, I respected and admired her more. She didn't let her problems ruin her (she obviously wasn't the 4 she could have easily been). She came out of it as a more determined and focused woman. I was, however, shocked that a babe as beautiful as Troi had been through the crap that she'd been through. I always thought babes like her just hung out and looked good. I didn't know they got played just like everybody else.

She asked me about myself, but I wasn't about to talk.

"Look Troi, it's already 10:00, and they close in an hour," I said.

"So?"

"So," I nervously replied. "Why don't we talk later?"

She wasn't having it. I told her I was born in 1962.

"Is that it?" she asked.

"Pretty much," I told her with a straight face.

She told me she would have to ask me what she wanted to know and warned me everything was fair game.

I explained that my mother and father fell for each other the first time they met. I also told her that me and my dad rarely talked, although we understood how to communicate with each other. "If he wanted me to clean my room," I recalled, "he'd just tell me that Dr. J kept his room clean." I told her my dad always talked about being strong and smart like Malcolm X and that he trained me to be an athlete from day one. She smiled when I told her he took me to all types of games and introduced me to Hall of Famers like Frank Robinson, who played baseball for the Baltimore Orioles, and Charlie Taylor, who caught touchdowns for the Redskins. "You can be them if you concentrate and work at it," he'd remind me. "He never understood I just wanted to be like him. To me, he was greater than any athlete he'd ever introduced me to," I said.

I also told her he had me hitting baseballs and catching footballs by the time I was three. I played on my first basketball team when I was just five years old. "He would take me out and make me shoot so much that it was second nature when I went out for the team," I said. "I was five, playing on a team of ten year olds. I was the star of the whole league."

"Are you serious?" she asked in disbelief.

"Very," I answered. I told her my father and I spent so much time "working on my game," that I just believed I was supposed to be a ballplayer. I wasn't supposed to miss shots.

"Did you want to play or was he making you play?" she asked.

"Of course I wanted to play," I responded. "I loved the attention, plus I saw how proud my dad was."

I told her my father was one of the most respected CPAs in Maryland, and that he stressed monetary accountability and financial restraint to me. "My father understood everything in the world," I wistfully said, "because all of our neighbors sought him out for advice and counsel."

She smiled at the waiter, who interrupted us and asked him for a glass of water. She laughed when I told her our pastor would listen to everyone else's problems and would then come to my dad for the answers. "I'm surprised my dad didn't charge him," I said laughing. "Because he firmly believed that time was money. If he gave you his time, he'd pop open his old cigar box and expect you to drop in some money."

"What's he doing now?" she asked.

"I'm not exactly sure."

"You're not sure?" she asked puzzled.

"No," I softly stated. "Because I never really understood what you do after you die." She gasped and said, "I'm sorry Shawn, I didn't know. What happened?"

"It was really weird," I said. "I was ten years old, and I made the sixteen-and-under AAU team."

"What's AAU?"

"It stands for Amateur Athletic Union," I answered. "And when you play AAU, you're playing with the top dogs." The waiter brought her water back and placed it down. He lit the short, green candle in the middle of our table.

"So you're playing AAU," she said reminding me where I left off.

"Yeah," I replied. "I finally make it to AAU, and my dad's freaking out."

"What do you mean you finally made it?" she asked puzzled. "You were only ten." "I know that," I said laughing. "But my father probably thought I was ready for sixteen and-under when I was six."

She shook her head and laughed.

"Anyway," I started. "He invites the entire neighborhood to my very first game and they're all yelling my name like I'm some star or something."

"Didn't that put a lot of pressure on you?" she asked.

"No way," I told her. "I'd been playing in front of big crowds since I was five. This was chump change." I told her the only difference was that it was the first time my mother came to see me play. "I liked that because I don't think she thought I could play," I said. "I don't mean to seem insensitive," she interrupted. "But what's this got to do with your father's death?"

"I'll get to that," I said. "The coach had to start me, because so many people were yelling my name."

"You started and you were just ten?" she asked surprised.

"Yeah," I answered casually. "I was only ten."

"How did your teammates feel about that, since they were so much older?"

"They felt good when I hit twenty points," I proudly stated.

"You scored twenty points against a team of sixteen year-olds?"

"Yeah," I quickly replied. "I hit twenty in the first half."

I told her I was having what was to be the very first of many "games of my life," and that even though I'd racked up forty-two points, we were still down by one with eight seconds to go.

"What happened next?" she anxiously asked.

"I left my man open, stole an inbounds pass, and drove the length of the floor," I said. "What happened then?"

"I rose off the floor and slam dunked for the first time in my life."

"You dunked when you were ten?" she asked astonished.

"Yeah," I casually answered. "My very first three hundred sixty degree slam."

"I can't believe this."

"Neither could my father."

"What do you mean Shawn?" she asked. "He saw you dunk it didn't he?"

"He saw it," I said. "And he was so shocked he had a massive heart attack right there in the stands."

"What did you do?" she asked horrified.

"I ran over to him, and he pulled me toward him to say something."

"What did he say?"

"He told me I'd played a good game, that I was a good son and he told me to take care of my mother."

"Then he died?" she gasped.

"Not exactly."

"What do you mean not exactly?"

"First he told me to work on the rotation on my jumper."

"The rotation on your jumper?" she asked puzzled.

"Yeah," I answered. "That was always a sore spot with him."

She just shook her head and smiled.

"Then he told me he loved me," I said softly. "And then he died."

"You saw him die?"

"Yeah," I replied. "But it was cool because he died happy."

"Why do you say that?"

"Because," I said. "We beat the defending champs, he saw me score forty-four points in my first AAU game, and I did it on his forty-fourth birthday."

"How did your mom deal with it?"

"She told me I played good too," I proudly answered.

Troi just shook her head and motioned for the waiter to bring her another glass of water.

I told her that basketball consumed my life and that I was a first-team high school All-American from the tenth grade on. "I wasn't interested in college, even though every big-time coach from Maryland's Lefty Drisell to UNLV's Jerry Tarkanian promised me the world if I went to their school," I said. "I just wanted to graduate and get out of school, because I hated going to class." I told her my proudest moment came in the Capital Classic All-Star game. It pitted a D.C. metropolitan team against a group of high school All-Americans. The All-Americans always blew our local team off of the floor and we were in awe when we watched them practice. "Everyone was talking about this skinny guy from North Carolina," I said.

"Who was he?" she asked.

"Michael Jordan."

"You played against *the* Michael Jordan?"

"The Michael Jordan," I answered in a huff. "I roasted the Michael Jordan like a bag of cheap peanuts."

I told her our overweight center was hurt in practice and he couldn't play. "They lost my shorts and wristband, so I had to wear his. The wristband was so big I had to wear it on my forearm, and the shorts had to be four sizes too big, so they were very baggy." I told her that baggy shorts defi-nitely weren't the rage back in 1980, but that it didn't matter because I put an NBA style whipping on Jordan and his boys.

"You beat the All-Americans?" she asked.

"We trounced them," I proudly stated. "I dunked on Jordan on the first play of the game then turned around and licked my tongue out at him." I told her I stuck my tongue out at him every time I slammed on him (which was often that night), and that I talked so much junk to him that he got frustrated and called a timeout after his team had exhausted its allotment of timeouts.

"What happened next?"

I told her they were assessed a technical foul because Michael called his imaginary timeout. Before I took the shots for the technical, I yelled, "Hey Jordan, watch this!"

"What did you do?"

"I closed my eyes, nailed both free throws, and won the MVP for the game."

"Did he say anything to you after the game?"

"No," I answered. "But I said plenty to him."

"Like what?" she excitedly asked.

"I told him he should stop wearing those cheap Converse sneakers he was wearing, and to get some Nikes like I had, and I told him that if he wanted to be like me he should drink Gatorade before each game," I added. "Then I advised him to take up another sport." "Another sport?"

"Yeah," I said. "I told him he should take up golf or base-ball, because he'd always be second best as long as I was around."

"You said that to *the* Michael Jordan?"

"I'd just scored forty-seven points on *the* Michael Jordan and barely broke a sweat doing it," I casually replied. "Then I pressed him about my twenty bucks."

"He owed you $20?"

"Yeah," I answered. "I talked him into a dumb bet."

"What was the bet?"

"I told him I'd score at least twenty points more than he did, and said I'd make the last two with my eyes closed."

"So he scored twenty-seven points?" she asked.

"That's right."

"Did he pay you the $20?"

"Nope."

"Well, what did you do?"

"Me and my buddy Donnie grabbed him in the locker room," I said, smiling. "Pinned him down, and cut off all his hair."

"You cut off Michael Jordan's hair?"

"Sure did," I replied, smiling. "Cut him completely bald."

She looked dazed. She shook her head in disbelief and said, "I don't know about this Shawn."

I didn't know what she didn't know. But I felt great. He'd decided to keep the bald head.

"There's more," I added. "When he got to his feet, I made him wear my jersey to the bus, so he'd always remember me."

"Why?"

"Because," I answered. "Before the game he pointed at me and told his boys that he was going to eat number twenty-three alive."

"Number twenty-three," she said surprised. "That's his number."

"No," I boasted. "That was *my* number. He didn't get it until I *made* him wear it to the bus!"

She looked away as the busboy, waiter, hostess and cook presented a birthday cake to the table right beside us. I was tired of talking. But she wanted my life story, so I had to finish.

"Two weeks later Jordan called me and asked where I was going to play college ball," I told her.

"Where were you going?" she asked.

"I told him I wasn't sure where I was going," I said. "I only knew I wasn't going to North Carolina."

"You're saying that Michael Jordan went to Carolina because you weren't going there?"

"You figure it out," I answered, smiling.

"Why didn't you want to go to Carolina?"

"Because Coach Smith sent my mother roses."

"Roses?" she asked. "What's wrong with that?"

"I told him to send carnations."

"Why carnations?"

"Because the only extravagant thing my old man ever did for my mom was to buy her a dozen roses every Friday," I answered. "So I always told the coaches who insisted on sending her flowers to send carnations. Roses were too painful for her."

"That's sweet," she whispered.

"I guess it is," I said. "But I figured Coach Smith confused me with another recruit, and I didn't need to be with a coach who couldn't even send the right flowers."

"Shawn," she said smiling. "If another man even tried to tell me a story as farfetched as that, I'd cuss him out for lying to me."

"I'm not lying Troi," I interrupted.

"I know that Shawn," she said. "I don't think you would ever lie to me."

I would if you called and said "we have to talk," I thought. But I knew she was right. I'd never really lie to her, and knew she'd always be straight with me. That's how it works when you're with a 6.

"What about your mom?" she asked. "What's she do?"

"I'm not sure," I solemnly answered as I lowered my head.

"I'm sorry Shawn," she said. "I didn't know."

"It's not your fault Troi," I softly stated. "You said that everything was fair game."

I told her my father was the greatest man I had ever known, and that after he passed, my mom was the greatest mother *and* father that anyone could hope for. I told her my mother openly talked to me about all types of stuff, and that she could make me understand any and everything. "My mom was one of the first black female bankers in the region," I said. "So like my father, she understood money. She taught me the value of a dollar."

"My mother's voice is constantly in my head," I told her. "Before I do something totally stupid, she usually bails me out."

"I wish she would have bailed you out before your tie fell off at the black-tie dinner," she said giggling.

"I do too," I replied, laughing. We held hands. I told her my mother was and is my most trusted ally, and that the earth was a better place because my mom walked on it. "She was the strongest, most complete woman I've ever known," I confessed. "You remind me of her." She started crying, but I didn't understand why. I was talking about *my* dead mother.

"Shawn, I've been told that I was the prettiest, the most attractive, and the most beautiful this and that by all sorts of people for my entire life," she said between her tears. "But I've never received a compliment as meaningful or as beautiful as the one you just gave me." She then kissed my cheek, and whispered, "Thank you."

She told me of her deep interest in basketball. She even said she was surprised she'd never heard of me.

"So am I," I said. I told her I didn't want to leave my mother alone, so I went to the University of Maryland. I was a first-team All-American as a freshman. "I blew my knee out in the first game of my sophomore season," I admitted. "And was never quite the same after that." I told her I transferred to Elizabeth City State College in North Carolina. I promised my mom I'd give up the game and concentrate on graduating.

"The coach saw me jogging around the gym one day and said he'd like me to workout with the team when practice started," I told her. "So one thing led to another, and I ended up playing."

"What did your mom say?"

"She wasn't happy," I admitted. "But she knew I wanted to play." I told her our first game was against North

Carolina, and Michael Jordan. He had turned out to be a fairly decent player. "They'd just won the national championship so I wanted them bad," I said. "Donnie called me an hour before the game, and said the whole neighborhood would be at my mother's place to watch me play." "Take 'em for bad cuz!" I remembered him yelling through the phone. Donnie told me my mom didn't look well, but that wasn't unusual. She was always nervous before my games.

"How did it go?" she asked.

"It went great!" I proudly answered. "I talked trash all afternoon, scored forty-four points, and we beat big, bad Carolina on national TV!"

"You're kidding."

"I wish I was."

"What's wrong Shawn?" she asked, noticing my sudden change in mood.

I told her I called my mother's house right after the game.

"I took Jordan for bad!" I yelled to Donnie when he answered the phone.

"Shawn," he replied sobbing. "Moms is dead!"

I told her I just dropped the phone and ran across campus in my uniform. I cried so hard for so long that I missed myself being featured on ESPN's *Plays of The Week*.

I didn't understand why Troi was crying over my dead mother. I was equally surprised when I turned around to find the waiter, the hostess, the busboy, and the cook all weeping directly behind me.

"What happened to her?" asked the hostess.

"Well," I started. "After the funeral, Mr. Butler, who was an old friend of the family and who is now my boss, told me she had a massive heart attack when I stole an inbounds pass and did the three-sixty-degree dunk, which sealed the game."

"Just like your father?" inquired the busboy, as they all sat down.

"Just like him," I said, nodding my head.

The waiter asked, "Did she say anything when it happened?"

I told them Donnie said she whispered, "Tell my boy that he played a good game, and that he was a good son."

"She said that?" asked the cook.

"That's what Donnie said," I answered. "Then she told him to tell me she loved me *and* to work on the rotation on my jumper."

"You're kidding?" gasped Troi. "That's what your father said."

"I know," I replied, slowly. "It was a sore spot with her too."

I told them that at the funeral, Mr. Butler confided my parents loaned him the money to start his company. He promised me I'd never have to worry about a job.

I'd never discussed what happened to my parents with anyone before. But, just as Troi's fire liberated her, talking about them seemed to free me from the guilt I'd lived with since I was ten years old. I withdrew and shunned the real world after my mom passed. I believed that my making game-winning, three-hundred-sixty-degree slam dunks essentially killed my parents. I told them I hadn't so much as picked up a basketball since my mom's heart attack, and that I was content knowing I had significantly contributed to the legend of the greatest player ever to play anything. Michael Jordan.

"Have you ever been in love Shawn?" Troi asked.

"I don't think so," I replied. "But I noticed after I stopped playing ball, all the girls seemed to lose interest." I told her I had pretty much isolated myself because I couldn't stand the thought of losing someone I felt close to again. I hadn't had a real relationship since my mom died ten years ago. I wasn't sure whether the cook, the waiter, the busboy, and the hostess could sense this was the first time that I felt alive since my mom left. Troi's caring eyes reassured me she knew and that's all that mattered to me.

The staff hugged us, and the hostess tore up the check. I liked that. It was my turn to treat. We walked back over to the ledge of the restraining wall, and chuckled when we saw someone turn out the last light still lit in the White House.

"I guess they're finish talking," I said to her smiling.

"I guess we are too," she whispered. "Let's go back to our room."

15ᵗʰ Message

"I'M GONE—I'M OUT OF HERE."

MESSAGE SENT ON
OCTOBER 19TH AT 9:55 P.M.

I was glad we talked that night. I found there was some truth to the line, "If you can't close the deal after the Hotel Washington, the deal can't be closed," because when we got back to "our room" (as she'd put it), we enthusiastically closed the deal. She came at me so fast, I almost forgot that we didn't use protection again. It's kind of different when you sport a condom. After I blew my knee out, my doctor made me wear a knee brace. It wasn't heavy, and though I imagined that it would be restrictive, it was actually pretty comfortable. It did change my game though. I just didn't feel the same. That's how it is with a rubber. You can still play the game. You just feel a little different while you're scoring.

Our conversation at the Hotel Washington had me thinking about everything. After my mom passed, I just didn't want to get involved with anything or anybody. I'd allowed the past ten years to pass right by me because of the guilt I carried. I used to wonder if it was the three-sixty-degree slams that caused the heart attacks. I now realized it really didn't matter. A simple tomahawk slam might have been just as bad. I figured my parents would have wanted me to be happy and wished they could have met Troi. They would have loved her and she would have loved them.

Before we hit the sack that night, Troi hugged me and whispered, "Thanks."

"Thanks?" I asked. "Thanks for what?"

"Thanks for being here, and for making this such a wonderful week," she said smiling.

"Thank you," I said. "This was a great week."

She then kissed me, and said she'd miss me when she went back to Chicago.

"I'll miss you too," I told her. I'd especially miss the bomb sex.

I knew she would eventually have to leave, but I really didn't want her to go. It made me think of our first night together when she didn't want me to leave. She pretty much told me I was staying. *You should tell her she's staying too,* I convinced myself. I'd be better off telling her I cracked the genetic code. I wondered if she wanted to stay an extra day. The way I saw it, we hadn't had enough of each other. I felt closer to Troi than anyone I'd ever known (besides my mom). I smiled as I realized we went together well. Kind of like pork chops and applesauce. Troi brought out the best in me. I felt I had the same impact on her. I knew that Troi's leaving shouldn't have bothered me like it did, but I didn't want her to go back to Chicago feeling as though she just had a little R & R in the nation's capital. We'd had a wonderful time, but besides saying thanks, we'd said nothing that defined our experiences.

I wanted to know our time together meant something. That we would use it as a springboard to something more tangible than good sex and hearty dinners. I worried she'd say, "We'll keep in touch" or "I'll never forget you" when she left. I wanted to hear, "Let's get together *real* soon" or "I'm glad we started like this." I wasn't sure what I was going to hear. I just wanted to know what we'd done eclipsed having fun and actually meant something significant to her.

On Saturday night, the last we were to spend together, we finally made use of the spacious in-suite jacuzzi. We ended up in each other's arms in the bed. I don't know if it was the intensity of our lovemaking or the sweltering steam that was rising from the hot tub, but I was out like a drunken bear in hibernation behind his favorite woodlands drinking hole.

I had a crazy dream. It started with Troi showing up at my office in one of those shiny, bright-red raincoats. Kelly led her to my office, closed the door, and left after Troi walked in. I looked up surprised and said, "Hi."

She said, "Hello handsome," before closing the blinds and removing her raincoat. It didn't make sense. But she stood in front of my desk and started undressing. Grace Jones' runaway hit from 1985, *Slave To The Rhythm,* played loudly in the background. I looked around the room trying to figure out how to turn the music down when suddenly, Mr. Butler knocked on the door.

Troi hid underneath my desk and started to unzip my pants. Butler walked in and handed me a package. He slowly said, "I-t-'s—n-o-t—h-e-r-'s," before walking out and closing the door behind him. I opened the package. His girlfriend's ponytail fell onto my desk. Troi, who was now completely naked, stood up and seductively whispered, "Bring home the bacon, Shawn, not the Sizzlean."

"Troi!" I yelled, puzzled. "We can't do that here, people don't have sex at work!" "Where have you been?" she asked surprised. "People have been having sex at work for years." She jumped on my lap, grabbed the ponytail, swung it over her head like a cowboy swinging a lasso, and yelled, "It's okay if we do this Shawn, because it's only a dream!"

None of this made sense to me, but like she'd said, it was only a dream so I went with it.

Even though it was a dream, I was surprised Troi didn't

mind having sex with so many people in the room. Sammy Davis, Jr. and Scatman Crothers were resplendent in their black tails and top hats as they performed a strenuous tap-dance routine in one corner of the room. Don Cornelius stood in another corner with a bottle of Johnson's Ultra Bleach and Glow in his left hand and a microphone in his right. He was wearing a purple jumpsuit and red stack-heeled sneakers with yellow piping. He just kept repeating, "Thanks for riding the *Soul Train*. I wish each of you love, peace, and s-o-o-o-o-u-l!" James Brown was on a tiny stage in the center of the room ruining the *Star Spangled Banner*. Like Don Cornelius, he wore a jumpsuit, except his was covered with stars and stripes.

My eyes, which were usually closed while we were being intimate, were wide open in disbelief. I couldn't believe she just sat on top of me and kept going while the Godfather of Soul was destroying the national anthem.

When James Brown finally screamed himself to the line that says, "the bombs bursting in air," Jimmie "J.J." Walker from the '70s hit sitcom, *Good Times* poked his head in the door. He, of course, yelled, "Dy - No - Mite!" Just as he said it, a spectacular display of fireworks filled the room. We came to an exhilarating climax and J.B. finally finished. He disappeared through a trap door just as Elvis Presley popped in and recited his trademark line, "Thank you—thank you very much."

That's just like Elvis, I remembered thinking. *Always ready to take credit for something a brother did.*

Troi zipped me back up and quickly dressed herself. She handed me two boxes she'd brought in with her. I hastily opened the larger one and found it contained a copy of Michael Jordan's first NBA *Sports Illustrated* cover. It read "A Star Is Born." It was inscribed with his signature and a note that read: *To Shawn-Wayne—The Real #23—I Couldn't Have Gotten Here Without You—Thanks!* I opened it, and a $20 bill, which he had also signed, fell onto my desk. It read: *M.J. always pays his debts.*

Big deal, I thought. *It only took him ten years.* I showed the package to Troi and excitedly said, "See Troi, I told you it was true."

"That doesn't mean a whole lot Shawn," she fired back. "Like I said, this is only a dream."

I knew she was right, but I was glad to have them anyway.

The other box was much smaller. When I opened it, I found a beautiful solid gold puffed heart.

"What's this for?" I asked.

"It's my heart," she said smiling. "And I'm trusting you to take care of it. As long as you have it, you have me."

I could deal with that, but her next line concerned me.

"Lose the heart," she said with a sharp edge. "And you lose me—I'm gone—I'm out of here!"

I placed it in my pocket and promised myself I'd lock it in my safe when I got home.

Before I knew it, we were whisked away to Houston's restaurant in Georgetown. The cute buxom woman who was going to keep me from entering the CBC dance because I'd lost my ticket was the hostess. She happily led us to our table. To my surprise, Danielle, who had stiffed me on Memorial Day, was our waitress. She, of course, recommended the surf and turf combo of filet mignon and lobster. She also suggested a nice white wine to complement the meal.

"That's okay," I said smiling. "We'll pass on the wine."

Another attractive woman brought us our sodas. I was shocked when she said, "Hi Shawn-why won't you return my calls?" It was Jasmine!

Troi stared at her, and snapped, "He's been busy girl-friend, so why don't *you* get busy and bring us some straws."

I liked that. It was classic Troi. Direct, to the point and tempered with just the right touch of feminine forcefulness.

Another attractive woman, whom I immediately recognized as Butler's girlfriend, brought us our soup. I carefully inspected both bowls to ensure she hadn't left any ponytails floating around. "Our chef would like to present a special appetizer to you," said Danielle. I looked to Troi and said, "Sure, why not?" I couldn't believe it when I saw old-man Butler himself decked out in culinary whites and a baker's hat, walk out with a tray full of hot wings.

"Take them back!" I ordered. "We don't do hot-wings."

It didn't surprise me when Danielle slipped a few in her pocket. She actually asked Butler for some extra sauce. I was flattered that the entire wait staff argued over who was going to serve us. My ears swelled as each of them said, "I'm taking him his food." Troi grew impatient. She quietly excused herself and said she was going to the ladies room.

I sat there, and thought it was strange that these people, all of whom I knew, were working in the same restaurant on the only night I'd ever been there. *I guess it's because it's a dream,* I thought smiling. *And since it's your dream, it's only fair that Troi foot the bill.* I reached in my pocket to look at the beautiful heart Troi had entrusted me with. It struck me that Troi had been gone a long time.

"Dammit!" I yelled.

I couldn't believe it. I couldn't find the heart! I looked all over the place. I ran to my ride and searched it without success. I dashed back inside and nearly flipped the table over in a mad attempt to find it there. I ran to the bathroom and said to myself in a panic, please, please, please let this be a dream! I broke through the door. She wasn't there. I just fell to my knees, put my hands to the sides of my head, and repeatedly yelled, "Please come back Troi—please come back!"

"It's okay Shawn," she said while shaking me. "I'm back."

"You're back!" I excitedly yelled, as my eyes popped opened. "Troi, you're back!" "Yes Shawn," she calmly stated. "I'm back."

"You really came back?"

"You see me here don't you?"

"But what about the heart?" I asked.

"What heart?"

It was then that I realized I'd just slid out of a bad dream and was making even less sense than I usually did. I tried to compose myself, and casually asked, "Where did you go?" "I went to get some ice for our sodas," she told me. "The steam from the jacuzzi made it really hot in here."

That was an understatement.

"Shawn," she excitedly said. "I pushed my flight back, so I won't have to leave until 10:45 tomorrow night.

"Really!" I happily answered. "Why did you do that?"

"Because," she started. "I wasn't ready to leave you."

Jackpot, I thought. She felt the same as me.

"I want to spend the entire day together," she said thoughtfully. "Then we can go to dinner and leave for the airport from there."

"Sounds cool to me."

"Good," she replied. "I was thinking that we could go to Houston's."

"Hu-Hu Houston's," I said stuttering.

"Yeah, Houston's in Georgetown," she calmly stated. "I hear they have great surf and turf."

This could only happen to me, I thought. I have what amounts to a nightmare, and she needs to make a site visit, so I can really lose it.

"Okay Troi," I said. "We can go to Houston's under one condition."

"One condition?" she asked.

"Yup," I smugly replied. "You can't go to the ladies room."

"I can't go to the ladies room!" she yelled. "Why can't I go to the ladies room?" "I'll tell you later," I said exhausted. "Let's get some sleep."

16th Message

16th Message

"I MISS YOU ALREADY."

MESSAGE SENT ON
OCTOBER 20TH AT 11:12 P.M.

 Although I was exhausted, I could hardly sleep on our last night together. I was worried I'd have another bad dream and would then have to put up with seeing Danielle and Jasmine again. It had only been a week, and though it didn't make sense, I felt Troi had become a part of my life. I was happy she wanted to spend more time together because that's exactly what I wanted. After that crazy dream, I wasn't exactly thrilled about going to Houston's, but I vowed our dinner would be light and care-free.

There was a long line outside the Wisconsin Avenue entrance of the restaurant, but we barely had to wait. Houston's didn't take reservations, but Troi apparently had clout. She approached one of the hostesses and whispered something. They smiled at each other, and we were placed near the top of the waiting list. Kelly went to Houston's all the time. She raved about the food and the atmosphere. According to her, it was the place to be. I'd never been there.

Houston's is in Georgetown, a part of D.C. I rarely visited. Georgetown's an okay place, but it's expensive as hell. I didn't know if Houston's was expensive, but it didn't matter. She was treating. I couldn't tell exactly how it looked because the lighting was pretty awful. The peppery smell of Hawaiian flavored steak, barbequed babyback ribs, and blackened seafood swirled about the room. It made me think of Taco Bell. We could have gone there. They give free refills on sodas. Houston's was a little noisy. The remnants of non-stop jabbering, casual laughter, forks hitting plates, and clanging glasses permeated the eatery. Kelly was right about it having atmosphere. It had all the atmosphere of a bowling alley. The decor was tree-trunk brown on tree-limb brown. Just right for those outdoorsy types who watched the Discovery Channel. We held hands as we waited at the greeting station. After just a minute, we were seated by a very friendly hostess with lots of teeth and lots of hips. I was surprised that Troi once again insisted on talking.

"Shawn," she said. "Tell me more about you."

"Like what?" I asked, realizing that I had no intention of volunteering anything.

"Like what?" she anxiously replied. "Like you, and what you like."

That was easy enough.

"I like basketball."

"I know that," she smugly replied. "But what else do you like?"

"Nothing," I casually answered.

"Nothing?" she said, looking puzzled. "How does someone like nothing?"

"It's easy," I explained. "I never do anything, which amounts to nothing, and I think I like that."

She looked at me perplexed (which was unusual for Troi). "You know Shawn, if anyone else had said that, I'd have shot it down, but coming from you, it makes sense. It's believable," she commented.

"How can you say you don't do anything?" she asked.

"You go out don't you?"

"Go out," I said amused. "Of course I go out. I go out of my house to my office, out of my office to the gym, and out of the gym, back to my house."

She laughed and said, "You know what I mean. Like on dates and stuff."

"Stuff," I said as I recalled using that on her during our first conversation. "I don't think I know what you mean by stuff."

"Okay Shawn," she sighed. "You got me on that one."

I figured I'd gotten over. I was surprised when she said in frustration, "Why can't you just tell me what you like, and what you do?"

"I don't know what you're getting at Troi," I answered calmly. "I already told you I like basketball and that I don't do too much of anything."

"Nobody can be like that," she said throwing her hands in the air.

"Well I can't speak for nobody," I said smiling. "But, I'm like that."

"Okay Shawn," she said, pushing her water aside. "If you are like that, why are you like that?"

"Because," I happily replied.

"Because?" she yelled. "Because what!"

Everyone looked over at us like we were two of those cheesy wanted criminals who leer out at you from the bulletin board posters at the post office. You look at them with disdain, because you know they're the pettiest of petty. You hate the fact that you may someday run into them. I understood how they felt. I waved and said, "We're not crooks, she's just a little upset."

"Shawn," she whispered. "How could you do that?"

"Do what?" I asked.

"How could you tell those people I was upset?"

"You are upset."

"I am not upset."

"If you're not upset Troi?" I asked smiling, "then explain

to me why you're trying to yell and whisper at the same time?"

She shook her head and started tearing up her napkin. Troi was clearly frustrated.

I understood why she was frustrated. I wasn't making sense, and my dad once told me one of the hardest things anyone can do is attempt to make sense out of someone else's nonsense.

The waiter came. Troi, ordered two surf and turf combos and two Cokes. We'd discussed what we would get on the way to the restaurant, and I could deal with the surf and turf deal. Especially since she'd already committed to treating. The waiter came back and dropped the sodas off. She looked over at me and asked, "Are you hiding something?"

"Am I hiding something?" I said. "Do you mean like under the table or out in my ride?"

"No!" she stated. "I mean is there something about you that you don't want me to know?"

"Of course not," I told her. "I've told you all there is to know." Just then the waiter showed up with our food. His timing couldn't have been better. There was no way she could expect me to yap while we were eating.

Unfortunately, we were at the end of a busy day, so we blazed through the food like two kamikaze dieters who'd just left their weigh-in at a Jenny Craig weight reduction center. As soon as she finished her last piece of steak, she again asked me, "What is it that you don't want me to know?"

I imagined she was taking a stab at my inheritance since I told her my parents died before I was twenty-one, but I wasn't *about* to talk about that.

"You're not making much sense Troi."

"What do you mean I'm not making sense?"

"If I were really hiding something," I said casually. "Do you think I would just confess it because you asked me?"

"Maybe," she replied, uncomfortably.

"I think you *may be* wrong," I said laughing. "Look Troi,

I've told you everything there is to know. I like basketball, and I don't go out that often." I looked at her and could see she was frustrated. This was our last evening together and I wanted it to be a memorable one. I felt I'd told her everything she wanted to know. It hit me that I hadn't told her everything she *needed* to know. I didn't give her the details she needed about my life. Since we'd talked at the Hotel Washington that night, I thought of my father more often. This episode made me think of him, and a poor shooting performance I'd had one night.

I was eight years old and was playing ball in the county twelve-year-old league. In our first game, I got ten open shots and made just one of them. Needless to say, my dad was furious when we got home. It was 9:30 on a cold November night. He pulled into our driveway, left the car headlights on, jumped out and told me to shoot. I quickly shot and methodically made ten in a row.

"Look at yourself!" he yelled. "What are you doing differently?"

"Differently from what?" I asked as the chilly night air ran up the legs of my warm-up suit.

"Differently from that ridiculous shooting performance you just made me sit through," he fired back.

"I don't know," I told him.

"Look Shawn," he said, while grabbing the ball from me and hoisting it toward the basket. "If you don't follow through properly, you won't have sufficient rotation on your shot, and it will not, I repeat, will not fall consistently."

It was now 9:45 and I was freezing. The only rotation I was thinking about was into my pajamas and underneath my covers.

"Look son," he said as he placed his arm over my shoulders. "Life is about details." I was cold. I wanted to detail my butt into the house. "You play the game well," he told me, "because you usually take care of the details."

That made me feel better, though not warmer.

"But you have to do it all the time," he reminded me. "You have to make sure you are thorough in your preparation and comprehensive in your tendencies if you want to succeed." We started walking toward the front door, and I felt relieved. "Details are important both on and off the court," he added. "And I want you to succeed regardless of what you do, so you must pay particular attention to details."

He closed the door. The heat scattered up my legs, like a mouse cutting across a kitchen floor when the lights are turned on. I gave him five and said, "Thanks dad." I imagine he thought I was thanking him for the advice. I was appreciative of the fact that he had let me go inside.

"Remember son," he said as he tucked me into bed. "Take care of the details, and they'll take care of you."

I was much warmer, and therefore much happier. "I got you dad. Details," I said. We smiled and slapped each other five. He turned off the light and closed my door.

I felt a smidgen of poetic justice as I left the house for school the next morning. I noticed my dad inside his car getting a jump-start from our next door neighbor, Mr. Spencer. "What happened?" I asked.

Mr. Spencer smiled and said, "I think your old man left his lights on last night. It's no big deal, it happens all the time."

I thought about how cold I'd been the night before and smiled as I walked toward my father's car. As he turned the key in the ignition, I knocked on the window, waved, and yelled, "Details dad. It's all about details." I ran off before he could say anything, but I found he was right. I scored twenty-eight points in our next game when I followed his advice.

I knew it was time to follow it again. I had to give Troi the details, even though I felt there wasn't much to give.

"Okay Troi," I said. "I have an idea."

"An idea about what?" she answered.

"Why don't you ask me what you want to know?"

"Why don't I ask you?" she shot back. "Why can't you just tell me?"

"How should I know what you want to know?" I asked grinning. She laughed and agreed with me. The waiter dropped by with a wonderful dessert tray, but we told him, "Not yet," and kept talking.

"I know I'm bringing some of my baggage into this Shawn," she said exasperated. "But I truly don't understand why men have such a hard time talking."

I knew she'd left her luggage in my ride, and I'd made it a point to speak correctly while she was around, so I couldn't relate to her dilemma.

"Well Troi," I said confidently. "As you can hear, I don't have much difficulty talking."

"What are you talking about?" she said. "You won't talk about anything if I don't force you to."

"I've told you everything Troi, but I'm willing to tell you more."

"That's more like it Shawn," she said smiling. "Now tell me what you like."

"I told you," I quickly replied. "I like basketball." I told her basketball was my life for most of my life and that I got a lot from it. I'd lost much more though. I'd lost my parents.

"You didn't lose your parents by playing basketball," she told me. "You didn't have anything to do with it."

I looked at her puzzled and said, "What do you mean I had nothing to do with it? They both died when they were watching me play."

Troi reached across the table and held my hand. She smiled and whispered, "Shawn, God decided it was time for your parents to take their place in heaven. God's will is bigger than any slam dunk you ever made, or ever could make."

I remembered my mother ran that same exact line on me after my dad died. It didn't make sense then. It made even less sense after my mom passed in the exact same way that he did. I wondered if Troi knew who God was and if she stayed in touch with God. She'd been through a lot, and she seemed cool. My mother said God helped her to accept my father's death. She constantly reminded me to thank God for giving me the natural talent to play ball. I didn't get to say much. My coaches were always doing it for me. Every time I'd hit a game-winning shot (which was often), they'd look toward the ceiling of the gym and run off the court yelling, "Thank God! Thank God we won!"

"Trust me Shawn," she reassured me. "It's not your fault. You can stop feeling guilty."

I was worried. Troi was starting to make sense too often. Just like my mom.

"As long as you feel guilty, you'll never do anything to get beyond it," she said. "You'll never play ball, you'll never dunk, you'll never allow yourself to really live." She was sounding way too much like my mom, which made me feel totally weird. I interrupted and asked, "Are we getting dessert?"

"Why do you do that?" she asked annoyed.

"Why do I do what?" I replied. "We always get dessert."

"Why do you insist on running from anything meaningful by asking meaningless questions at the wrong time?"

"Meaningless?" I said. "It wasn't meaningless when you wanted extra bread pudding at Georgia Brown's on Wednesday."

"That's not what I'm talking about and you know it," she angrily replied.

I knew she was right, but I was stalling for time. She had to be at the airport in an hour, and I didn't really want to talk about my parents anymore. I wanted to focus in on us. She had a point about the guilt stuff. I had plenty of time to contemplate it, but I only had an hour with her and I realized I needed details just like she did. Only I needed them about us.

"Troi," I said, while avoiding her question. "I'm not trying to avoid anything, I just want to talk about something else."

"Something else?" she smugly replied. "Something else like what?"

"Something like us."

"Us?" she answered surprised. "What about us?"

I wasn't exactly sure what I meant about us, so I asked, "What is it that we're doing?"

"What is it that we're doing?" she said smiling. "We're getting ready for dessert."

We both laughed, but I quickly understood how she felt when I was ducking her questions because she really ordered dessert and actually started taking note of the time. She told me she'd had a wonderful time, that she would miss me and that she expected to see me play basketball when she came back to town. I liked that. Not because she wanted to see me play, but because she said she was coming back. She saved me from asking about it.

I still had a funny feeling. She absolutely refused to discuss anything about us. We'd had a wonderful week. But I had no clue as to what Troi saw in me. I'm a decent guy. But Troi was about twenty steps above decent. If Halle Berry was a solid ten, Troi Stevenson was a solid fifty (plus she seemed like a 6). She was smart, sexy, beautiful, and completely honest. Troi was the total package. She was the type you rushed home to meet your parents. I'd never been around such good marrying material. Not that I wanted to marry her. That never even crossed my mind. I just wanted to know where I stood.

"Why do you like me?" I asked, nervously.

"Why do I like you?"

"Yeah," I said. "What do you see in me?"

"What do I see in you?"

"Is there an echo in here or something?" I asked smiling.

"Funny Shawn," she said, while turning her wrist to look at her watch.

I reached for her hand, looked her in the eye, and once again said, "Tell me why you like me."

"I like you because you're sweet," she said smiling. "You're decent. I feel safe with you. I know you would take care of me, and I'd never have to worry about you."

"Is that it?"

"Of course that's it," she said surprised. "Isn't that enough?"

It wasn't enough. It reminded me of a particularly bad blind date I'd been on. Kelly set me up with a friend of hers who was especially overzealous in her pursuit of food. She ran up a $60 tab, and spent half the evening talking about some guy who'd just dumped her. When I dropped her off, she thanked me for listening and told me I'd given her the courage to call him. Kelly called and asked what I thought. "She was very honest," I told her. "She was decent, and I felt safe with her."

"That's great," Kelly happily answered.

She was decent all right. Unlike Danielle (who broke me at Jasper's), she at least offered to share her food before she devoured it. She was also nice enough to ask if I wanted the rest of mine before she reached over and slid it onto her plate. I felt safe because she was as thick as a any NFL linebacker that I'd seen. Nobody was going to bother us. Troi may not have realized it, but she said the worst things you say to a guy. Whatever happened to handsome, sexy, riveting, compelling, and just plain cool? I doubted she saw any of that in me. But I'm a guy. Guys like to hear that stuff. She pretty much told me I was a decent date. I wanted more than that.

"Let me get this straight," I said. "You like me because I'm honest, and because you feel safe with me."

"Sort of," she answered. "I didn't actually say I liked you. Those are just qualities I like about you."

"Oh, so now you're saying you don't like me."

"I didn't say I didn't like you Shawn."

"You didn't say you did."

"Of course I like you," she said. "You're a wonderful man, you impress me."

"I impress *you?*" I asked surprised.

"Of course you do," she said, smiling. "I still can't believe you pulled off those tickets for the black-tie dinner," she added. "Only a man who truly has it going on could have managed that."

That was more like it. That was better than honest and

decent. Casper the Friendly Ghost was honest and decent. I wasn't trying to be Casper. He never got laid.

"You are quite a catch Mr. Shawn Wayne," she said. "You're funny, you're sexy, you're a wonderful lover, and strange as it may seem, I'm drawn to your innocence," she added while reaching for my hand. "I am really going to miss you."

"I'm going to miss you," I whispered.

We sat and looked at each other for what seemed like an eternity. I didn't say anything and she didn't utter a word. We were taking stock. Reminiscing. Wondering. Fantasizing. and, hopefully, considering a future that included each other.

The fifteen-minute ride to the airport was sobering. It was obvious neither of us wanted her to leave. She held my hand so tight my foot fell asleep from lack of circulation. We nearly sideswiped a limousine on the 14th Street Bridge. The driver rolled down his heavily tinted window and chomped on his cigar. He extended the middle finger on his right hand. I saw one of my coaches do that before, but the ref threw him out before the coach could tell him why he didn't like the call. I figured the driver was probably a frustrated coach. I sped away because my foot woke back up and because we were pressed for time.

We got to the airport at 10:35 and rushed through the terminal, but found her plane was running fifteen minutes late. She checked her bags. As we approached the loading deck, she pulled two boxes from her purse.

"I'm glad the plane is late," she said smiling. "These are for you." I was nervous. It made me think of the two boxes in the dream. We'd never discussed the dream, so I figured the chances for Jordan's first *Sports Illustrated* cover were slim. But I knew I didn't want to see that heart again. I only wanted the real one.

I opened the first box and laughed. It had three pairs of beautiful silk socks.

"I figured I owed you since I threw yours over the balcony," she said grinning. She then turned toward the huge airfield observation window, and said, "Tell me when you're finished with that one."

I didn't understand that move, but I figured she just wanted to look at the planes. I opened the slender box, and found a beautiful black silk necktie, and a stunning black bow tie. I just held them up, and said, "Troi these are beautiful-you didn't have to do this." "Yes I did," she answered as she turned back around. We broke out in laughter. She had put on my clip-on necktie, which had fallen to the side, just like it did at the black-tie dinner. I was surprised when I heard a familiar laugh coming from behind me.

"That's cute sister," said the man who was walking toward us.

I turned around and was shocked. I looked up and once again saw Jesse Jackson. He had on the same Nike warm-up suit he was wearing when I first met him on the elevator.

"Son," he told me while reaching to shake my hand, "I learned something from you." I didn't know exactly what he meant, but I hoped that he wasn't referring to what I'd said about Troi on the elevator.

"Will we see you at next year's conference?" he asked.

"You sure will, Reverend," interrupted Troi. "We'll be there." I looked at her surprised. We stood closer together. It felt funny standing in front of a preacher with Troi at my side like she was. It had to look like a wedding scene, but I knew it wasn't. Troi would never wear a clip-on tie to anyone's wedding. Especially ours.

As the passengers embarked onto the plane, a short guy walked up with a beautiful set of leather luggage. "It's time to go Reverend Jackson," he said. Troi and I looked up. We had to laugh. It was the limousine driver I'd almost run into on the bridge. Troi kissed me and told me she'd call. She made me promise I'd come see her. My head was above the clouds her plane was preparing to fly through. She was leaving, but everything seemed cool. She made it a point to assure me (and herself) that we were getting back together.

Our week hadn't been hit and run. It had been real for her, just like it had for me. I knew I'd finally found my 6.

I watched the plane take off and made my way back to my ride. I turned on my cellular to call Donnie, but I figured I'd check my messages first.

"Please hold," said a mechanical voice I didn't recognize. "You have a call from the American Airlines air phone.

"Shawn," stated the caller slowly. "I miss you already." It was Troi, and I already missed her too, but I wasn't about to call her in an airplane to tell her so. That would have cost a bundle from my cell phone. I looked in my rearview mirror and noticed someone had blocked in Jesse Jackson's limousine. My curiosity was getting the best of me. I jumped out, walked back to the limo, and knocked on the window. The driver rolled it down, leered at me, and spat out, "What do you want?!"

"I was just wondering what team you coached," I said.

"What team do I coach?" he asked. "What the hell are you talking about?" I extended the middle finger of my right hand and walked away. The limo driver pulled up next to my ride. He blew his horn, rolled down his window, and again extended his middle finger toward me. I rolled my window down and yelled, "Nice meeting you coach!" before extending my middle finger back to him. It didn't make sense, but he just shook his head and pulled off.

I was feeling pretty good even though Troi was gone. I called my machine to hear Troi's message again. I'd saved it. I had actually saved every message she'd left, except the one that said, "We have to talk" (I had erased that one before I left work that day). I played her last message, "I miss you already," six times (she was my 6, so I figured it was appropriate) and recounted our week over and over in my head as I drove up I-95, and across the Woodrow Wilson Bridge. I remembered every moment like it had just happened. I wondered if what she told me about my parents was true. Troi was like them. She was smart, she was thoughtful, she made sense, and she understood me. Most important, she cared about me.

I sat in my driveway and listened to our song, Pat Metheny's *Cathedral In A Suitcase,* six times before I forced myself to go inside. This was the first night I slept at home in nearly a week. I wanted to be sleeping somewhere with Troi. Not just somewhere with her, anywhere. I listened to her last message again as I undressed. After turning out the light, I sat at the edge of my bed to wait for *SportsCenter* to come on. I looked down at my feet and smiled when I realized I still had my socks on. It hit me that in just one week, Troi had given me enough good memories to last me the rest of my life.

You're going to miss her, I thought. *You're really going to miss her.*

17th
Message

Troi's first night away was the toughest I'd had in years. As I slept, I kept turning over with hopes that she'd be there. She wasn't. I lay awake and thought about what she was doing and wondered if she was thinking about me. I hoped she still missed me. I played her messages again while I watched the 3:00 a.m. encore of *SportsCenter.* Amazingly, Troi had made quite an impact on my life. It didn't seem to make sense because we'd only been with each other for a week.

I wanted to call her, but I thought about what Kelly had told me and realized calling someone at three in the morning would look pretty desperate. She could call me anytime she wanted to. Two in the morning, three in the morning, it wouldn't matter, as long as she called. I forced myself back to sleep and couldn't wait for the sun to rise and wake me up. Fortunately, the phone rang at 6:00 a.m. before the sun came through. A smile jumped across my face. I knew it had to be her.

"Good morning," I happily answered.

"Good morning to you too," replied the sweet voice on the other end. "I was just wondering," she continued, "could you come by a little early to pick me up?" It was Kelly. As usual, her early morning call was directly related to a ride to work.

"Sure," I said, softly. "What time?"

"What's wrong with you?" she asked. "Let me guess. Miss *thing* has gone back to Chicago, and now you're stuck with dealing with us regular folk."

"That's not exactly it."

"Well, what is exactly it?" she asked.

"You wouldn't understand," I slowly answered.

"What do you mean I wouldn't understand?" she said frustrated, "I understand everything else!"

Maybe she would understand, I thought. But I didn't understand Kelly.

I noticed that every time Troi's name came up, Kelly seemed to get upset. This time was no different. I couldn't see why Kelly didn't care for Troi, because Troi really seemed to like her. Kelly and this guy she met at a CBC reception joined us for drinks one night. She nearly lost it because her date was fawning over Troi. He basically ignored Kelly and asked Troi how long she'd be in town. He told her he'd show her around if I were too busy.

I didn't like his move, but I loved her response.

"Shawn would never be too busy for me," she told him smiling, "and if he was, I'd have no problem waiting for him. He's worth the wait."

Kelly was fuming, but she really got upset when he offered a toast. He romantically gazed at Kelly and said, "To the most beautiful woman at the conference." He then looked toward us and stated, "To you Troi. May you be successful in your endeavors, and may God continue to bless you."

Troi and I were raising our sodas and I didn't see what happened next, but somehow Kelly's drink ended up in her date's face. She grabbed her coat and marched toward the door. I remembered thinking she must have really hated that drink. Troi said he deserved it.

"Deserved what?" I asked, while sipping my soda.

"Forget it Shawn," she said. "I think we'd better leave."

I shook Kelly's date's hand and said, "It was nice meeting you. Maybe we can do this again soon."

We left him wiping his face at the table.

When I picked Kelly up for work the next morning, she said Troi brought it on by acting so "prim and proper." She told me I should have intervened.

"Why should I have stopped him?" I asked laughing. "He was with you." Besides, he committed to paying the very moment he saw Troi. I thought he could have said almost anything as long as he was treating and as long as he didn't disrespect Troi.

Kelly just didn't like Troi. She almost seemed happy that she'd gone back to Chicago.

"Shawn," she said, bringing me back to reality. "I know you're not stuck on Troi."

"I'm not stuck on her," I said. "But I do miss her."

"Miss her!" she yelled. "How can you miss her? She just left!"

"I know she just left," I said. "But I was missing her before the plane took off."

"This is ridiculous Shawn!" she said. "Do you think she misses you?"

"She said she did."

"When did she say that?"

"When she called," I told her.

"She called?"

"Yeah," I answered. "She called me from the plane."

"She called you from the plane?" she gasped.

"She sure did," I answered proudly.

There was a deep silence. Kelly then jumped in and said, "She called from the plane because she hadn't gotten home yet, but I guarantee you won't hear from her after she settles back in."

I thought about it and hoped she wasn't right.

"I bet she didn't even call to let you know she made it back," she said sarcastically.

I didn't like what she'd said. She was right. Troi hadn't called again, and I knew she had to be back in Chicago. I'd listened to the news and hadn't heard about any plane crashes.

"Look Shawn," she said, softly. "I'm sorry."

"Sorry about what?" I asked.

"I shouldn't have said those things about Troi," she said. "I know how much you like her, and I know she's probably a beautiful sister. But, I'm your friend. I don't want to see you get hurt."

"What makes you think I'm going to get hurt?" I asked hesitantly.

"Because," she started. "Troi came to town looking for fun."

Looking for fun? I wondered.

"She probably needed to get away from her routine in Chicago," she said. "So you provided her the break, but now she's back to the reality of her real world." We suffered through another one of those long silences before she said, "Face it Shawn, you may never hear from her again."

I shuddered. Maybe she was right. Kelly was usually on target when it came to women. I couldn't imagine what it would be like if I didn't hear from Troi again.

My concern grew to fear when I didn't hear from her on the first day. It escalated to panic when she didn't call for the first week. I knew she was busy. But nobody's so busy that they can't pick up a phone to call. I tried to call her, but she never answered. I left cute little messages. They didn't work. I even called her job. Her uncle answered. He was nice the first time. After about the eighth time, he told me he'd given her my messages. "Apparently, she doesn't want to speak with you," he said before introducing me to Mr. Dial Tone. I hated being hung up on.

Slowly, I dwindled into a protracted slump.

I couldn't believe she hadn't called. We'd made so many wonderful memories in our short time together, and I couldn't shake any of them. I called my answering machine and checked my messages constantly. I sat and stared at the phone some nights waiting for it to ring. I would pick up the receiver to make sure the phone was working. I even convinced an operator to make an emergency cut-in when the line was busy one night. It didn't work. She'd left the phone off the hook. I couldn't force myself to wear the ties she'd bought for me. I did wear the socks though. All of my other socks were rotting in the hamper.

I couldn't work out and I didn't want to eat. I felt like a discarded croaker at Red Lobster. I didn't like fish, but my mom did. She always ordered croaker when we ate out. She'd eat it to the bone, would commend the chef, and often gave the waiter a generous tip after she finished. What bugged me was that the remains of the fish invariably ended up being trashed. It brought my mom a good deal of pleasure, the waiter a good tip, and the chef a worthy compliment, but it ended up with nothing but its bones in the trash. It had been used for someone else's benefit. That's exactly how I felt.

I was Troi's well-done, half-eaten croaker.

She'd complimented me, just like my mom complimented the chefs. Though I knew it was a stretch, I reasoned the socks and the ties were a tip of some sort. After she "tipped me," my usefulness had expired, she tossed me out just like the bones of a freshly digested croaker. I knew once the fish was cooked, it had to be eaten. When it was eaten, the bones had to go. But had it been left alone in the first place, it wouldn't have ended up being tossed in the trash. My mother once told me it was better to have loved and lost than to not have loved at all. I didn't buy that. Feeling like a croaker wasn't getting it for me. I wanted to be a goldfish or something. At least people keep them around. I felt worse than the fish. I knew someone would pick up its bones (along with the rest of the trash) and ultimately put the lonely bones out of their misery and into an incinerator. Nobody was going to pick me up and put me out of my misery.

I honestly felt that way until my phone rang when I was getting into the shower one night. I let it ring. I imagined it was probably Donnie or Kelly trying to cheer me up again and I didn't want to be cheered up. It didn't make sense, but I wanted to feel bad and lonely. I figured it was the only way for me to get over her. My machine picked up anyway. When I heard that wonderful melodic voice flow through the speaker I bolted from the shower, and ran right into the door.

It was Troi!

"Shawn," she said. "I got your messages. I apologize for not calling, but I've been so busy."

I picked myself off of the floor, but once again tripped over the soap I'd dropped when I fell the first time.

"I miss you so much, but I'm stuck on this project, and I can't get away," she continued. "I was wondering if there was any way that you could get up here."

I raced to the phone, picked up the receiver, and excitedly yelled, "When?!"

"Shawn," she said. "Is it really you?"

"Of course it's me," I answered while drying myself off. "Who did you expect?"

"It's so good to hear your voice," she said. "How have you been?"

"I've been like a croaker," I replied half-heartedly.

"A croaker?"

"Just like a croaker," I answered dead-panned, "I'll tell you about it later."

"So are you coming up to see me?"

Am I coming? I thought amused. *She's got to be kidding.*

This was just like when she was in town and asked me if I was coming back to see her at the hotel. Despite the resentment, anger, and pain I'd suffered over the three weeks she hadn't called, there was no real decision to be made. All of those bad feelings seemed to be a million miles away. I couldn't relate to *if* I was coming. I just wanted to know when she wanted me to be there and how long she wanted me to stay.

"Of course I'm coming," I said. "What's good for you?"

"This weekend looks good for me," she answered. "I'll Fed-Ex you a ticket tomorrow, and I'll pick you up from the airport Saturday morning."

"That's a bet," I enthusiastically stated.

"Shawn," she seductively whispered. "I hope you're ready to bring home the bacon."

I smiled. "Only if you bring out the pan."

"The pan's always out for you," she replied before blowing me a kiss and saying goodbye.

I couldn't believe she'd called, in the exact same way I couldn't believe she hadn't called. I felt the same way I felt when she made me promise to come see her and when she left the message that said, "I miss you already." I felt special, I felt needed, and I felt complete. All of which confirmed that Troi was my 6. I thought about how bad it felt when I was feeling like a croaker and smiled because I was once again feeling like watered down Play-Doh. It felt weird because my feelings had never been exposed like they were now. I didn't understand how I could go from being a cooked croaker to wet Play-Doh in such a short time. She had apologized and said she missed me. That was all I needed to hear. The fact that she even called was enough for me. The moment I heard her voice the bad feelings all but faded.

I jumped back in the shower and had my first good night's sleep since she'd left. I don't know if I normally slept with a smile, but I know I did that night. I couldn't help it. I was happy, and it felt good to feel that way again.

I couldn't wait to see her. Being a goldfish would be nice.

18th Message

"I WAS OUT OF LINE."

MESSAGE SENT ON
NOVEMBER 17TH AT 7:24 A.M.

When I picked Kelly up the next morning, I told her Troi called and that I was going to Chicago to see her on the weekend. "Hold it Shawn," she interrupted. "You promised you'd take me to Home Depot to help me pick out some mini-blinds."

"Kelly," I calmly answered. "I didn't promise anything. And I wasn't going to help you pick them out, I was only giving you a ride."

"You did promise!" she said, "and you were going to help me. You said that you would."

"Kelly, you know I never said I would help you pick out anything," I told her. "You wouldn't even trust my taste enough to help you pick out anything," I added. "So I don't know where that's coming from."

"You have very good taste Shawn," she said sarcastically. "Except when it comes to women."

"We don't even need to go there today Kelly," I said.

"No Shawn," she responded forcefully. "You don't need to go there."

I wondered what she meant. I'd never seen Kelly this upset. Over the past few weeks she had proven to be an especially understanding and loyal friend. She listened as I talked about how much I missed Troi. She even came by to clean up my place and wash my clothes. She knew I was depressed. One Saturday she came by with a picnic basket and two tickets to a University of Maryland football game. I remember her smiling and saying, "If this doesn't help, nothing will." She had on Maryland's traditional colors, red and white and it was a wonderful day, until the game actually started. They got pounded by Florida State. I didn't say a word on the way home. The way they were blown out reminded me of how I'd been blown out by Troi. Kelly didn't mind though, she just held my hand and said, "It's going to be all right. She's going to call before you know it." I don't think she actually believed Troi was going to call, but she said it so often that I started to believe it.

I couldn't figure out why Kelly spent so much time convincing me that everything was going to be cool. She said Troi would call and when she finally calls, Kelly's not happy for me. It didn't make sense.

We were at a stop light on Rhode Island Avenue. I looked at her and asked, "Whadda you mean I don't need to go there?"

"You don't need to go," she quickly replied, "because you don't need to go."

"What's that mean," I asked, "that I don't need to go?"

"Shawn," she explained cautiously. "Troi didn't think to call you for three weeks." *That's true,* I thought.

"She didn't return your calls, she didn't write, she didn't do anything for or about Shawn," she continued. "Miss *thing* got so caught up in whatever she was doing, or *whoever* she was doing, that keeping in touch with you wasn't even an issue."

I didn't like the sound of this. It sounded too true. Especially the "whoever she was doing" part.

"Shawn, you were so out of it you couldn't even watch *SportsCenter* for a week," she stressed. "You can't let someone have that level of impact on your feelings without getting something back."

What Kelly didn't understand was that I didn't want or expect anything back. I only wanted Troi.

"You can't let her walk over you like that," she insisted as we finally pulled into the garage at work. "You can't just let her call you out of the blue and go running like a trained puppy."

"Kelly," I said cautiously. "I don't understand why you're so upset."

"I'm upset!" she yelled while taking off her seat belt, "because you're going out there and I'll have to get my mini-blinds alone. And while you're out there with her, I'll be putting up my mini-blinds alone. I care about you, and she doesn't, but when she says jump, you say how high and how long, and if I even asked you to jump, you'd turn around and ask me why."

We looked at each other over the top of my ride and I said, "I'm sorry Kelly, you're right. Why don't we go get the mini-blinds tonight?"

She slammed the door and stomped off. She didn't even hold the elevator for me.

I honestly didn't understand why she was so distressed. I figured the mini-blinds must have meant a lot to her.

Kelly didn't ride to work with me, wouldn't speak to me, and stood me up on our regular Thursday turkey lunch date at the Wall Street Deli on E Street. It was a bittersweet three days. Troi called at least twice everyday. I was so excited. I wanted to tell Kelly about it, but couldn't. She wouldn't return my calls. She finally called and left a message on Friday morning.

"I was out of line," she confessed to my machine. She then apologized, and said if I took her to Home Depot after work, treated her to dinner, and helped her with her mini-blinds, we could call a truce. I knew I needed to pack. I had to be at National Airport by 8:00 the next morning, but I missed Kelly and wanted to tell her the good news about Troi.

The evening was relatively pain free until Kelly asked, "Are you still going to Chicago?"

"Yeah," I answered, cautiously, "I'm leaving in the morning."

"Okay," she said. "I wish you luck."

"What do you mean you wish me luck?" I asked concerned.

"Because," she replied, "you finally seem like yourself again. I hate to see what's going to happen when you come back."

"What makes you think that something's going to happen?" I asked.

"Because," she stated, firmly, "she's going to hurt you."

"Why would you say something like that?" I asked. "You're supposed to be my friend."

"I am your friend," she deliberately stated, "and that's why I'm saying it now, so you won't go out there with the wrong expectations."

I wasn't sure what she meant about the wrong expectations. I only expected to define our relationship. And to have great butt-naked sex, of course.

I thought about what Kelly had said when I dropped by Prince George's Plaza to pick up some undershirts from Hecht's. I knew tee-shirts at Hecht's were probably expensive, but I'd received one of their gift certificates from my co-workers last Christmas. For once, the cost really didn't matter. I knew I was taking a chance by going out to Chicago. I felt being with Troi justified the risk. As I left Hecht's, I walked by a jewelry store. It had a big neon-orange going-out-of-business sign in the doorway. I never much paid attention to jewelry stores. I didn't wear jewelry. It costs too much. I was struck by this one though. In the window was a beautiful gleaming puffed heart. But it wasn't just any heart. It was the exact same gold heart Troi had entrusted me with in the dream.

That heart was like a magnet. I walked in without knowing why I walked in and instinctively motioned to the heart. "How much is it?" I asked.

"How much do you want to pay for it?" asked the salesman. That line alone quickly brought me back to my senses.

"Not much," I quickly replied.

"Well how much is not much?" he asked smiling.

"How much does it cost?"

"Well it retails for two hundred," he slowly stated. "But since we're going out of business, I'll give it to you for $50."

"You'll give it to me for fifty bucks," I said grinning. "I don't think I can afford for you to give it to me for $50."

He laughed and said, "Well this is our last day. What will you pay for me to give it to you?"

I moved my head back and held the heart in my left hand. I considered the risk Kelly eluded to. *If it doesn't work out you can't get a refund,* I thought. I definitely didn't want to sink major bucks into something that might not work out.

"I'll pay $8 for it," I said.

"Eight bones," he said laughing. "Are you sick?"

"Nah," I answered smiling, "I feel fine."

"Look bro," he started, "I like you, and I'll work with you, but $8 American ain't getting it."

"Okay," I said as I turned to walk out of the store. "It's no big deal."

He ran around the counter, and said, "It is a big deal. You wouldn't have come in here if it wasn't a big deal."

He was right. I wouldn't have gone in if it wasn't a big deal, but I didn't care how big a deal it was. I only had $8 on me so I had no room to bargain.

"Look cuz," he said, sounding like Donnie. "This joint will be closed forever in about an hour."

"And?" I interrupted.

"And I'll give you a break, but you can't carry me like this."

"Look cousin," I said, as I realized that I meant to say, "cuz." "I've got $8 on me right now, and that's all that I've got."

He leaned back and tapped his right forefinger on his chin. "You sure you only got eight bucks?" he asked in disbelief. I took the bills out of my pocket and plucked off the lint. "This is what I've got, nephew," I said.

He just laughed. He put the cash in his front pocket and said, "I shouldn't do it, but what have I got to lose?" He looked over my shoulder and whispered, "Look cuz, you don't need a receipt or nothing like that do you?"

"Nah, I'm cool," I said, wondering what "nothing like that" could be.

He handed me the heart, and said, "Good luck, main man."

"Don't I get a box or a bag or something?" I asked.

"For eight bucks," he said laughing. "The only thing you can get is your butt up out this store."

I got his hint. I scampered out of there like a first-grader rushing to a playground for afternoon recess.

I didn't have to pack much. Troi had booked a super-saver flight that required me to return to D.C. within twenty-four hours of my arrival in Chicago. I didn't like the idea at first. But, when I found the ticket was only $25, I dug it. *We could definitely keep seeing each other at twenty-five bucks a pop,* I thought. *Even I could swing that.* It was difficult to sleep that night. It reminded me of when I was a kid waiting for Santa Claus to show up at Christmas. I kept looking at the clock and begging it to get to 7:00 so I could jump up and dash for the airport, just like I used to run to the tree on Christmas morning. I couldn't wait to get to the airport. There was no way I was going to make it to 7:00. I got dressed at 5:00 a.m. and watched the 6:00 edition of *SportsCenter.* 7:00 couldn't get there fast enough. I was ready. I'd put on a pair of black denim jeans, the black leather bomber jacket Kelly had given me last Christmas, a simple red Ralph Lauren Polo sweatshirt (with a cool black horse), and a pair of well-kept classic red, white, and black Air Jordans-the same that Mars Blackmon wore in Spike

Lee's hit debut flick, *She's Gotta Have It!*

I owned a collection of Air Jordan sneakers that was probably more awesome than the assortment Michael Jordan had himself. My gallery of Jordans included every pair ever made. From the classics I was wearing, to the more sophisticated high-tech ones with the abundant padding and sleek Italian styling. I'd never worn any of them. In fact, I'd never even taken them out of their boxes. I'd vowed never to let them touch any floor, anywhere, unless the situation called for it. I didn't see them as mere sneakers. They were works of art that could be appreciated by those who had an undying love for the game, or had a heavy dose of respect for M.J. My annual November 1st purchase of new Jordans was an eagerly anticipated ritual. I knew they were overpriced, and though I never balled in them, I knew if I ever did I'd want to play in the same shoes that Jordan wore. Every other player's shoe came out and it wasn't a big deal. When Jordan's shoe hit the shelves, the stores were packed. I knew guys who missed work to ensure they got theirs before their size was sold out. I'd heard that guys who wore them to the gym would get picked to play (even if they had no game) because they had the balls to wear Jordans to the gym in the first place.

I never imagined I'd wear them. But this was a special occasion, and Troi deserved the best that I had.

I drove to National Airport, parked in the satellite parking lot and immediately wondered why a satellite would need a parking space in the first place. The plane was on time, and I was out of D.C. and in Chicago before I knew it. As I walked off of the plane I wondered what she'd be wearing and what it would feel like to have her in my arms again. Knowing Troi, she probably sprung for some flowers. She might have even ordered up a limo. She was like that, and that's why I liked her. She'd do unique little things that showed she cared. Although Kelly didn't see that in her, I did. Troi always went out of her way to make things special. That's why she was so neat. I decided to be the last off the plane to surprise her. The

surprise was on me. When I walked into the passenger greeting area, she wasn't there. I figured we had our times mixed
up since I'd changed time zones. I checked my Timex. It was
10:00 a.m., her time. I knew I was supposed to get there at
11:00 my time, which was 10:00 her time. I figured she
thought it was supposed to be eleven her time. I just grabbed
my bag and decided to wait it out.

It was eleven her time before I knew it, which made it
twelve my time. I stood up and waited for her to parade in
with some flowers or something. She didn't show. *She must
be running a little late,* I told myself smiling. I lost my smile
at 12:05, her time. I knew she couldn't be that late. I decided to call. She wasn't at home, but I left a message on her
answering machine. I couldn't believe she was late by both
of our times. I figured it was a stretch, but I decided to call
her office. Every time I called in the past I got her uncle or
voice-mail. I knew I might not even get an answer on a
Saturday, but I had to try something.

"You've reached Myers and Stevenson, this is Troi
Stevenson," she said.

"You're there!" I yelled.

"Yes I am," she casually replied. "With whom would you
like to speak?"

"Troi," I said. "It's me."

"Me?" she asked. "Me who?"

"Me, who?" I interrupted. "Me, me!"

"Shawn!" she said. "Are you on your way?"

"On my way!" I fired back. "I'm here!"

"You're here," she said. "You're where?"

"I'm here at the airport," I replied.

"You're in Chicago?" she asked.

"Yeah," I answered. "You were supposed to pick me up
two hours ago. Remember?"

"Oh my God!" she gasped. "I'm so sorry Shawn, I lost
track of time."

"Don't sweat it," I said. "How long will it take you to get
here?"

"I'm about an hour-and-a-half away," she answered. "But here's what you can do." "What's that?" I asked.

"Get a cab to my condo. I'll call ahead to have my building manager let you in, and I'll meet you there."

"Okay," I replied. "When will you get there?"

"Give me a minute," she answered. "I have to put the finishing touches on this piece."

I didn't feel comfortable with this arrangement. I didn't want to pay for a cab, but it made more sense to meet her at her place than to wait at the airport for another ninety minutes.

"I'll hurry," she assured me before hanging up.

The ride to her condo was quick. I didn't get to see much of Chicago. It had streets, stop lights, churches, and liquor stores just like D.C. As far as I could tell, the only thing Chicago had that Washington didn't have was Michael Jordan. We had the president, but I'd take M.J. and the Chicago Stadium over Bill Clinton and the White House any day of the week.

The Sumo-wrestler sized cabbie parked outside her condo. He wanted to charge me $15 for a ten-minute ride.

"$15!" I exclaimed. "That's more than a dollar a minute."

"Look Mac, the fare is fifteen bucks. You can pay it, or I can take it from you—you decide."

I wondered who Mac was and realized he was serious about the $15. I pulled out all the money I had, a $20 bill, and handed it to him.

He shot me back a five, and said, "Ain't you gonna give me no tip?"

"I'll give you a tip," I said while stepping away from his ride. "Lose some weight!" He blew his horn, extended the middle finger of his right hand (just like Jesse Jackson's limo driver), and yelled, "Up yours!"

I extended my middle finger back toward him and yelled back, "Up yours too. Take care coach!"

He shook his head and slowly pulled away.

The building manager met me at the door. In a delightful

British accent he said, "You must be Mr. Wayne."

"Yeah," I told him, "I'm me."

"It's very good to meet you sir," he said. "Miss Troi called ahead and informed me you'd be arriving." We stepped on the elevator and he said, "She indicated that she'd arrive shortly. She asked me to make mention of some sort of bacon sir."

"Bacon?" I asked.

"Yes sir," he answered. "I believe she wanted to be certain you brought some bacon."

I had to laugh.

"Would you be requiring the grocer to deliver a spot of bacon sir?" he asked, while placing a key in the gold-plated doorknob.

"That won't be necessary," I said trying to mock him. "I've brought my own."

"Very good sir," he replied. "Don't hesitate to call should you require assistance."

I stood in Troi's dimly lit foyer. I couldn't believe I was actually in Chicago. I pulled the heart out of my pocket and buffed it on the sleeve of my sweatshirt and chuckled as I thought about how her building manager would feel if he knew just what type of bacon Troi was talking about.

She'll get the bacon alright, I thought. Because when she gets here, we're going out Oscar Mayer style.

19th
Message

 I was pretty drained from the excitement of just being there and from having gotten up too early, so I decided to drop my bag and cop a nap before Troi arrived. My father taught me that thorough preparation was a key to good performance. He said proper rest was a vital component to sound preparation. I knew I needed to be prepared because Troi made it clear she expected a lasting and impressionable performance. A quick nap was my only option. I wasn't sure whether I should hop on the sofa (if she had one) or jump in the bed and cool out there. I thought I'd look a little too anxious if I were on the bed. The sofa was going to have to work. I dropped my bag to the floor, took off my bomber and reached for the light switch. I quickly found I wouldn't be sleeping on the sofa because I didn't see one. I carefully stepped out of the foyer and into the living room.

I wasn't even sure if labeling it as a "living room" was appropriate. This place didn't appear to be fit for human habitat.

I felt like I'd gotten off at the Port Authority bus station in New York City. Kelly was from New York, and she described it as earth's final checkpoint to hell. "You see people there who cannot be living, and who are in no way qualified for a pass to heaven," she told me. "If they checked everyone who was at the Port Authority at any given time, I'm sure they'd find most of them are dead, and are en route to hell."

I laughed when she said it because I couldn't even imagine what she was talking about. But, there was nothing to laugh about here. Clothes were on top of clothes, which were on top of underwear. They led to a bunch of papers, which were stacked on top of more clothes. *This can't be what they mean by the layered look,* I thought as I instinctively started placing papers with papers and forming piles to separate the colors from the whites.

My mom once told me you can't get a complete read on a woman until you've seen how she lives. "The lipstick and the nails may look good on the outside," she warned me. "But the inside of their home makes a statement about how they see themselves and the world around them."

"The world around them?" I asked.

"That's what I said," she answered flatly. "A woman who can sleep among chaos will be willing to treat you and others in a chaotic manner."

I didn't understand that at the time.

"And if she's not willing to make her own existence comfortable, your existence will be of little consequence to her," she added.

"What if she's like Miss Porter around the corner, and she's too busy to keep her house up?" I asked.

"If she's like Miss Porter, you don't need to be bothered in the first place," she said laughing. "But a woman who *claims* to be too busy to keep her own place up is having a problem identifying her priorities," she explained. "And a woman who can't identify her own priorities will not make you a priority."

I was worried she was right. Troi's place was beyond hope. I couldn't believe it was so foul. I tossed clothes in the right piles, stacked papers in orderly mounds, and recalled how nice her hotel room was. One of the reasons Troi impressed me, was that her hotel suite was flawless whenever I showed up. She even had little chocolates on the pillows. The toilet paper would be folded with a neat little triangle at the end. The waste-baskets were always empty, and the towels were always fresh and folded just right. I couldn't figure out how she changed the linens everyday, washed and folded towels, dusted, kept her suite in immaculate condition, and still had the energy to go to meetings all day and make love to me all night.

I figured she was nothing short of amazing. I knew her condo was nothing short of amazing. But, it was amazing for all the wrong reasons.

I looked at my Timex. She'd be there soon. I decided to catch her at work to pin down what time she was leaving. When I called, she told me she was waiting on a fax from D.C. She'd be a little longer than she expected.

"Cool," I said smiling. "See you when you get here."

What struck me was that she never mentioned the condition of her place. I figured she would have said, "Excuse the mess, but I've been busy," or something like that. The only thing she said was, "Just make yourself comfortable."

I laughed when she said it. I knew the only thing that could have gotten comfortable in there was one of those dead people from the Port Authority bus station Kelly had told me about.

It was obvious Troi had been very busy. It explained why she couldn't call for three weeks. I thought about what my mom had told me about busy women and their messy places. She was usually right. But moms are entitled to mistakes too. I knew I couldn't handle this catastrophe by myself and remembered the building manager told me to call, "should I require his assistance." *You'll require his assis-*

tance and his assistant's assistance, I thought laughing. I picked up a silver-plated receiver.

To my surprise, the building manager answered on the other end. He said, "How may I help you Mr. Wayne?"

I wasn't exactly sure how he could help me, but I'd noticed that Troi had the phone numbers of a maid and laundry service stuck on the side of her refrigerator. It was stocked with every type of spoiled delivery cuisine imaginable and a carton of milk that was so old it didn't even have a picture of a missing kid on the side.

I liked that he remembered my name. "Miss Troi will be requiring the services of your top launderer and most proficient household technician, " I said.

"Very good sir," he replied. "When shall I schedule an appointment for Miss Troi?" I laughed to myself and responded, "You may schedule an appointment for Miss Troi right now."

"I see sir," he stoically stated. "You are, of course, aware that we do not provide these services on Saturdays."

I wasn't aware of anything, except that her place was a wreck and that there wasn't going to be any bacon passed to any pan if it wasn't straightened out in a hurry.

"You are, of course, aware that Reverend Jackson will be dining with us this evening," I told him, lying.

"The Reverend Jesse Jackson?" he asked excitedly.

"Is there another you know of?" I asked, while wondering if there was indeed another Jesse Jackson.

"Very good sir," he replied hesitantly. "We shall attempt to accommodate you."

"Very well," I said before hanging up. I located a bucket underneath the sink and a mop tucked inside the full-length pantry. I went right to work. *They haven't built a maid who could handle this mess alone,* I thought as I rolled up the sleeves to my sweatshirt. I found a tiny food-stained clock radio sitting beneath a soup bowl. It had been left upside down. I flipped it on after I cleaned it off. The way things were going, I figured the '70s hit, *The Clean-up Woman,* would come on. I was pleasantly surprised when one of my favorite tunes, Patrice Rushen's *Remind Me,* graced my ears. It made me think of Troi, and I smiled. I answered a knock at the door.

"My goodness, no," said the cute Mexican accented woman as she walked past the foyer. She stepped in the "living room" and placed her hand over her heart. "Storm hit here, no?" she asked.

"I'm not exactly sure," I told her smiling. "But we've got to do something about it."

"I Carmen, no?" she said while extending her hand.

"I Shawn, yes," I replied smiling, "and we need to get to work."

Before I could say another word, she took over. She picked up the silver-plated receiver and two other women and some guy arrived within minutes. Carmen sketched a map of the condo. They gathered around her and maneuvered about with the precision of a major military operation. They cleaned, washed, folded, dusted, rearranged closets and dresser drawers, and wouldn't allow me to lift a finger. One of the women even placed the papers in proper order and filed them in a cabinet she found in Troi's bedroom. I knew they were done when they high-fived each other, and suddenly left without even saying "so- long." Carmen hung around and asked if I was satisfied.

"Definitely," I said.

"I know I should not say," she said in something that resembled English, "but not good to live like this, no?"

"Yes," I answered. "Not good to live like this."

She walked toward me, and said, "You not live here, no?"

"Yes," I replied trying not to confuse her or myself. "I not live here."

"You have friend here, no?" she asked.

"Yes," I answered confused, "I have girlfriend here, no."

We both laughed. She then deliberately stated, "Girlfriend who not keep clean not be good girlfriend."

I didn't like the way she said that. It was the first thing she'd said without adding, "no" to the end. She said it like she meant it, and like she knew what she was talking about.

"She call Carmen next time, no?" she said, reverting to her familiar refrain.

"Yes," I said flatly. "She call Carmen next time."

"Carmen get tip, no?"

"Yes," I quickly answered. "Carmen get tip, no."

She then gave me a spiteful look and fired off in perfect English, "I did all this work, and you not trying to give up a tip. Are you sick or something?!"

"Nah," I replied somberly while reaching into my pocket. "I feel fine." I gave her the $5 bill I'd received from the cabbie. She smiled and walked towards the door. "See you again sir, no?" she said while standing in the doorway.

"No," I answered forcefully. "Not see you again."

"That's your loss mister," she said, while throwing her head back and closing the door behind her.

Troi's place was now clean. I actually found her sofa and realized Carmen and her little army spent all day revitalizing this war zone. One problem though. Troi still wasn't here. I wanted her to be surprised and actually didn't want her to arrive before they finished. But I'd lost track of time. I was shocked when I checked my Timex. It confirmed it was 7:00 p.m., my time, and 6:00 her time. I couldn't believe it was that late and she hadn't arrived or even thought to call. I figured she had some big surprise planned. I called her at work again. The surprise was again on me. She was still there.

"Troi," I said stunned, "what are you doing?"

"Hi honey," she answered sweetly. "I'm just running a little behind."

"A little behind!" I exclaimed. "You were a little behind when you left me at the airport for two hours!"

"I know sweetie," she casually stated. "But I'm about through."

I couldn't believe what she was doing. She acted like I'd just walked around the corner to see her, and that I should just act happy and wait.

"Shawn," she said. "You know what I'm working on, and you know it's very important to me don't you?"

"Yeah," I answered in frustration.

"Then why don't you let me finish?" she said with a noticeable edge. "The more you call, the longer it will take."

"I haven't called in six hours Troi," I reminded her.

"I know baby," she answered while typing in the background. "That's why I got so much done."

"Okay Troi," I replied. "I guess you're right."

"I'm really sorry hon," she said, still typing. "But I am hurrying."

"Troi," I said while picking up the remote control to the huge wide-screen television in her living room. "What channel is ESPN on?"

"It's channel twenty-three," she answered.

I turned it on just in time to catch *SportsCenter* and instantly felt more at home. I didn't know what to say and was tired of hearing her peck on her keyboard. She interrupted the silence. "Shawn, am I good for one of your massages when I get home?" she asked. "Of course," I said.

"Good," she replied. "I'll hurry." She blew me a kiss and hung up before I could say anything.

I didn't understand why she called me back in Maryland and told me to come see her if she knew she'd be as busy as she was. *She couldn't have thought it was going to work out like this,* I convinced myself. Something big must have come up. I sat across her comfortable leather sofa and tried to adjust the volume on the screen. It was too loud and I was exhausted. I wasn't exactly sure if it was the lack of food or the anxiety I'd built from the events of the day, but something hit me hard. I was out of it before the *Did You Know?* segment of *SportsCenter* hit the screen.

I didn't wake up until I heard some keys jiggle at the door. I looked up and couldn't help but smile. It was Troi. I reached for her hand, but she walked right past me and fell out in a chair in her spacious master suite. I then picked her up, carried her to the huge king-size bed, gently laid her down and carefully removed her shoes.

"Are you okay?" I whispered.

"I'm so sorry Shawn," she said, starting to cry. "I didn't mean for this to happen." "It's okay," I reassured her. "You're here now. That's all that matters." I held her in my arms and gently rocked her, just like I did when she first told me about her father. Through her tears, she told me her old man was attempting to force his way back into the company.

"We may lose it," she said weeping, "but we have to fight him with everything we've got."

It was strange, but I felt a sense of relief. Not because her father was trying to take over their business. But I now understood why she was so late and why her condo was in a condemned state when I first arrived. She had been so focused on fighting her dad, that little else mattered. I slowly removed her baggy blue jeans and oversized gray sweater and slipped her into a frilly red gown, which I'd found hanging behind the door. I smiled when I realized she didn't have on an ankle bracelet. *This is the first time you've seen her without one of those,* I chuckled. I knew that if Miss Troi Stevenson left the house without an ankle bracelet, something was terribly wrong. I unfastened her watch and shuddered when I saw that it was 1:32 a.m. Her time.

"Shawn," she whispered. "Can I still get my massage?"

"You can get anything you want," I replied softly, "or anything you need." I sat on the side of the bed and gently stroked her back. The heart I'd bought for her was hitting the side of my pocket. I figured this wasn't the best time to give it to her. She made my decision easier. She was sound asleep within two minutes of my touching her.

I climbed off the bed and turned off the big screen in the living room. I then returned to the bedroom and slowly undressed before neatly folding my clothes and placing them on the inviting wing chair near her closet. It didn't bother me that she was so late. It didn't even bother me that she'd fallen asleep before I could "bring home the bacon." It didn't matter that I'd come all the way from Maryland to clean up her place, to watch her sleep, and to lose my modest bankroll to a too large cabbie and a two-tongued maid. The only thing that mattered was that we were together, as I hoped we would be. She called me to come to Chicago because she needed me. I was happy that she had. I wanted to be there for her.

I sat at the head of the bed and turned her bedroom TV to channel twenty-three, hoping that I could catch the 2:00 a.m. encore of *SportsCenter*. Troi slid her head onto my chest and softly whispered, "Thanks for being here." I said nothing. I let her sleep. She didn't have to thank me for being there. I would have been there or anywhere she wanted me to be. As long as it meant we'd be together.

It didn't matter that it was 2:05 a.m., her time, and thusly, 3:05 my time. Being there with her in my arms made it our time. *And that's the only time that counts,* I muttered as I fell off to sleep.

20th Message

"THE PLACE LOOKS WONDERFUL."

MESSAGE SENT ON
NOVEMBER 19TH AT 2:34 P.M. (MY TIME)

Fortunately, we had a deep restful sleep, much like the one we had on her last night in D.C. I woke up at about 8:00, walked around her spacious condo and laughed as I thought about Carmen and her cleaning crew. They had done quite a job, because they made Troi's place look beautiful. The living room, which was now fit for real living, featured a buttery-soft calfskin burgundy sofa. Adjacent to it was a matching love seat. A sheet of understated, yet elegant rectangular beveled glass sat comfortably on the base of a freshly polished brass coffee table. It rested on a classic beige virgin-wool border rug. Two soft-tan ceramic swirl table lamps with brass bases and hand crafted shades sat atop the brass-legged end tables. They separated the sofa and love seat from a contemporary leather recliner and companion ottoman. A stunningly beautiful white marble fireplace, which was covered with a shiny brass-edged glass face-plate, was nestled in one wall and her big-screen TV sat on another wall next to a sleek nickel-plated Bang and Olufson stereo system.

It's as laid as her hotel suite was, I thought as I opened the door to her space-age stainless-steel refrigerator. I noticed that "Carmen's Army" had cleaned it out and dispensed of the rotten food. A pat of Philly brand cream cheese, a tiny four-ounce can of Donald Duck orange juice, and a packet of saltine crackers from the gourmet oriental food delivery service, Chop-Chop Chinese To You, sat on the top shelf. That would have been cool. But there was nothing on the other shelves or in the crisper, except an open box of Arm & Hammer baking soda which I'm certain was left by Carmen's clean-up squad. I hadn't eaten since yesterday morning on the plane and I didn't believe in taking someone's last bit of food, but I was starving. I took everything out and placed it on top of the slick glass-top surface cooking island in the middle of her kitchen. The cream cheese, saltines, and bland orange juice didn't work for me and I knew it wouldn't work for her. Especially since I ate it all.

I remembered the building manager mentioned they had an on-site deli that delivered. "It's an amenity our tenants insist on," he told me. "They stock only the freshest foods and finest desserts, and they deliver at a moment's notice."

The clock on her microwave read 8:32, so I had to make a move because I needed to be at the airport by 10:00 (her time, of course). The building manager connected me to the deli and the woman who answered informed me they had a special breakfast-in-bed offer. It came complete with a long stem rose, a reusable serving tray, plastic stemware and a copy of the *Chicago Tribune* newspaper.

"How much is it?" I asked, realizing I had no money to pay for it anyway.

"How much does it cost?" she answered laughing. "Must you ask?"

"Yes I must," I said.

"Our tenants are assessed a monthly fee based on their use of our services," she casually told me.

"Oh," I said surprised. "I didn't know they did that here

too." I didn't know they did that anywhere. But their arrangement fell well within the bounds of my depleted bankroll. I went for it and ordered the special.

The food was there in fifteen minutes, and it looked almost too good to eat.

"I get tip, no?" asked the delivery person.

"No," I answered, smiling. "You get no tip." It was Carmen, and I smiled as I led her to the door.

"I had to try," she said laughing. "Enjoy."

I carefully carried the tray into her bedroom and sat it on the dresser. Then I searched for some candles to place on the nightstands. I still wasn't up on what the candle move was all about, but I knew Troi liked it, and I was willing to eat in the dark again if it pleased her. I found two round red candles in her designer-styled bathroom and gently placed them in two hunter-green teacups which had been hanging suspended from the stemware rack over her kitchen. After I lit the candles I woke her up and whispered, "Good morning."

"Hi," she said still half asleep. "Shawn!" she exclaimed. "This is wonderful. You didn't have to do this."

"Yes I did," I replied, smiling. "You didn't have anything for us to eat."

I sat beside her, and she gave me a quick peck on the cheek. I was glad she went with the peck. She hadn't brushed her teeth yet.

We once again fed each other and were finished eating in no time. We would have finished faster, but she was talking about her job and her father the whole time. I wanted to talk about us. I wanted to give her the heart. But she kept going. It was 9:30 before we knew it. She looked at the mirror-paneled clock on her wall and gasped, "Shawn, we've got to get you to the airport."

I couldn't believe it. I dug having breakfast with her. I enjoyed just spending time with her and being in her place. It didn't even bother me that the only bacon passed to any pan was the bacon that came with the breakfast. I'd traveled to Chicago to confirm that she felt as strongly about me as I felt about her. I wanted to see if she was really my 6. As it stood, the only thing I'd confirmed was that she was still stuck on her job and that she still liked to eat in the dark. The trip to the airport was more of the same. During the entire ride, she talked about her job and her father's takeover attempt. The only good thing about it was that Troi had an awesome midnight blue Lexus SC400 sports coupe with supple tan leather seats and a remote controlled Alpine CD system. It was an automatic, which really didn't surprise me. I knew Troi wasn't cheap. She would never drive a stick.

We were at the airport in ten minutes and I'm certain I could have posed as the poster child for "frustration." She could tell I was annoyed as we stood in the passenger waiting area. "What's wrong Shawn?" she asked. "You barely said a word in the car." *How could I have said a word?* I thought. *You ran your mouth for the entire ride.*

"Nothing's wrong," I sighed.

"Don't lie to me," she said, "tell me what's wrong."

"Troi," I said as I reached in my pocket to hand her the heart. "I came here for a reason."

"And what might that be?" she casually asked.

I knew exactly what it might be, but for some insane reason I couldn't tell her. I guess I was worried because I didn't know how she would react. Although I knew our time was short, I immediately went into one of my patented stall modes.

"Did you like the eggs this morning?" I asked.

"Did I what?" she yelled. "You are not doing this again," she said while grabbing my arm and heading toward two chairs near a bank of pay phones.

"Shawn," she said deliberately. "You are going to tell me what's bothering you right now."

"I don't know what's bothering me," I said.

"What do you mean you don't know what's bothering you?" she asked loudly.

"Sir, would you please tell her what's bothering you?" requested an older lady who was using one of the pay phones. "I can barely hear, and I'm on a long-distance call."

"I don't know Troi," I said slowly, "I guess I just expected this weekend to be a little different than it was."

"Are you upset because we didn't get to have sex?" she demanded.

"Sex?" I replied. "Is that how you see it, as sex?"

"Sex is sex," said the lady on the phone. "They've got me on hold," she whispered. "What do you mean Shawn?" Troi asked. "Of course I see it as sex. That's what it is."

"That's news to me," I replied. "I didn't know you saw it like that."

"What in the world are you talking about Shawn?" she asked.

There was a long silence. The woman on the phone looked at both of us and said, "You should tell her what you mean."

I didn't like her interrupting, but I knew she was right. I had to tell Troi what was on my mind.

"We didn't have sex Troi," I started. "Well, maybe the first couple of times it was sex," I said grinning. "But after that we made love."

"We made love?" she responded.

"That's what he said," interrupted the woman on the phone.

"Of course we made love," I told her. "What we did was special, it was real. It wasn't just sex. It was making love."

"Making love?" she said while reaching for a seat. "What do you mean making love?"

"You don't know what making love is?" asked the lady on the phone.

Troi nodded her head and said, "I think I know what making love is." She then looked at me with tears in her eyes and whispered, "Shawn, I've never met a man like you." That made me feel good.

"You are the nicest, most considerate man I've ever met."

That made me feel better.

"I think of you when we're apart, and you always make me feel better when things aren't going right," she added. "You make me laugh, I respect you, I know I can trust you, and I'm certain you'd take care of me."

"So what's not to like?" asked the older woman.

"Yeah," I chimed in. "What's the problem?"

"The problem is I don't love you Shawn," Troi said.

"You don't love me?" I asked surprised. "I don't think I was expecting you to love me."

Not that I would have minded her loving me. That would have been cool. I just wanted to know where we stood with each other. It didn't matter that she didn't equate "bringing home the bacon" to making love. I could deal with that as long as she felt what we'd done meant something, and that it would thrust us into a real relationship.

"Just because I feel we made love doesn't mean I think we necessarily love each other," I told her.

"Well, what does it mean?" she asked.

"Yeah," said the phone lady. "What arc you saying?"

"I'm saying that what we did was special, and I think we should define what we have," I said.

"What we have?" Troi asked.

"Yeah," I replied, smiling. "You know, like are we going steady, should we enroll in MCI's Friends and Families, or are we just doing the sex thing?"

She laughed and said, "Shawn, I don't know if we're doing anything that I care to define."

"What's that mean?" I asked.

I looked around and waited for the woman on the phone to interrupt. Thankfully, she had left.

"Shawn," she softly stated, "I'm happy we met, and I've already told you what I think of you. But I don't think I'm looking for a relationship."

I wasn't exactly sure what she was telling me. I only knew my heart suddenly felt like it belonged beneath my shoes. I was crushed.

"I don't think I know what you're saying Troi," I told her. "But it doesn't sound good."

"Sure it's good, she said smiling." "The fact that we met was good, and what we've shared has been good."

I understood that.

"But I don't think it means we should have a relationship," she continued, "I wasn't looking for a relationship when we met."

"What were you looking for?" I asked cautiously.

She shrugged her shoulders and smiled. She then said, "I guess I was looking for a little fun, a little excitement, and a break from the routine."

"A break?" I asked. "Like a coffee break or something?"

"Not exactly," she answered smiling, "but I guess you could put it like that."

I couldn't believe it. I'd flown halfway across the country to find that she saw me as a cup of flavor-rich Sanka.

She reached for my hand and looked me in the eye. "I know you weren't looking for a relationship, were you Shawn?" she asked.

"No," I said lowering my head, "I wasn't looking for anything. I just wanted to know where we stood."

"That's good," she answered. "Because what we have is perfect."

"What's so perfect about it?"

"It's perfect," she replied, "because we're not obligated to do anything. We do what we do because we really want to."

What's so good about that? I wondered.

"It's good that we don't have to call each other," she continued. "I like the fact that I can call when I feel like it, because I don't want to feel that I have to call." She giggled and said, "I know you feel the same way, don't you?"

"I guess so," I softly answered while sliding the heart back into my pocket.

"Good," she said. She then stood up and looked at her watch. "Looks like your plane should be leaving soon. I'm heading out to the office," she said. She leaned over, kissed me on the cheek, and whispered, "Thanks for coming. I'll be in touch."

I couldn't believe what was happening. She had broken my heart just like Bruce Lee broke a stack of bricks in the 1973 smash kung-fu flick, *Enter the Dragon.* Bruce stared those bricks down. He mumbled something in Chinese and broke them to bits before walking away with a huge grin. I don't know if Troi meant to demolish me like Bruce meant to destroy those bricks, but she'd done it big time. *And she walked away smiling just like he did,* I thought. I looked down at the floor. I just knew my heart was lying all over it, shattered into a million pain-stricken pieces.

I watched her Lexus pull away from the airport and realized she was really gone. I meant nothing to her. I thought about what Kelly told me when she said Troi was looking for fun and needed a break. I could see my mom shaking her head, pointing her finger, and saying, "A woman who has a messy place has a problem with her priorities and will never make you a priority." I could hear my dad telling me, "Son, life is about details." Had I followed his advice, I'd have known what Troi was about before I'd have even allowed myself to fall for her. What really got me was Carmen, the woman who'd cleaned the disaster area that masqueraded as Troi's condo. She warned me (without adding "no" to the end), "Girlfriend who not keep clean, not be good girlfriend."

I hated the fact that Carmen and everyone else came out right about Troi. I don't remember how I made it onto the plane, or how I got to my ride when I made it back to National Airport at 3:08 p.m. (my time). I only know that I crossed the Woodrow Wilson Bridge and missed the exit for Bladensburg. I couldn't force myself to take the next exit (which was also for Bladensburg). I later wondered how I ended up driving sixty-six miles around the Beltway and again crossing the Woodrow Wilson Bridge. It was 8:13 when I looked at my Timex. I'd been driving around the Beltway, which wraps around Washington, Maryland, and Virginia, for over five hours. *Get a grip,* I told myself. *Just get yourself home.* I was once again crossing the Woodrow Wilson Bridge and couldn't shake Troi from my thoughts. I pressed my foot down on the accelerator, but nothing happened. My engine stalled. It coughed like an old sailor with a nagging lung condition. I didn't know anything about cars, but I got out, popped the hood and tried to figure out what people look at when they look under their hoods.

I didn't know what I was seeing or what I wasn't seeing. I climbed back in and immediately noticed my gas gauge frowning at me from well beyond empty land. Damn, I thought, frustrated. *When it rains, it pours.* And rain it did. I jumped out to close the hood and ran back to the door, only to find that I'd locked myself out. I stood in the pouring rain, wondering what I'd done to deserve this. How could I have been so wrong about Troi? I walked to the side of the bridge, wanting to cry. I felt I'd lost the only person whom I'd allowed into my life since my mom died. I also wanted to cry because I knew I'd have to pay a locksmith at least thirty bucks to open my ride. I didn't understand why I couldn't force myself to cry. I think it was because I promised myself that I'd never cry again after my mom died. *When she died, you cried for days, and it didn't make a difference. It didn't bring her back, and it didn't make you feel any better,* I reminded myself. *Plus, you missed yourself on Plays of the Week.*

It was now completely dark. A policeman pulled behind me with his lights flashing and his siren blaring. "Place your hands over your head and get into your vehicle!" he yelled through the speakers atop his cruiser.

How does he expect you to get in your ride while your hands are over your head? I wondered.

"I can't get in because my keys are inside. I need some-one to pick the lock!" I yelled back.

There was a helicopter flying toward us. The officer yelled, "Did you say you had a glock?"

A glock nine millimeter pistol, I thought puzzled. *Why would I have one of those?*

The helicopter drew closer. It was so loud that I covered my ears with my hands. "Be careful!" yelled the policeman toward the helicopter. "He's got a glock. He's holding it to his head."

It was really dark, but I looked up anyway. I didn't see anyone with a gun to his head. I wondered who he was talking about. An older guy with a black shirt and a blue jean jacket leaned out of the helicopter and yelled, "Don't do it son. It's not worth it!"

What's not worth what? I wondered as I looked around to see where his son was. Traffic had come to a complete standstill. Even though the guy in the helicopter and the police officer were trading insults over who should handle the situation, my thoughts remained on Troi and how she had dumped me.

I thought about how we first met and our first dance. I remembered the first time I touched her, and the way we made love. *She may have thought it was just sex,* I lamented. *But we definitely made love.* I recalled how we constantly called each other when she was in town. How we dined out every night and how much fun we had at the black-tie dinner. I remembered our first real conversation and smiled because we had confided in each other and shared the painful details of our lives. I laughed when I thought about her yelling at my socks at two in the morning while she was out on the balcony with no clothes on. *That wasn't so funny,* I reminded myself. *Those socks did cost you five bucks.* I knew she'd replaced the socks with an even better pair, but lowered my head when I realized there was no way I could ever replace her with a better woman. It was cold, dark, and wet, but I was in no hurry to move off the bridge. It just didn't matter. Nothing mattered. I no longer had Troi.

While I lost myself reminiscing about the wonderful memories that Troi and I shared, the cop snuck up on me and drew his weapon. "Drop to your knees, and put your hands in the air!" he yelled.

What's this, a stick-up or something, I wondered. "I don't have any money," I yelled as the helicopter engine shut down. "I gave it all to a cabbie and a maid in Chicago!"

"What's the problem son?" asked the guy who had been in the helicopter.

"Watch it father," replied the officer. "He's dangerous."

I remembered thinking it was odd that they were father and son because the officer was noticeably white, and his dad was absolutely black.

The cop's old man walked toward me. He knelt down and whispered, "How can I help you son?"

I didn't say a word. I figured he was talking to his kid.

"Look friend," he stated. "You can talk to me. I will not judge you, I will only try to help."

"You can help?" I asked.

"Of course," he replied smiling. "What can I do for you?"

"I ran out of gas and my keys are locked in my ride," I told him. "Can you help me with that?"

He looked at me confused and asked, "You were going to jump because you ran out of gas?"

"Jump?" I responded surprised. "Into that?" I asked looking toward the choppy waters of the Potomac River. "Why would I do something crazy like that?"

He shrugged his shoulders and asked, "Well, what about the gun?"

"Gun?" I answered hesitantly. "You'll have to ask your son about that."

He looked over at the policeman. They just turned their palms up and shrugged their shoulders in unison.

"Do you have a slim-jim to open his door?" the father asked the cop.

"Yeah," he replied. "I have one in the trunk."

The father stood up. We looked out over the side of the bridge. "Are you all right?" he asked concerned.

"Not really," I answered. "I just got dumped."

"Is that why you're out here?"

"No sir," I answered. "Like I told you, I ran out of gas."

He walked over to the officer and whispered something to him. The officer yelled for a man in a tow-truck to bring over a gas can. As the guy emptied the gas into my tank, the officer said, "You know, technically I could take you in and have you observed for pulling a stunt like this."

"I didn't know that," I answered solemnly. "I didn't think running out of gas could get you in that kind of trouble."

The father walked toward me and gave me a tiny card with his phone number on it. He told me to call if I needed his help.

The officer pulled off and I wondered how a black father produced a son who was as white as he was. My engine turned over, and I eased into the traffic crossing the bridge. I flipped on my CD player and shook my head as the song that Troi and I had selected as ours, *Cathedral In A Suitcase*, played over my sound system. I couldn't bear to hear it. I turned it off and switched over to the radio. "This just in," said the golden-throated announcer. "A distraught man is apparently threatening to shoot himself on the Woodrow Wilson Bridge." *Jeez,* I said to myself. *You're lucky you missed that.* "Details are sketchy, but traffic is at a standstill as authorities try to reason with this crazed individual." *He must be crazy,* I thought. *It's one thing to be stuck out in this mess like you were, but to do it by choice. He's got to be off.*

Even though I couldn't get Troi off my mind, I made sure I didn't miss the Bladensburg exit. I didn't want to walk into my place and deal with this alone. I knew I now really was all by myself. Troi brought out both the best and worst in me at the same time. I couldn't understand how she just dumped me and then walked away smiling like nothing happened. I wondered if she felt as bad as I did as I checked my messages.

"Hi Shawn," the voice said. "The place looks wonderful. I don't know how you pulled it off, but I appreciate it." Apparently she wasn't feeling too bad. She sounded too good. "You're a real sweetheart," she whispered before hanging up.

If I'm such a sweetheart?, I thought, dejected, *why did you dump me?*

I didn't know what to do or what to think. The last time I'd felt this bad was when my mom passed and it took ten years and Troi's nudging to get me through that. I didn't know if I could go back into a shell for another ten years. When I thought about not having Troi, I realized I could do it for another twenty. Troi was the best thing that ever happened to me, and I knew it, though I doubt that she did. She forced me to put my parents' deaths into perspective and made me look at myself. We'd discussed where I was, and more important, where I was going. She talked to me, listened to me, laughed with me (and not at me) and made me feel relevant. I remembered rejoicing because I thought God had put someone on this earth who understood me and accepted me. She made me feel alive. Troi had done that, and so many other things for me, inside of a week. I thought we were connected. I obviously misread her feelings, because I believed that she wanted me as much as I wanted her.

I didn't want to sleep that night. I was afraid to wake up the next day and have to deal with the fact that Troi was really gone. *She was never really here,* I told myself as I sat in the dark. I remembered how she went without calling me for three weeks, and recalled how I went from feeling like a croaker to feeling like wet Play-Doh in a matter of minutes. I thought of how devastated I felt when she hadn't called and regretted she'd told me she actually preferred not having to call (like she was some screwed-up 2). I didn't believe I could ever get over Troi. I couldn't get it together. Before I knew it, an uncontrollable stream of tears ran down my face. I definitely wasn't trying to cry. Crying wasn't on my agenda. I didn't do crying. I didn't care, and it didn't matter. I was alone in the dark and the heart I was going to give to Troi was clutched tightly in my right hand. It was well past midnight and the phone rang. I didn't answer it. I knew that no one would understand the pain I was dealing with.

I searched my mind for answers. I couldn't find any that made sense to me, or that made me feel any better. I knew I was going to be without Troi. I would miss her beautiful voice, her soulful laugh, her incredible legs, her wonderful sense of humor, and her warm smile. *You'll miss her ankle bracelet, her White Linen cologne, and the incredible lovemaking too,* I sadly thought. But none of that seemed to matter.

I knew that more than anything, I'd miss her reassuring eyes. When things got too shaky, or when I really screwed up (like I did at the black-tie dinner), Troi could just look at me and instantly make me feel better. I knew I wouldn't feel better now. I was already feeling like a croaker. Only this time I felt worse than a croaker.

I felt croaked.

21st Message

MESSAGE SENT ON
NOVEMBER 20TH AT 12:13 A.M.

 I didn't want to wake up the next morning but my alarm clock didn't care, so it unmercifully rang out at 6:45 a.m. I reached over to switch the radio on and continued to lie across the bed. Al Jarreau sang the scorned-lover ballad, *When I Fell For You.* I didn't need to hear this song because I felt black and blue just like Al did when the babe he was singing to dumped him. I was glad we didn't have to work that day. There's no way I would have made it in. I never really understood what being depressed was all about. I knew it felt bad, and that it was worse than feeling like a croaker because I didn't want to move, didn't want to eat and didn't want to talk to anyone. Amazingly, I didn't even want to see the early morning edition of *SportsCenter.*

I finally forced myself to sit up. I stared blankly at the television. An ad for Troi's cologne, White Linen, was on. Ironically, it featured the silhouette of a woman driving through the streets of Chicago in a beautiful midnight-blue

Lexus sports coupe. I leaned forward to get a better look and adjusted my eyes as the woman prepared to step out of the car. There was a close-up on her shapely legs. I gasped when I saw she was wearing Troi's ankle bracelet and the satin shoes she'd worn to the black-tie dinner. They never showed her face, but I'd seen enough to be reminded of Troi. I quickly changed the channel and switched to Home Team Sports, the D.C.-based cable sports network. I smiled as they showed an old game between the Bulls and the hapless Los Angles Clippers. I laughed because Michael Jordan was beating the Clippers single-handedly while the fans in Chicago stadium were going crazy. One of the Clippers missed a wide-open lay up, and the ball bounced to the side of the court. A woman with a beautiful head of hair reached down from her courtside seat to return the ball. My heart stopped when the camera focused on her face. I couldn't believe it. It was Troi. She smiled as Jordan walked over and gave her a high-five after retrieving the game ball.

If I was going to get over Troi, I could see that losing myself in the tube wasn't the solution.

A loud knock told me someone was at my front door, but I didn't want to see anyone, so I decided not to answer. Whoever was knocking really wanted to get in, because after a few minutes, there was an even louder knock at the window.

"Wake-up cuz. Wake-up!" yelled a familiar voice.

It was Donnie. I figured if he was both awake and at my place at 7:15 in the morning, something was desperately wrong. I walked to the door to let him in and was surprised to find him looking fit and clear-eyed.

"What's up money?" he said, slapping me five. "How was the windy city?"

"It was pretty windy," I replied, trying to hide the fact I'd been crushed.

"That's it?" he asked, placing a toothpick in his mouth. "Pretty windy?"

"Yeah," I answered, "it was pretty windy."

"Things didn't work out, huh man?"

"Things worked out alright." I told him, "It was chill."

I knew it wasn't chill, even though I wasn't exactly sure what "chill" was. I did know things were screwed up, and that I was screwed up, but I wasn't about to let my main man know about it. I never thought it was cool to let another man know you've been hurt. It wasn't cool to look like a chump. I'd never even heard a guy complain about being hurt by a babe and I wasn't really interested in starting a trend. Most of the guys I knew who'd been dropped by their ladies usually took the stance that it was the woman's loss. They would quickly regroup, find a willing replacement, and would waste little time brooding over the lost lady.

I always felt women were at a disadvantage when it came to dumping men. My mother once told me women sometimes drop guys to wake them up, or to make a point. I knew that was probably true, because Dawn, whom I dated when I was in college, dropped me and told me I wasn't giving her or our relationship enough attention. I knew she was right, but I was a star basketball player. I always had at least five other babes who were ready to take her spot. One day, she called and said she'd had it. She hung up before I could lie and tell her I'd change. I was thinking of who to call while the dial tone was still fresh, and eventually called Danielle (the 2 who devoured the surf and turf platter at Jasper's). Dawn called me two days later and asked why I hadn't called. I reminded her that she'd dumped me and informed her I wasn't about to chase her. "I didn't really want to break up, and I don't want you to chase me," she said forcefully. "I just want you to get your act together."

There was only one problem. I'd already started *getting my act together* with Danielle. But Dawn was pretty cool, plus she was smart. Naturally, I decided to keep my act together with both of them. It worked pretty good until Dawn found out what was going on. She called, told me she knew about Danielle, and dropped me like Mike Tyson dropped Michael Spinks. I actually missed her and nearly called back two weeks later, but I knew she'd just blow me off and tell me to grow up. Dawn wasn't nearly as cute or as phat as Danielle, but she really cared about me. She always put our relationship first. I never let anyone know how much I missed Dawn and that she'd gotten to me by cutting me off. I knew no one would ever know that Troi had effectively broken my heart. Especially Donnie.

"If everything was chill," Donnie said, slowly, "when are you goin' back?"

"I ain't trippin'," I told him. "She knows how to get to D.C."

"My man!" he said laughing. "Run your house."

Yeah," I chimed in. "Run my house."

I knew I'd said something wrong because Donnie just looked at me and burst out laughing.

"You'z a trip cuz," he blurted out. "You don't have to front with me."

Front? I thought puzzled. *What the hell is front?*

"I ain't trying to front," I said, not even knowing whether I was fronting or not.

"Shawn," Donnie interrupted. "You been my man since before you was a man."

What does front mean? I still wondered.

"I know when sumthin's up," he continued, "I know when you ain't bein' straight." I knew I wasn't being straight and also knew I had no intention of being straight. I decided to change the topic, before he broke me.

"What are you doin' up at seven in the mornin'?" I asked. "You need some cake or something?"

"Who don't need cake?" he replied, laughing. "I'm chill, so I won't sweat your bankroll this time."

That's a switch, I thought grinning.

"I just wanted to kick it," he told me.

Kick it? I thought puzzled. *I wonder if that's the same as fronting.*

"Things have been real down for me," he stated.

"Down?" I asked, concerned. "What's wrong now?"

"Nutin's wrong," he answered proudly. "I just told you everything was down."

"How can nothing be wrong if everything is down?" I asked confused.

"What is you sayin' cuz?" he replied.

"If down is up, then fronting is faking," I said.

"Dat's right," he happily answered. "Down is up, and frontin' is fakin'."

I didn't get it, but Donnie sure did, so I let him explain.

"It goes like this cuz," he said. "If a nigga's down then he don't be frontin' when he's kickin' it."

"Let me get this straight," I interrupted. "If a dude is up, then he won't have to fake when he's kickin' it." I wasn't exactly sure what kicking it was, but I knew he'd explain it.

"Dat's close," he stated. "But what I'm sayin' is that when a nigga's frontin' when he's kickin' it, he ain't down."

"Donnie," I said exasperated. "Why can't you just say that a dude who lies when he talks isn't cool."

"Dat's what I said!" he fired, back laughing.

I still didn't get it. But I realized Donnie didn't get me either, so it was "chill" (I guess). When I was playing ball, I could talk "jive" with the best of them. But that was ten years ago. The "acceptable" words have changed since then. People used to tell me that I was the "baddest" ballplayer they'd ever seen. That never made sense to me. I always thought I was pretty good. I learned to accept being called "badd," because people usually smiled when they said it. I eventually found that being "badd" was actually pretty good. Nowadays, guys say Michael Jordan is "stoopid dope." This makes no sense to me. No one ever mentioned him being involved in drugs on *SportsCenter*. Being out of the loop for ten years had a price attached to it. One of the prices was missing out on all of the cool slang that evolved. When I did hang out (which was rare), I tried to talk slang, but it didn't usually work out. I was so busy trying to figure out what everybody was saying that I usually screwed up and said the wrong thing. I would pretend to be "down" (if that's the right word) with what was going on, but it didn't always work like I wanted it to.

Talking to Donnie reminded me of how men changed completely when they talked to women. Donnie always spoke to babes like he was a well-educated man. Around me and other guys, he talked like the parolee he was. I could always accept that from Donnie. I admired that he was being true to himself. But I often wondered why I and some of the other guys we knew talked to each other like we'd never passed an elementary school English class. All of us knew that any woman worth hanging with wouldn't stand for us calling each other niggas. We didn't dare do it in their presence. I never even understood why we used the term niggas. We knew full well that someone who wasn't "like us" could be stomped for invoking the "N word." I don't think we meant any harm. When we said it, it seemed easier than saying, "Hello." Saying "Hi there" was lame. "Wha's up nigga" worked. I didn't make the rules. I just tried to play by them.

Around a group of guys you could speak your mind. Any and everything went. It seemed that the worst you came out of your mouth, the better off you were. Guys probably figured you were very cool, or very crazy. Either of those were good enough reasons to leave you alone. Donnie once told me he talked that way because niggas in the hood just talked like that. I knew he wasn't from "the hood." I didn't know exactly where "the hood" was located. I did know that the slang guys used started somewhere. I just wondered where and when it would end.

Donnie walked into the bathroom and exclaimed, "Shawn, don't tell me nutin's up. Quit frontin nigga!" He stepped back out into the doorway and held my rain-soaked 1984 edition Air Jordans in his hands.

I lowered my head and whispered, "Nothing's up man, just drop it."

"If nutin's up," he stated, "Din what is it dat needs droppin?" We both grinned. He then said, "Man you ain't never worn your Jor - Danz."

"I still ain't worn 'em," I answered lying. "They just got a little wet."

"Yeah," he replied laughing. "Dey jus' got a little mud on 'em too!" He dropped the shoes to the floor and walked toward me.

"Shawn, you my man, and if you don't wanna kick it, we don't gotta kick it," he said. I understood what he meant by kicking it this time.

"But if sumthin's up, you know you can holla at me."

We looked at each other and smiled. Donnie (in his usual style) found something else to talk about. "You know I been clean since I got out," he started. "I got me a legit gig, and I been churchin' hard."

"Straight up?" I asked.

"Straight all the way up," he answered loudly. "I even been goin' to meetin's three nights a week."

"Whaaat?" I replied, making "what" sound like it was a five-second long word.

"Yeah money," he interrupted. "I'm tired of the life."

"The life?" I asked. "Exactly what is the life?"

"Tha' life that don't let you have a for-real life," he countered. "Cuz I been out dere for so long dat I forgot what real livin' was like."

This doesn't sound like Donnie. I knew he had an angle.

"Dis ain't jus' talk Shawn," he told me. "I seent what all dis crap has done to my peoples, and it ain't cool."

"It hasn't been cool for years," I reminded him.

"Word up," he fired back.

What word is up? I wondered.

This didn't sound like the Donnie I knew. Particularly because he was making sense. Over the past three years, Donnie's life had been worse than cold creamed chip beef on burnt toast. Donnie loved crack, and though I didn't care for his addiction, I tried to understand it. I wanted to be supportive and to be his buddy. But sometimes it appeared I was doing him more harm than good. He would give me amazing sob stories for cash and could get anything out of women he needed or wanted. Ironically, the only thing that Donnie used more than crack was women. He knew exactly how to get the most from them. He just never figured out when to stop, or more important, how to stop using either. His mother once called and told me that together, we were Donnie's worse enablers. I told her the only thing that "enabled" Donnie was the fact that he truly enjoyed being high, and that he was willing to do it Malcolm X style. By any means necessary.

I liked what Donnie was saying. He had never, not once, said anything about wanting to be clean. Donnie never "fronted" like he felt bad about being a junkie. He seemed perfectly happy with getting high and with taking advantage of others to get his drugs. He never wanted a long-term job. He didn't want to explain to a boss why he robbed him. It was easier to explain it to some neo-liberal judge who felt that Donnie was somehow failed by some mysterious system. He once told me he'd never go to meetings because he already knew what being high was all about and he didn't need to hear anyone else talk about dope. Donnie wasn't a church goer either. Even *he* felt guilty about how easy it was to rip them off. He'd simply hit the plate for the tens and twenties and would literally walk out before it got back to the ushers.

Donnie dug crack as much as I dug basketball, and for most of my adult life I believed we both lost too much because of our vices. We both lost our parents and ourselves (Donnie's parents were still alive, but he'd lost them long ago, though his mom still cared).

"Shawn," he said. "I'm tired of running, and dat's why I'm gettin off."

"That makes sense," I said.

"Yeah," he answered grinning. "It makes more sense din the way I been carryin' it." I still wondered what he was up to. I was waiting for him to hit me up for some cash.

"I do need sumthin' from you cuz," he stated.

Tah-dah, I thought. *Here comes his big pitch. I knew he was still full of it.*

"You always been there for me," he said. "But now I really need you."

"How much do you need Donnie?" I casually asked.

"I told you I don't need no bank," he replied. "I need you to be there when shit don't seem right."

"When is that?" I asked puzzled.

"Whenever dat monkey is climbing up my back."

"Monkey?!" I said confused. "Whadda do you mean, monkey. I never seen you with no monkey."

"You ain't seen him Shawn," he responded laughing, "but I seen him, and heard him. He's a mean ass."

I really didn't know what Donnie was talking about and I was worried he'd stolen a poor little monkey from somewhere. I figured he tried to sell him for drugs but couldn't find a buyer.

"Look Shawn," he said. "I started hittin' the pipe 'cause I hated myself."

"Why did you hate yourself?" I asked. "You were the man."

"I wasn't nobody's man," he answered. "I was frontin' like I was da man."

He sat down.

"I didn't have nutin' goin on Cuz, but when I was high I felt like I had it all goin' on." "Why did you feel like that?" I asked.

"Cause I felt powerful, I felt strong. I felt like I had control."

"You didn't control nothing," I said. "You were always out of control."

"I know dat," he laughed, "but dat monkey makes you *think* you in control."

"Donnie," I asked concerned, "have you gotten in trouble with somebody's monkey?!"

"Man I been in trouble for years 'cause of somebody's monkey," he sternly told me, "but I ain't f'ing wit dat monkey no more."

I was pretty confused. It sounded like Donnie was saying he was really going to stop getting high.

"Shawn," he told me. "Everybody's got sumthin' they need to get over."

I could definitely relate to that.

"You got your thing, I got mine, everybody's got an issue."

"So what's your point bleed?" I asked realizing, that I meant to say "blood."

"My point *bleed*," he answered laughing, "is that we all have problems, and we all need something or someone to help us get past them."

I didn't know what was weirder. Donnie making complete sense, or him uttering a complete sentence without totally butchering *some* King's English.

"I love you cuz," he told me, "and I got a problem to lick, but I'll always be there for you just like you been there for me."

"Thanks," I said, surprised.

"It seems like it took me forever to even admit I had a problem" he stated, "and it was one of the hardest things I've ever done."

"That makes sense," I replied shaking my head.

"It makes sense for you too cuz," he said. "I know you trippin' off sumthin', and I hope you at least know it, 'cause if you don't, you ain't never gonna deal with it."

I just nodded, and we slapped each other five. Donnie then stood up and reached in his pocket. Surprisingly, he handed me a crisp $20 bill.

"What's this for?" I asked.

"I been owing you for years nigga," he said. "This is just something small."

"I know it's something small," I said. "You owe me a lot more than this!"

He laughed as he walked toward the door and said, "Shawn, I guarantee you didn't think you'd ever get that."

He was right. I'd written off his debts long ago.

"Donnie, are you serious about staying clean?" I asked.

"Look Shawn," he said, pointing toward me. "I ain't fooling myself. This ain't gonna be easy, and I can't fall 'cause I can't afford to fall."

He's serious alright, I thought.

"And that's why I need you," he continued. "You was there for me when I was druggin', now you need to be there while I'm not."

"I'll be there," I told him.

"I'm here for you too, cuz," he replied before hugging me and closing the door behind him.

I never imagined Donnie would ever be anywhere for me. But I could tell he meant it. Especially since he gave me that twenty spot. It didn't matter whether Donnie would ever be there. He'd already done enough. Besides my parents and Troi (for a short while), I'd never had anyone who inspired me. I knew Donnie was a cold-blooded junkie. I admired him recognizing his life meant little if he remained on crack. He said everyone had a problem, and we all needed someone to help us along. I knew he could tell that something was wrong, but he didn't press me. He made me realize I had to press myself and that I could rely on him if I needed him. *You could probably even rely on Kelly,* I thought as I checked the message I couldn't bear to hear last night.

"Welcome back Shawn," it started. "I know that you had a ball with your sweetie. So when's the big date? I just know that you're getting married," she said, laughing. It was Kelly, and though I didn't think she really thought that Troi and I were getting married, I realized there was no way I could rely on her to help me deal with my heartache. I wasn't about to deal with her, "I told you so's."

I sat down on the sofa and decided I'd better eat some breakfast. I still didn't want to, but I had to. I needed the energy to deal with Donnie's monkey. He had left him, and he was now on my back whispering Troi's name over and over. *Donnie's been on crack for years and he loved it,* I told myself while opening a can of Spaghettios. *If he can drop crack, you can get over Troi.*

That made sense. It sounded easy, but I knew it would be difficult to forget about Troi, or to drop her from my thoughts. Especially since she dropped me first. I knew Donnie was right. I had to deal with my problem. I guess it was just hard to accept, because the only thing Donnie was ever right about was drugs. More than anything, I knew he was on target about needing someone to help me past it. *But who,* I wondered.

I didn't know exactly who it would be. I just hoped she'd be as fine as Troi.

A moment with the marrying one—Profile of a 5

"My biological clock is ticking—I need a husband."

MOTTO OF A 5

Keep your guard up if you're dealing with a 5, because 5s will treat you so good you'll think they're 6s. And then one day (usually out of nowhere), your 5 will slip in a casual question or comment about marriage, babies, and a long-term commitment. A few days later (after you've lied and said you had nothing against marriage, kids, and commitment) she'll hit you with a more direct question, like: "Since you're not afraid of marriage, when are we getting married?" You will have just finished making passionate love and for some bizarre reason you'll continue to lie and say, "I don't know."

It's only a lie because you do know. You know you're not getting married and you immediately start to feel weird because you know those two lies will come back to haunt you. You feel so weird because you realize that your 5 has started to weave a web of entrapment that exceeds the one the feds pulled on Marion Barry—only he got off easy in comparison to what you're about to deal with. Not that marriage is anything at all to fear. Marriage can be wonderful (especially if you're married to your 6). But marriage with a 5 is often difficult because you go in feeling that you never had a real say in the matter. You quickly realize that real love (and all the cool stuff that comes with having a happening wife) has little to do with your empty, destined-to-be-a-failure marriage.

5s are so amazing because they have the whole marriage thing down to a specific (and well practiced) science. They always wait to hit you with the move when you're most vulnerable. Either during or directly after a zesty session, or following an incredible meal (which is summarily followed by a zesty session). 5s know you are at your physical low point at these stages. They understand that guys are such physical creatures that they'll fall for just about anything when they're drained, stuffed, or otherwise satisfied.

But it's not just about the perfectly timed questions with 5s. It's part of the process, and it's a process that works.

Do you think that Buffy, Jody, Sissy, and Uncle Bill had it sweet when Mr. French catered to their every whim on the '70s bubblegum sitcom *A Family Affair?* Old French hooked them up big-time because he was definitely trying to hang around (just like a 5). And where do you think Mr. French learned how to rope in an entire family? He learned from a 5! And 5s have passed that tradition down to daughters, nieces, first, second, and third cousins, and any other babe who was willing to listen. Not that all babes took the bait. A whole lot of them aren't pressed about being married. But 5s are pressed. So they cook, clean, sew, wash, and make sure the refrigerator stays full of whatever you like to eat or drink.

They don't bother you about hanging out, because they realize if you're out late and you show up at their place, you're staying over. And while you're watching *SportsCenter,* they'll literally feed you and wash your dusty clothes and neatly arrange them in the drawer that's suddenly been designated as yours. You have great sex and fall asleep (like any guy would). You wake up to more *SportsCenter,* more food, and of course, more sex. Your clothes are cleaned and pressed. You have a toothbrush (that you didn't buy or bring with you) in the bathroom, and you are allowed to read the sports section of the morning paper in peace. You are fat. You are happy. You are comfortable. It all seems so cool.

But is it?

It can be if your 5 is about sex when you walk in the door, action films without plots, and round-the-clock TV sports. If she's not, it can be pretty foul. It gets screwed because 5s often put a premium on getting you and place little emphasis on keeping you. They'll book you and suddenly gain weight. They'll stop cleaning. And you can forget about hanging out with the fellas. You now have to come home. That new toothbrush isn't so new anymore, and she snores so loud that you start watching *SportsCenter* in the basement. Soon thereafter you realize you were hooked by good food, good sex, and a pretty darn good game plan. You learn how to use a microwave (she stopped cooking right after the wedding), and your bi-weekly trip to the dollar movies is especially gratifying. It's the only time you get to commiserate with your other miserable buddies (who also got booked by 5s). Eventually you become disillusioned, but it amounts to little. She gives you some at least once a week, and your money's so tied up that you just shut up, deal with it, and get used to sleeping with the remote on the basement couch.

If a 5 decides she really wants you, make it a point to protect yourself (literally). 5s still believe they can hook you with a baby. If a 5 is on the pill, watch out for the classic pill protest move (i.e., "I'm tired of the pill, I'm getting off of it for a while). It's a legitimate maneuver. But a wise 5 will have unprotected sex with you and *then* announce her protest. It works out well for the 5. The way she sees it, if she can't have you, she has the closest thing to you—your baby, and ultimately your bucks for child support. And don't fall for the old, "I don't want anything from you," line. That's bull. They'll later hit you with the "It's not for me, it's for the baby" move. It can, and usually does, get ugly. 5s don't believe in adoption either. They can't really tie you down if they give their baby up. Just get the pampers and get with the program, because 5s will show just how little say guys have when a babe decides that she wants to be pregnant. You have no say, and 5s have no problem showing you that.

Being married to a 5 isn't totally awful because you still get to watch *SportsCenter* (in the basement of course), and because your 5 is happy because she has you—her husband.

Shawn
Wayne
on "I've never dealt with a babe who was pressed about marrying me. I guess they'd keep their cable up and they'd put up with *SportsCenter,* but

I'm not so sure they'd deal with the extra value meal move. I dig extra value meals, and if a babe can't get with an extra value meal, she's probably stuck up. Who wants a chick who's stuck up anyway?

22nd *Message*

"I TOLD YOU SO."

MESSAGE SENT ON
DECEMBER 16TH AT 12:45 P.M.

Three weeks passed before I saw or heard from Donnie again, so I was shocked when I caught him wrapping Christmas gifts at Landover Mall one afternoon.

"Shawn, what's happening!" he yelled as I walked pass the center court circle that featured an old white Santa Claus. I didn't have a problem with white Santas. But I wondered why Landover Mall, which was the mecca for black shoppers in Prince George's County, insisted on forcing black children to ask a white Santa for Christmas gifts. I knew families who traveled halfway across the county to P.G. Plaza. They had both a black and a white Santa. I didn't care what color Santa was, as long as the gifts were under the tree on Christmas morning. But I understood why it bothered some people. I thought about it as I walked toward Donnie, and wondered why I'd never seen a white kid sitting on a black Santa's lap. Some things just don't make sense.

"Donnie," I whispered as we shook hands. "What are you up to?"

"What am I up to?" he said smiling. "I'm up to my neck with the Lord."

He was handling the cash at a stand for Glendale Baptist Church. I just knew I'd caught him in the midst of one of his grandest hustles. Donnie had so much personality that he could have convinced the Pope to reconsider his stance on abortion. I figured he'd conned some poor church into allowing him to handle their money, which I knew would ultimately find its way into some crack dealer's waiting pockets. I hadn't heard from him in nearly a month, so I figured he was back in jail or still hung up on crack. That's the way it always worked. But Donnie looked even better than he did when he announced that he'd kicked the habit.

The whites of his eyes were actually white. He always looked chiseled. But now he looked like he'd put on at least ten pounds of solid muscle. A close-cropped fade haircut replaced the cool dreads he'd worn for the past three years and it was the first time I'd seen him with a clean-shaven face since we were sixteen. He'd dumped his trademark toothpick. His voice was clear and not nearly as raspy as it usually was. He looked me dead in the eyes and not at the ground when he spoke. A pair of pleated, neatly pressed khakis replaced his chronically wrinkled oversized jeans, and a long sleeve rugby-style jersey enveloped his upper body. There was something about him I couldn't quite figure out. He seemed so different. He actually seemed happy. This bothered me. I knew the only time Donnie James Lee was happy was when he was high. Although I spent little time at church, I didn't want to see Donnie rip them off while he was tripping on crack.

"What are you doing?" I whispered as I pulled him aside. "What kind of hustle is this?"

"Shawn," he answered laughing. "This is the only hustle that lasts."

I inched my head back and whispered, "What the hell are

you talking about?"

"What the hell am I talking about?" he happily exclaimed as André Crouch's version of *Oh Happy Day* played through a tabletop boombox. "It's the Lord's hustle, and believe me Shawn, it's no hustle. It's the real thing!"

"How much have you hit them for?" I asked, reaching for my meager bankroll.

"I've hit them for everything they can give me and then some," he answered smiling. "They helped me put my life together Shawn. They helped me get rid of that monkey."

The monkey moved into my place. I knew he was serious about dropping him. That monkey and I had some long battles about Troi. Sometimes it seemed the only thing that kept me from getting over Troi was that damned monkey. Other days it was something else. It didn't really need to be much of anything. As I thought, getting over Troi was a task I wasn't up to. Donnie had disappeared for three weeks, so I naturally assumed he was strung out. I rationalized not dealing with my situation by convincing myself that Donnie hadn't dealt with his. I was wrong. He'd dealt with it. I just wondered what it took to get rid of that monkey. I wanted him off of my back.

"Shawn," Donnie said. "I wish I could say I was back, but I can't. I was never really here."

"You've been here," I reminded him. "We've been to Landover Mall a zillion times."

"Not here like here, but here as a member of God's family on God's green earth," he said.

"Shawn," he stated. "I've never been a part of anything that really meant anything." He paused and smiled. "Now I have my church family. They believe in me and accept me with all of my faults and sins," he continued. "And if I fall, I know they'll pick me back up."

I knew he was working an angle. I just couldn't figure what it was.

He told me he'd joined their Narcotics Anonymous group. He was to receive his sixty-day chip in a week. He proudly showed me his thirty-day chip and explained that some twelve-step program, and his pastor, Anthony Maclin, were on a mission from God to save his life. He even introduced me to his pastor. He reminded me of Jesse Jackson without the rhymes. He was smart, he was cool, and just like Jesse Jackson, he didn't have on one of those collar things. Pastor Maclin told me Donnie was a tireless worker and that he'd been a big help around the church. "He's a positive influence," he said. "And the kids really look up to him."

"They look up to Donnie?" I asked. That didn't make sense. Donnie was my man. But he was a junkie's junkie.

"I know what you're thinking," Pastor Maclin said. "But Donnie never misses service. He comes to Bible study, he helps out with our Boy-Scout troop, and he knows how to reach the kids on their level."

I looked over at Donnie proudly and watched as he helped two older women load their bags. What struck me most was that Donnie now talked like he had sense, and like he had been recently blessed with an impressive command of the King's English. He was a different man. He really seemed to be beyond his problem. I knew he had changed when the two women offered him a $5 tip. He turned it down. "Buy your grandchildren something nice," he told them, smiling. "God's looking after me."

When I saw him hand the five bucks back, I was convinced. He'd either changed or gone crazy. Nobody gives up five bones like that. Especially Donnie.

Donnie and I hugged. He asked me if Troi was coming to town for the holidays. "She's kind of tied up," I answered.

"Then why don't you go out there?" he said. "I know you're not trying to be alone on Christmas."

I definitely wasn't trying to be alone on Christmas. I wasn't exactly looking forward to spending Thanksgiving by myself either. But I'd done that and survived. I was prepared to make it through Christmas alone too. "I'll be cool," I told him. "You know I've never been too big on Christmas anyway."

He knew that was a lie too. I was always into Christmas. Until my mom died. My parents died ten years apart and they both passed right before Christmas. I learned to deal with it after my dad's heart attack. It never seemed the same after my mom passed. I didn't really deal with too much of anything well after she died. I absolutely could not deal with Christmas.

I was accustomed to being alone at Christmas. This one would be no different. I guess I programmed myself to *think* I deserved to be alone during the holidays. I believed I'd caused my parent's deaths. I never counted on meeting Troi. But when I did, and when things appeared to be going perfect, I just imagined we'd be together throughout the holidays. It didn't matter when she didn't call for three weeks after she first left. It didn't matter that her uncle told me she didn't want to hear from me. I just believed we'd be together. It seemed so right. I was convinced she was my 6. I hadn't heard from Troi since I'd left Chicago. I hadn't dealt with getting over her like Donnie had confronted his addiction to crack. I didn't know if Glendale Baptist had a group called "Broken Hearts Anonymous," but if they had one, I'd have joined. I was totally impressed by what they'd done for Donnie. I knew it was nothing short of a miracle.

Kelly had invited me to her place for Thanksgiving. I declined and told her I was too tired to eat. She didn't question me. She reminded me I was always welcome at her place and told me I could call whenever I needed her. We never talked about what happened with Troi, but she knew something had gone wrong. She pressed me about it for a week. When she saw I wasn't budging, she called and left an interesting message. "Shawn, I'm your friend, and I will always be here for you," she started. "I would do anything for you, if I thought it would make you happy," she said. "Don't shut me out, because Troi shut you out," she continued. "Regardless of what happened, I promise I won't say, 'I told you so.'"

Kelly sounded sincere, but there was no way I was going

to tell her she was right about Troi and later down the line have to listen to her gloat about it. Although our friendship thrived, Kelly and I didn't seem to get closer. We went to a few Maryland basketball games and went out to dinner twice in three weeks. We didn't talk like we used to. Kelly insisted I was ignoring her. She invited me to spend the night at her place one evening, but I said, "That's okay, I wouldn't want to mess up your sofa."

"You don't have to sleep on the couch," she told me.

"Well where will I sleep then?" I asked.

"In my room silly," she replied smiling.

"That's kind of you, Kelly," I said. "But where will you sleep?"

"In my bed," she whispered.

"I'll pass," I told her as I looked around her room. I realized I'd be sleeping on the floor, while she rested in the bed. We seemed to be missing each other because I had Troi on my mind, but Kelly had something else on her mind. I could never figure out exactly what it was.

I was in Landover Mall to find Kelly's Christmas gift one night. I knew she liked leather. She had given me a beautiful black calfskin leather bomber jacket last year. I gave her the $50 Nordstrom's gift certificate my co-workers had given me two years ago (I just went and had the name changed. It cost only seventy-five cents). She seemed to appreciate it, but she told me she expected leather this year. It appeared I was lucky because D.C.'s cowhide boutique, Georgetown Leather Design, had a store in the mall that was having a big holiday sale. As I walked down the aisles and absorbed the smell of fresh leather, I noticed a jacket with a $950 price tag. *What kind of sale is this?* I wondered. *Who's going to pay nine-hundred-fifty big ones for somebody's dead cow?*

This Christmas, the funky holiday groove by the late Donnie Hathaway, played over the store sound system. I headed toward the purses and the brief cases and glanced at the price tag on a beautiful brown purse. It was out of my range too. *A hundred seventy-five for a purse,* I thought startled. *If somebody bought one of these, they wouldn't have any money to carry around in it.* I looked up. To my delight, I noticed a stand with some slick leather gloves. They were on sale for $19.99. Kelly had several leather coats, but her deep-brown waist jacket was by far the toughest. I found a cute pair that looked to be Kelly's size. As I reached for them a raspy voice said, "I was just about to get those, thank you very much."

I looked up and walked toward the register without saying a word. The woman who said it looked like she could have been a bouncer at The Classics nightclub in Camp Springs.

"Excuse me," she said tapping me on my shoulder. "I told you I was going to get those, thank you very much."

"You're excused," I replied. "But I got them first, so I'm buying them, thank *you* very much."

I understood her persistence. They were the last pair of brown gloves on the rack, and she was there before I was, but I reached first. I figured they were rightfully mine. With tax, the gloves came out to $20.99. I gave the cashier $21. He gave me a penny in change, but I dropped it on the floor. My eyes were glued to it as it rolled around. It ended up under someone's left boot, and I bent over to pick it up. I looked up. It was her. The big lady who wanted the gloves. She didn't budge. She laughed and stated, "God doesn't like ugly."

I knew I'd seen her somewhere before, but I couldn't remember where.

"Could you move your big foot?" I asked.

"My big foot was there before your penny was," she said. "Isn't that how you operate?"

"Look miss," I answered.

"Don't call me miss," she interrupted. "Don't even act like you don't know who I am."

I stood and looked her over. I didn't have to act like I didn't know who she was, because I had no clue as to who she was.

"I know you?" I hesitantly asked.

"Don't even try it Shawn Wayne," she shot back. "You haven't changed a bit."

If I hadn't changed a bit, she must have. I didn't know who she was.

"You really don't know who I am," she said, surprised, "I can't believe this."

"Where would I know you from?" I asked.

"From college."

"What college?"

"From Maryland," she said. "What other college did you go to?"

"I transferred to a school in Carolina."

"That's what happened to you," she said surprised. "I always thought you left school for the NBA or something."

I knew I didn't leave Maryland for the NBA or anything. But I still didn't know who she was.

She lifted her big foot and I retrieved my penny. I quickly stuffed it into my pocket. "Thanks," I said. "What's your name anyway?"

"My name?" she replied, laughing, "I don't think my name is important."

What's she trippin' on?, I wondered.

"But I'll make sure to tell my roommate that I saw you."

"I know your roommate?" I asked.

"Shawn," she answered giggling, "I doubt that you know too much of anything."

"Well I do know this," I said, insulted. "If God doesn't like ugly, then he definitely doesn't like you." I stepped toward the front entrance and deliberately stated, "You know something?—I probably would've recognized you if you hadn't put on so much weight-thank *you* very much."

I walked through Hecht's and made my way to the parking lot. I thought about Donnie as I located my ride and realized I had to make a move to get over Troi. I decided to call and give her one more chance. *If she turns you down, you know it's over and you can go on,* I convinced myself. And if she doesn't turn you down, you're back in. There was a cute bronze Mazda MX6 parked next to my ride. I could barely get in because it was parked so close to me. I tried to squeeze in, but couldn't help but graze the passenger door of the Mazda. The MX6's alarm screeched so loudly that it startled me. I instinctively opened my door again, and scraped it even more. I once again hit the door of the MX6 as I forced myself out of my ride. I wanted to see if I'd done any real damage. I concluded it was okay as I ran my hand across the deep groove that ran across the door. It looked like it could be rubbed out. Besides, no one saw me do it anyway. I jumped back in my ride and pulled off in a spurt. As I sat at the stoplight to exit the mall, I could hear my mom saying, "I raised you to be fair and to be honest." I did-n't know how she knew I'd just left the scene of a "minor accident, " and wondered what was worse, listening to my mom or putting up with that monkey?

I checked my rearview mirror and made a quick u-turn. I knew it was wrong to leave someone stuck with something I'd damaged even if I'm going to have to pay for it. To my surprise, the woman who'd stood on my penny in Georgetown Leather Design was standing beside the Mazda with a nasty glare in her eyes. "You did this," she yelled as I pulled next to her, and she recognized my ride.

"I did what?" I asked, trying to appear surprised.

"You screwed my roommate's car up," she yelled, "and I know she's going to blame it on me!"

"Well it is your fault," I said. "You parked too close to me."

"It's not my fault," she countered. "You didn't have to scrape it that bad!" I walked to the passenger side and she yelled, "Look at it. It's ruined!"

I did look at it and she was right. It was pretty much ruined.

I stood up and told her I was sorry. I wrote my name and insurance number on the receipt for Kelly's gloves. She snatched it and said, "This may make it even worse."

"Whadda you mean, this makes it worse?" I asked. "I came back. I didn't have to do that."

"You didn't have to leave!" she yelled.

"You're right," I said, "and you didn't have to park so close to me. Make sure you tell your roommate that."

She smiled and said, "You're right Shawn. Thanks for coming back."

I was glad she'd said that, because I was upset myself. My deductible would get eaten up if she made a claim. I didn't need this crap at Christmas.

I didn't need it anytime. Now it seemed worse. For some ridiculous reason, I blamed the whole situation on Troi. Had I not been thinking about her when I opened the door, I'd have easily squeezed in. I blamed Troi for everything that was going wrong in my life (which seemed to be plenty). After I got home, I just laid across the bed and looked at the ceiling. *The last time you laid like this,* I reminded myself sadly, *you were counting ceiling fan turns with Troi.* At that moment, I knew I had to call her. I reached for my phone book, and flipped to the "S" page for Stevenson.

You can invite her up for Christmas and relive the magic all over again, I happily thought. She probably missed me too. But knowing Troi, she was too proud to call. I was too proud, too. But my pride had run its course weeks ago when I realized I didn't want to be without her. Besides, I liked the idea of spending the holiday with Troi. *It'll be like old times,* I convinced myself. Unfortunately, it was a little too much like old times. Once again, I ended up with her answering machine. I called her job and was connected to her voice mail. I hung up without saying a word. I should have left a message at both places. I couldn't. My mouth turned to mush as soon as the beep tone instructed me to speak. That annoying beep reminded me of the many messages I'd left when Troi first left Washington, and of my calls that she failed to return for three weeks. Troi didn't make a dent in my life, she made a full-scale collision. I allowed myself to fall for her. I thought she was falling for me. I was convinced she was my 6. She wasn't. I knew I needed to accept it. I wanted her in my life, because for a week she made it seem to matter. Troi was probably too attractive and too dynamic for me anyway, but I felt that we found a happy medium in each other.

When I was nine years old I had an incredible game where I scored thirty-eight points and didn't miss a single shot. My dad sat me down on my bed when we got home. He didn't say a word. He just helped take my shoes off and walked out of the room. I didn't understand why he did that because he always dissected my games and told me what I'd done wrong. I couldn't think of many mistakes I'd made during that game. I chalked his lack of conversation up to my strong efforts. At breakfast the next morning he said, "Son, you played a good game, but you'll play better ones."

"Thanks dad," I said as I poured milk over my Wheaties.

"You're never as good as your best game," he told me. "And you're never as bad as your worst." That made sense then, but I really understood it now.

Troi may have been the best woman I'd ever been with, but that didn't mean she was the best I'd ever be with. *Danielle was the worst, and you definitely weren't as bad as she was,* I thought laughing. *And like dad said, there'll be better ones.* I knew my old man was right. Donnie was right too. It was time to rid myself of Troi Stevenson. I knew it would be hard, but I was ready for it to be done. I wasn't going into 1994 with Troi hanging over my head. But, I was happy I had at least two weeks to change my mind in case she called.

I still didn't want to spend Christmas alone. Everything was screwed up. I was about to get stuck with paying for a paint job on that woman's roommate's Mazda. I stared at the ceiling and wished Troi would just call and make things right. I knew it didn't make sense, and I knew it wouldn't happen. But I wanted it to happen anyway. Christmas was a week away. It hurt to know this would be the loneliest Christmas I'd have since my mom's death. I wouldn't have my mom. I wouldn't have my dad. I wouldn't have Troi. It was going to be me and that no-good monkey.

I stared at the phone until two in the morning. I wished it would ring.

It never did.

The late-night edition of *SportsCenter* was coming on, but I turned it off. Sports made me happy. I wasn't interested in being happy. Especially with so much going wrong.

Ho-ho-ho, I thought as I turned out the lights. *This is going to be one unmerry Christmas.*

23rd Message

"ONLY YOU COULD RUIN MY CHRISTMAS."

MESSAGE SENT ON
DECEMBER 17TH AT 7:03 A.M.

 When the sun rose the next morning I didn't want to rise, just as I hadn't wanted to rise for the past month. I tried not to think about Troi, but the more I tried not to, the more I thought about her. I hadn't watched *SportsCenter* in nearly two weeks. I wasn't really interested in keeping up with the NBA anyway. Michael Jordan finally followed my advice and retired. He left to play baseball. Maryland's basketball team was doing pretty good. They'd finally played Georgetown and won on the Hoyas' home court. I had tickets to the game, but I missed it. I wanted to be home in case Troi called.

She never did.

I knew this would be a double-dose-of-bad-news type of day. I'd decided to kick the Troi habit (just like Donnie kicked his). I also knew I'd have to deal with the lady and her Mazda. She didn't give me much time to work up a good story, where I could have somehow blamed her for the situation, for when I stepped to my mailbox to retrieve my weekly copies of *Sports Illustrated, Basketball Digest,* and The *Sporting News,* she left a message.

"Mr. Wayne," she started. "It took me five years to save for a new car, and I finally decide to buy one as a Christmas gift for myself."

This was going to be trouble.

"I ordered it two months ago and had to wait for delivery because I got a special paint job," she continued. "I just picked up my brand new car, the first car I've ever owned, two days ago. And now, thanks to you, my paint job is destroyed," she said. "Only you could ruin my Christmas."

You've heard that voice before, I told myself.

"The only thing that surprises me is that you came back after you screwed it up," she said. "That's a switch."

What's that supposed to mean? I wondered.

"I'd prefer not to deal with you," she stated. "But I'm forced to. I want my door repaired immediately."

This is going to be a mess, I thought. *She's pissed.*

"You may reach me at 555-1434."

I knew I was in for trouble. Anyone who'd leave a message as long as hers, would be expecting l-o-n-g money for the repair. I couldn't figure where I knew the voice from. It made me feel uneasy. I thought of when Danielle called and I didn't remember her.

It was almost 7:30 a.m. I opened a Coke, downed the Raviolios I'd prepared for breakfast, and walked toward the phone to face the music.

"This is Miss Truesdale," said the woman who answered on the other line.

She's a miss, I thought. *This may not be so bad after all.* I decided to crank up the bass on my vocal cords. I put on my "official" sounding voice to impress her.

"This is Shawn Wayne," I said.

"And?" she replied, obviously not impressed.

"And?" I answered. "And, uh, this is Mister Shawn Wayne."

"You've said that already Shawn," she scoffed. "Paula was

right. You haven't changed a bit."

"And who might be Paula?" I asked, sounding more like a buffoon than any buffoon could've possibly sounded.

"Paula might be my roommate," she responded laughing. "And you still haven't grown up have you?"

What's that supposed to mean? I wondered.

"Well Mr. Wayne," she said, doing an outstanding impersonation of me. "It appears that we have a problem."

"That we do," I answered, unsure of whether I should stick with the "official" voice. "Cut the crap Shawn," she snapped. "You won't joke your way out of this one."

What's she talking about? I wondered. *She acts like she knows you.*

"Look Shawn," she said flatly. "I didn't have time for your games ten years ago, and I don't have time for them now."

"What games ten years ago?" I asked puzzled. "Did you play basketball?"

"What are you talking about Shawn?" she yelled, frustrated.

"What are you talking about?" I fired back.

"I can't believe you're still playing games," she said exasperated.

"I don't play basketball anymore," I said.

"You're not making sense Shawn," she quickly stated, "but that doesn't surprise me." *Who is she?* I wondered. *You've heard that voice.*

"Shawn," she said, sharply. "I want my car repaired immediately."

"That's cool," I answered. "Get an estimate, and I'll take care of it."

"I got an estimate yesterday. It's going to be $2,385," she told me.

"Miss Truesdale," I retorted. "I only scraped your door, I didn't bang it or anything."

"That may be so," she answered, "but like I said to your machine, I have a special paint job. They can't repaint it. They have to replace the door."

"Who told you that?" I asked surprised.

"Mazda told me that."

"Well what did you expect them to tell you?" I responded. "They just want your money."

"That may be true as well," she stated. "And I want your money. I want my car fixed now."

I couldn't believe it was going to cost twenty-three hundred and some change. I figured I'd bargain her down to one of those cans of touch-up paint. They cost a buck ninety-eight. I didn't want to use my insurance company. My dad always told me that nothing beats a failure but a try. The prospects looked bleak, but I had to try something. "I'm pretty decent with a can of paint," I said. "And I think we could get your car done quicker if I get on it right away."

She laughed and said, "You're kidding, right?"

"Of course not," I answered. "I'm good with my hands."

"I remember that," she said. "But they already have a door waiting, and the thought of you finger painting my door nauseates me." We both laughed. Then she quickly stated, "I'm going to call your insurance company at 9:00 to get this settled."

She had me. I didn't have a reasonable alternative, so I said, "Okay Miss Truesdale. Good luck."

"Thanks Shawn," she said. "By the way, how's Danielle?"

"Danielle?" I asked. "I don't know any Danielle."

"You can stop that Shawn," she coolly stated. "I saw you two together at Jasper's back around Memorial Day."

"Oh," I said, slowly. "You mean that Danielle."

"Yeah," she answered. "You know which Danielle I'm talking about."

I definitely knew what Danielle she was talking about. But I wondered how she knew which Danielle she was talking about.

"I don't know how she is," I told her. "We were actually meeting on a blind date." "That's a good one," she said sarcastically.

"Seriously," I said. "I hadn't seen her in ten years and I hope I don't see her for another ten."

"You didn't marry her?" she asked surprised.

"Why would I marry her?" I asked. "She wasn't all that."

"Well you certainly thought she was all that ten years ago," she stated with a noticeable edge.

"Why are we having this conversation Miss Truesdale?" I asked.

"Because we should have had it ten years ago," she answered. "And why do you insist on calling me Miss Truesdale?"

"That's who you said you were when you answered the phone," I answered.

"Well, you know who I am," she said. "And even though you ruined my car, you can drop the formality bit and call me by my first name."

There was a long silence (the kind Troi and I used to have). I didn't know her first name. I couldn't figure out why she thought I'd know her.

"Shawn," she said breaking the silence, "it's Dawn."

"I used to date a Dawn in college," I told her.

"No kidding," she replied smugly. "I'm her."

"You're Dawn?!" I exclaimed. "My Dawn?"

"I'm not your Dawn," she answered bitterly. "But I am the Dawn you used to date."

I didn't know what to say. I was in a temporary state of very real shock. But her name wasn't Truesdale before. She was a Smith. A plain ordinary Smith. She said she was a Miss. Maybe she'd been married. She kept her husband's name when they divorced. Maybe she was still married. She could be another Jasmine. Maybe she has a husband and a boyfriend. I didn't know what to think.

I hadn't seen Dawn in nearly ten years, but I thought of her often. I knew that besides Troi, she was the only woman who'd ever had a real impact on me. I met her when I signed my letter of intent to play ball at the University of Maryland. Dawn was a student reporter for the campus newspaper, *The Diamondback.* She was assigned to do a feature piece on me. "Let's get something straight," she said when we first met. "I hate sports and I don't particularly care for jocks."

"Why's that?" I asked, grinning.

"Because jocks don't work for anything," she replied annoyed. "Everything's fun and games to them." She then went right into the interview. Oddly enough, we became fast friends.

Dawn was the only woman my mother really took to. "She may not be as fancy as the other girls," she told me. "But she's smart, she's thorough, she's thoughtful, and she's actually kind of cute." I knew my mother was right, but I had fine babes literally chasing me around campus, so I didn't take to her at first. "Dawn is a strong young lady," mom said. "She'll stick by you, but she won't take any crap off of you." I found that to be true too. Dawn didn't fall for anything. And after we hooked up, I didn't even try to run anything past her. "She's got spunk," she added. "I admire a young lady with a well-placed sense of spunk. She's the one for you," she told me, laughing. "Don't let her go, she'll be hard to replace."

As usual, moms was right on all accounts. It was indeed difficult to replace Dawn.

I fell in with Danielle the day Dawn dropped me. I actually called Danielle "Dawn," on our first date. If Danielle was butter, Dawn was margarine. The butter may have tasted a tad bit better, but the margarine tasted pretty much the same. And it was much better for you all across the board. It was low-fat, low-sodium, and it digested better. That's what I liked most about Dawn. She was easier to take, and to deal with than any woman I'd ever been involved with. *She was your Land-O-Lakes sweetheart,* I thought smiling.

There had to be a couple thousand cars parked at Landover Mall yesterday, I thought shaking my head. *And you pick hers to screw up.*

"So Dawn," I said in my regular voice, "how've you been all these years?"

"I was fine until you messed up my car."

"I didn't mean to do it," I told her. "I'm really sorry."

"I know that," she answered in an "aw, shucks," kind of style. "And I'm sorry for coming down so hard on you," she said. "But as soon as Paula told me what you'd done, I kind of lost it."

We laughed, and she asked, "So who are you playing for?"

"I'm not playing," I answered.

"*The* Shawn Wayne is not playing in the NBA," she slowly replied. "What did you do, retire or something?"

"I didn't retire," I responded solemnly. "I quit."

"Well, what's the difference?" she asked laughing.

"My dad once told me you can't retire from something you've never been a part of," I told her. "He told me that you can't leave work at night, if you didn't show up during the day."

"That's interesting," she interrupted.

"Yeah," I stated. "So I couldn't retire from the NBA, because I never played in the NBA. I never showed up."

"You're kidding?" she gasped. "What happened?"

"It's a long story," I answered. "I don't talk about it much."

That topic, of course, took us straight into another one of those intensely uncomfortable silences, but she came to the rescue again. She asked, "So if you're not married to Danielle, who are you married to?"

"Married?" I replied laughing. "Are you kidding? I'm not married."

She told me she'd almost gotten married, but she chickened out. She didn't know if she wanted to look at the same guy for the rest of her life. She said she transferred from Maryland after we broke up because she didn't want to have to deal with what she described as "the legend known as Shawn Wayne." She laughed when I told her I transferred right after we broke up too. I didn't tell her it was for different reasons. I told her about what happened to my mom, and that I'd finally gotten over it. She told me about her job, she was a reporter at the Washington Post. Truesdale started as her pen name. She got used to it and legally changed her name from Smith. Strange as it may seem, she told me that she was single and was very available. I didn't know why she told me that, and was further confused when she asked, "Shawn, why did we break up anyway?"

"You broke up with me," I answered, surprised.

"I never broke up with you Shawn," she said, coyly. "I just wanted you to make a decision."

"A decision?" I asked. "A decision about what?"

"You didn't really think I was going to stand by while you dated that teenager did you?"

"How did you know she was a teenager?" I asked, "I didn't even know that."

"She was in my sister's tenth-grade home ec class," she replied.

"Why didn't you tell me?" I asked surprised.

"I thought you knew!" she blurted out.

We both laughed before I, in one of my most illogical twists of logic said, "Since you never broke up with me, and I never broke up with you, then we are technically still together. Right?"

"I wouldn't put it like that Shawn," she replied. "I gave you a choice, and you made it."

"But you hung up before I could say anything," I reminded her.

"That's true," she said slowly. "But you had my number. You could have called me back."

She had me on that one. I searched my mind for a snappy response. I almost gave up when I realized what the logical answer was. *Blame it on the roommate,* I surmised. "Dawn, what if I told you that I did call back, and that I left a message with your roommate?" I asked shrewdly.

"What if I told you my college roommate, Paula, is still my roommate, and that I'm going to let you run that one by her?" she replied, and then put Paula on the phone.

I didn't know what to do because I hadn't called and left

a message ten years ago. And I knew not to piss off her roommate. She was like a Sherman Tank with stretch pants.

"What kind of lie are you telling on me?" she asked forcefully.

"Hi," I replied. "How are you?"

"I don't have time for your nonsense," she quickly stated. "Make your point."

I didn't have a point to make. *Or did I?*

"Hey Paula," I said, "seems to me that Dawn didn't get the whole story on exactly how close you parked to me yesterday."

I could tell she was looking around. I wasn't surprised when she whispered, "I don't think she knows that, and I don't really think it matters."

"If it doesn't matter," I said, "why are you whispering?"

"What do you want from me Shawn?" she asked upset.

"It's simple," I stated. "I called Dawn ten years ago and left a message with you, but you forgot to pass it on."

"I can't tell her that now," she whispered. "She was asking if you called every five minutes."

"She was?" I asked, pleasantly surprised. "Anyway," I said refocusing, "it's that or I call my insurance company and lay the blame on you for parking across lines." She sighed and I asked, "Are you even insured to be driving *her* car?"

"I wasn't driving it when it happened," she replied. "But I got your point."

She agreed to tell her I'd called and told me she wanted to say one thing before she hung up. "Shawn," she said. "You're still a jerk!"

"Paula," I quickly countered, invoking her trademark line, "thank you very much."

I could hear Paula recounting the story to Dawn. I smiled when she squealed, "He really called? Why didn't you tell me?"

"Because he was a jerk," Paula directed toward the receiver.

Yeah, yeah, yeah, I thought impatiently. *I was a jerk.*

"And he's still a jerk!" she yelled before stomping out of the room.

"I guess I owe you an apology," Dawn said as she picked up the receiver.

"You don't owe me an apology," I said, "but you do owe me a date."

"I think I can manage that," she said, laughing. "What are you doing for breakfast?" "I'm eating."

"That's too bad," she countered. "Because I was going to treat you to brunch at Hogate's."

"That's cool," I responded.

"But you said you were eating."

"I am," I answered, "I'm eating with you."

She laughed and told me to meet her at Lane Mazda, which was just down the road from where we met at the University of Maryland. "I'll drop my car off and we can pick it up when we've finished," she told me. "See you in about thirty minutes?"

"In a half," I shot back before hanging up.

I couldn't believe it. I was really going to see Dawn after ten years. If I could have drawn up the perfect woman, it would have been Dawn, with Troi's body. I couldn't believe she was still in the area. I was shocked that she was single, and "very available," as she'd put it. I knew that I'd eaten a can of Raviolios for breakfast, but it didn't matter. I didn't like Hogate's anyway (it cost too much). My appetite was of little consequence.

We'd talked on the phone for nearly an hour. It was the very first hour I hadn't thought of Troi since I met her back in September.

I knew forgetting Troi wouldn't be easy. But I knew that Miss Dawn Truesdale could make Troi Stevenson a distant memory if she were even slightly interested. I knew Dawn probably wouldn't be looking for anything, and I figured I probably wasn't ready for anything, but I knew seeing her would be special. I knew if Troi called and said to meet her at a gas station in a half-hour, I'd be there filling up on the most expensive brand of high-test. I didn't know if Troi was Dawn without a heart, or if Dawn was Troi without a body-I honestly didn't know, and I didn't care. The only thing I cared about was making it to College Park in thirty minutes.

I couldn't wait to see her.

24th
Message

Breakfast with Dawn that morning was like desperately needing a haircut and being the next in line at a crowded barbershop. It was perfect, and it was right on time. As Kurtis Blow's *Christmas Rappin* played in the background, we easily picked up where we left off ten years ago. She was as smart and as sharp as she was when we first met. We decided not to go to Hogate's. Instead, we spent the day walking around Maryland's campus. We reminisced about our college days and how much fun we'd had. We held hands as we walked into Cole Field House, where the Terps played their home basketball games and headed toward the collection of old team photographs.

"You were something else," she said, as we found the pictures from my two years at Maryland.

"How would you know?" I asked surprised. "You never came to see me play."

"I always came to see you play," she said, standing back.

"I just never let you know about it."

"Why?" I asked.

"Shawn, you didn't realize it, but to me, you were larger than life," she said. "That's why I was so attracted to you. I didn't want you to feel like I was just another co-ed who wanted you because you played ball," she said, "I didn't even like basketball."

"So what made you come then?"

"I came because I'd never seen anyone who played like you," she confessed. "You made watching basketball fun."

"Are you serious?" I asked.

"Yes Shawn," she sighed, "I'm very serious."

We sat down in the bleachers and she asked, "You know what I liked the most?"

"What's that?"

"You got all this attention, but you stayed the same as when we first met."

I wished that I'd stayed the same, I thought.

"I remember when you scored 38 points against Duke as a freshman, and you came by my dorm afterward. You acted like you'd just mowed the grass or something," she recalled. "We called your mom, went to McDonald's like we always did, and people were all over you. But you weren't even phased."

"You remember that?" I asked.

"How could I forget?" she said laughing. "You ordered a cheeseburger Happy Meal, because it was cheaper than buying everything separately."

"I don't remember that," I said flatly.

"You did it all the time," she said, laughing.

"I used to call you my little combo man."

"Combo man?" I asked.

"You were the combo man," she said grinning, "because if you could save two cents by ordering a combo of something that you didn't even want, you'd do it."

"Who wouldn't do that?" I asked.

"I honestly couldn't tell you," she answered sighing,

"because the only person I was thinking about was you."
She then leaned her head against my shoulder and we just
sat and stared at the basketball court.

That quiet moment came to define many of the
moments that we started to share. We would sit and talk
sometimes. When it got quiet, it wasn't like the strained
silences I'd experienced with Troi. It was more like thoughtful contemplation. Where Troi made me horny, Dawn made
me think. Where Troi laughed with me, Dawn both challenged and provoked me. She called me everyday.
Sometimes two and three times a day (just like Troi did
when she was in town). But unlike Troi, I knew Dawn
would keep calling. I read all of her articles in the *Post,*
which opened me to other parts of the paper besides the
sports page. We actually started going to plays and other
social events that cost too much money. Fortunately, her
buddies from the Style section at the paper hooked us up.

Donnie was staying true to his word. He was even coach-
ing a basketball team in his church league. Dawn and I went
to one of their games, and it was pretty pathetic. Donnie
knew hoops, but his players played like they thought hoops
were earrings and nothing more. It was all in good fun
though. Donnie didn't mind the losing because the games
kept him busy, and anything that occupied his time kept
him away from drugs. He told me that he grew stronger as
time passed and that he sometimes went for days without
thinking about crack.

"What happens when you think about it?" I asked.

"I call somebody," he answered smiling. "I'll call anybody
who'll listen."

"And what if nobody's around?"

"Then I pray like hell," he told me laughing. "Because
God will always listen."

He then pointed toward me and commented, "You
should call on him Shawn, because he'll be there for you."

I immediately wondered why Donnie thought that God
was a "him" in the first place. We went to a game one night

and one of Donnie's players got hurt during the pregame lay-up drill. That's the kind of team he had. *Who can get hurt doing lay-ups? I* wondered. *These guys are stiffer than those figures at the Blacks In Wax Museum that Dawn took you to in Baltimore,* I thought. Donnie walked toward me. I turned to Dawn, but she wasn't there. I figured she went to get a hot dog.

"Shawn, remember when you said you'd be there if I needed you?" Donnie asked.

"Yeah," I cautiously answered, "what's up?"

"Well I need you right now bro," he calmly stated. "Lace em up."

"Lace 'em up?" I asked surprised. "What are you talking about?"

"We only have four players, and we have to start with five," he said. "The other guys will be here, so I just need you to get us started."

"I can't do it," I told him.

"What do you mean you can't do it?" he asked. "You said you'd help if I needed you, and I need you. What's the problem?"

"There are two problems," I replied. "First, I haven't played ball in ten years, and second, I don't have any gear to play in in the first place."

I looked up and to my surprise saw Dawn walking across the floor with a black Nike gym bag. She dropped it in front of me, crossed her arms and said, "You've got something to play in now, so what's your new excuse?"

I looked over at Donnie, who looked at Dawn, who was still looking at me. I couldn't think of anything to say that would allow me to save face. Dawn smiled and said, "What's the problem? Suit up!" I snatched the bag and stomped towards the locker room. I was surprised when I opened it to find one of Donnie's team's jerseys folded neatly on top of my classic 1984 edition, red, white, and black Air Jordans. I unfolded it and found the number twenty-three stitched on the front, and my last name sewn in an arch across the back. There was a black wristband that fit snugly across my forearm, and a pair of baggy red shorts were tucked under the shoes.

Donnie walked in and yelled, "We need you player. Tip-off is in five minutes!"

What was I doing? I hadn't played ball in ten years.

I walked onto the floor all decked out in my '84 Jordans (which were a perfect match for my uniform). The crowd immediately cracked up. "Look at baby Jordan!," yelled one man. Another exclaimed, "All you need is a haircut, and you'll look just like him!" I looked at Dawn and shrugged my shoulders. She whispered, "You'll do fine."

From the outset, it appeared that she was wrong. I was terrible. I honestly wanted to do well, but I'd lost it. I was no longer a ballplayer, I was just another guy playing basketball. It didn't much matter though. Donnie still believed in me. He called a timeout and told his team to get me the ball.

"That clown has already shot three air balls, plus he missed two wide-open lay-ups!" yelled one of the players in frustration. "Why should we get the ball to him?"

"This clown is Shawn Wayne," Donnie replied, "and he's an All-American!"

"I don't care if he's *John* Wayne," quipped another, "if he's an All-American, then we're All-universe."

They all laughed. As the huddle broke, one of them tugged at my jersey and whispered, "Just stay out of the way and let us do this."

I felt like crap. When it came to basketball, I'd been the man from age five on up. I couldn't believe this group of no-talents thought I was holding them back. I shuddered when I realized they were right. I was holding them back. As we walked back onto the floor, Dawn yelled, "Shawn, you need to adjust the rotation on your jumpshot!"

The rotation on my jumper? I thought puzzled. *Where did she get that from?*

I quickly found it didn't matter where she got it from. She was right. I made the adjustment and went on a rampage. I made four three-pointers in a row and closed the half with a thunderous follow-up slam off a missed free-throw. The game was nip and tuck, and we were behind by a point with eight seconds left. I stole the ball from my man, drove the length of the floor, and without thinking, took off, yelled loudly, and pulled off a perfect three-sixty degree slam dunk. The buzzer sounded and I just stood underneath the basket and looked around to see if anyone had suffered a heart attack or some other major medical catastrophe. When I saw Dawn and Donnie running toward me I was instantly relieved. I knew that we'd won, and that everything and, hopefully, everybody was okay.

Dawn and I grew to know and trust each other. We spent Christmas delivering gifts to kids at Children's Hospital in D.C. We ate dinner with Kelly and her new boyfriend at his place and went to a splashy ball at the tremendously expensive Four Seasons Hotel on New Years Eve.

"It's black tie," she warned me. "So rent a tux."

"Rent a tux," I answered laughing. "What makes you think I don't have one?"

"If I know you Shawn," she countered. "You probably don't even have a black tie." "If only you knew," I softly answered.

"What's that mean?" she asked concerned.

I knew what it meant, but I didn't feel a need to discuss it with Dawn. I hadn't thought about Troi for nearly two weeks, but as soon as she said "black tie" the memories came right back with the monkey. We'd gotten closer in two weeks than Troi and I would have ever gotten. Dawn was an open book and I was a willing reader. But I knew it was time to "give her the book" on Troi and me.

I told her everything. How we met, how we made love, how she left town, how I went to see her, and finally, how she dumped me. She was very understanding. She said she'd been through something similar. "I had problems recovering too," she told me. She said she sensed I still had feelings for Troi, and nearly proved her point when she asked, "What would you do if Troi called, told you she wanted you, and asked you to come see her?"

"I'm not sure," I answered, shaking my head, "I really don't know."

I worried that my answer, coupled with the fact that Dawn just wasn't the type to play a tidy second fiddle, would change the course of our blossoming relationship. But I knew that I'd never hear from Troi again. Troi was a 2, and 2s don't waste a lot of time calling guys unless they want or need something.

We went to the ball anyway. It was the first time I'd seen Dawn without a pair of floppy jeans and an oversized sweater or blazer. The subtle, well-situated ballroom lighting perfectly highlighted her smooth chocolatey-brown skin. Her deep brown eyes seemed almost hypnotic from the moment I picked her up. Dawn had striking features. Most would have described them as perfectly ethnic. I knew better. I saw them as just plain perfect. I marveled at her brand-new impeccably maintained braids, which were called cornrows in the '70s, and admired how they sat gracefully over her sensuous, sloping shoulders.

She wore an incredible black silk chiffon dress that had exquisite jeweled hand-sewn sequins and twirly beads attached to the plunging collar. It left me guessing about her shapely bustline. Was it real or was it Wonderbra? The beaded sheer sleeves were the perfect showcase for her slender feminine arms. Her enchanting legs appeared to jump from the front slit of her dress, which rose about four inches above her knees. She carried a sassy black satin envelope clutch bag, and a pair of festive glitzy rhinestone cluster and pearl earrings graced her ears. Her elegant black satin pumps completed the outfit. The only thing missing was an ankle bracelet. It was the first time I'd ever seen her body presented with such impact. *It's the first time you've ever seen her body at all,* I reminded myself, laughing.

Dawn and I had never slept together. She dressed so cleverly that I never knew what type of figure she had. She was convinced a woman shouldn't have to flaunt her body to secure a man. "I want a man who will make love to my mind," she told me one night. I'd made love to her mind so often I was having wet dreams from my brain. It was time for some real action.

She's Dawn with Troi's body, I thought as she returned from a table with some of her gossip-driven co-workers. *Hold up, I told myself. She's Troi with Dawn's body.* As she reached for my hand and dragged me toward the dance floor, it struck me that she was Dawn with Dawn's body. She didn't need an ankle bracelet. She was as sexy as a new Corvette on a used-car lot, and as soft as church music at a South Florida nursing home. We slow danced to O'Bryan's soulful torchlight ballad *Lady I Love You,* and it felt weird at first. A familiar voice whispered, "I'm outta here." My eyes were closed, but I opened them and looked toward the door.

I watched as the crowd appeared to part, like it would have done if Michael Jordan had strolled through the ballroom. I smiled as a tiny, furry hand reached for a drink at one of the floating bars. I couldn't believe what I was seeing. It was the monkey! He'd finally decided to leave.

I didn't understand it, but I immediately felt a tremendous sense of relief. When midnight struck, we embraced and kissed like two parents who'd just found their child had been awarded a four-year college scholarship, *after* they'd spent their entire lives sacrificing and saving so the kid would be able to go. We were happy, we were focused, we were together, and most important, we both heard bells during that kiss.

1994 had arrived and it couldn't have started off in a more superb fashion. Donnie was cleaner than Ivory soap, and he'd met a wonderful woman at his church. "I prayed about it, and God hooked me up," he said as only he could say it. "We're both recovering, so if we ever get down, we call each other."

Donnie's really changed, I happily thought.

"And if we're out of quarters, we just drop and pray," he told me smiling. "God's chill like that, cuz."

Some things never change, I thought laughing.

Kelly and her new boyfriend had gotten really close. I think she actually had sex for the first time in years. She left a message that was stranger than her usual strange messages. "I'm climbing the walls," it started. "I think I'm in love with Alan—he's such a man."

Alan was a cool customer, plus he was a doctor, which I'm certain didn't hurt his chances with Kelly. She met him through Butler's girlfriend Amanda, who was now his secretary. Butler's wife dumped him (for a man half her age). She took half his money in the process. He didn't seem to care though. He cherished Amanda, and she had so much influence on him that he evolved into a more understanding and likable boss. "She's a hell of a woman, *and* a hell of a worker," he confided to me in the elevator one morning. "By the way," he asked as we walked toward our office, "how's that beautiful young lady from Chicago? Troi's her name isn't it?"

"Troi who?" I answered laughing.

"The young lady from the dinner," he said.

"Oh her," I answered, grinning, "I'm sure she's still beautiful."

I was certain Troi was still beautiful. But who cared? It didn't matter to me. Dawn and I appeared to be going in the right direction, though neither of us seemed to be rushing to admit it. She made it a point to watch me play ball (I'd joined a league and scored forty-four points in my first game). She convinced me to hookup with some of her coworkers who were members of a happening community service group called Concerned Black Men. They were concerned about a lot of stuff, and they did an awful lot of good, so there was always plenty to do. I tutored kids in math, took them to games, and showed them how to shop for bargains. I felt I was making a real impact. Especially with the bargains. Before I knew it, every one of those kids started showing up at 7-Elevens with coupons. The guys were actually cool, plus they had free food after their meetings. I easily fit myself into their agenda.

Dawn's editor asked her if she'd be interested in writing a column. She jumped at the opportunity. We celebrated by going back to the McDonald's near the University of Maryland (which we'd affectionately dubbed our McDonald's). We ordered *two* cheeseburger extra value meals. I thought that one would do, but she reminded me we were celebrating, so we really splurged and supersized them.

Everything seemed to happen so fast (just like it had with Troi), but I knew that Dawn and I were the real thing. Our relationship was deep, vital, and uniquely substantive. We pushed each other and in our quiet moments shared our dreams, our fears, and even our regrets of the many mistakes we'd individually made over the years. I admitted I never called her back ten years ago, and she admitted that I wasn't the one who scraped her car. "Paula got drunk one night and told me she'd done it, and that you hadn't called," she confessed. Things progressed easily. We both realized the candles that were lit in our hearts ten years ago had ignited the moment we actually saw each other again at the Mazda dealer. We seemed determined to keep them aflame. We cared for each other just like my mom and dad did. We talked so often and spent so much time together doing so many different things, that she'd gotten me down to watching *SportsCenter* just twice a day. She turned me on to Washington's top political talk show hosts, WAMU's Derek McGinty and WDCU's Ernest White, and I hipped her to Tony Kornheisher and Michael Wilbon (who also work with her at the *Post*), and Ric "Doc" Walker at D.C.'s hot sports-radio station, WTEM.

My life was good. My mom was right. Dawn was the right woman for me. I really believed it when she called me one day and said, "Let's go for a ride."

"Okay," I said, "I'm on the way."

"I suggested the ride," she interrupted, "so I'm on the

way." She arrived in about ten minutes. I carefully opened the brand-new door to her cute Mazda MX6, and she pulled off like a formula-one racer sitting on the pole position at the Indy 500.

She has a stick!, I gasped as we rolled onto the Beltway, and headed toward the Woodrow Wilson Bridge. I had to laugh. I sat back and grooved to *Lone Gone,* the hot jazz tune by trumpeter Pharez Whitted. I concluded that Dawn driving a stick wasn't that big a deal.

Kelly once told me that finding the right person wasn't nearly as important as being the right person. As we headed into Virginia, it struck me that she was right. I thought of all the wrong babes I'd dated for all the wrong reasons. I smiled because it felt great to finally feel like the right person (though I wasn't altogether certain just what being the "right" person actually meant). I do know that I felt right because Dawn brought out the best in me. She made me deal with myself as no one else had (or could). I wondered how we managed to lose each other for ten years. I laughed as I realized we'd be together for the next ten even though she had a stick.

I'd finally found my 6.

You too can hit the jackpot— Profile of a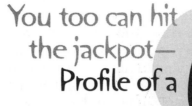

"I'm single, I'm available and *Yes,* I'm interested."

MOTTO OF A 6

There's not a whole lot to say about 6s, because when a woman is right she's just plain right. She doesn't have to look a certain way, she doesn't need to wear a certain type of perfume, and she absolutely need not drive a certain kind of car. She doesn't do anything exceptionally different or phenomenally well, except make your life and your very existence fulfilling, compelling, vital, and utterly complete.

6s don't play games. They don't have to. They tell you they're interested because they are, and they sense you are as well. They don't manipulate, because they know you'll do nearly anything for them (just as they would do for you). 6s don't just listen to you piss and moan about your rotten day and your know-it-all boss. They hear you out and they understand. They motivate you to succeed at whatever your highest level may be.

They don't baby you, nor will they put up with your crap. They won't worship the ground you walk on. They won't cater to your every need, and they won't give you your way just because you're a guy and you think it should be that way. They won't have your meal ready when you walk in the door. They won't have your slippers out or your cigar lit, and they won't wear pearls and pumps to wash the dishes. They won't do any of that. They don't have to. They're 6s. And all of the unreasonable, unrealistic expectations that guys have about women fade when they find a real 6.

6s will bring out the best in you, and you in them. 6s don't waste time with stale, meaningless arguments. They discuss relevant problems, and together you find solutions. 6s understand that guys want to be respected, that they want to be dealt with honestly and fairly, and that men want to be loved as much as women do. Lots of women understand that. 6s do something about it.

6s aren't perfect. Nobody is. But love with a 6 is as close to perfection as perfection can get. Growing and togetherness are important to 6s. So when you find your 6 (and you will find her), love her, keep her (don't possess her—you won't have to), cherish her, and make the commitment to make her world as beautiful and as meaningful as you possibly can. She will do no less for you.

Shawn
Wayne
on

If a babe was a 6, I don't think I'd care whether she had cable or not. It wouldn't even be a problem because she could come over and check out mine whenever she wanted to—it's like that with 6s. You want to share everything with them and you know they deserve cable, even if it means you have to foot the bill.

Last
Message

"I HAVE GOOD NEWS."

MESSAGE SENT ON
JANUARY 24TH AT 7:48 P.M.

Dawn and I totally recaptured our magic of ten years ago. Everything was literally perfect. She'd started her column, which was appropriately titled *Dawn of A New Day.* Her common sense approach to complex issues endeared her to so many readers across the country that she became a nationally renowned sensation. I won MVP in my basketball league, and though Dawn made it to all of my games I hated the rides home. She was a bigger critic than my mom and dad combined. Kelly and Alan continued to be a hot item (he sent her flowers constantly and taught her how to cook). Donnie landed a full-time job as a substance-abuse counselor in the same prison system he used to "live" in. Mr. Butler contributed major dollars to Concerned Black Men *and* contributed a fat diamond to Amanda's ring finger.

Dawn called me one evening and said we needed to talk. "About what?" I asked defensively.

"About us," she replied, "I want to know where you stand."

"I'm standing in front of my TV right now," I said as the theme to *SportsCenter* played in the background.

"Ha-ha, combo man," she countered, "I want to know how you feel about me and about us."

"I want to know too," I said.

"You want to know how you feel?" she asked.

"No sweetheart," I said, "I want to know how you feel."

"I think you should come over because we need to say it face to face," she said.

"I'm on the way," I replied.

I knew what she was going to say, and I knew what I was going to say because when you're ready to say it, and you're ready to hear it, you know it.

The phone rang before I could jump in the shower. Surprisingly, it was Dawn.

"Shawn," she said, "don't come over here and say something that you don't mean or that you can't back up."

"I won't," I insisted, "and don't you do it either." A distracting beep interrupted us. I had another call. "Get your line and hurry up and get over here," she said before hanging up. I clicked over and immediately recognized the voice that belonged to the blind date from hell, Danielle.

"Hi Shawn," she said in a sweet voice. "I was just calling to see if any jobs opened up at your office."

Another beep alerted me to another call. I made it quick.

"Danielle," I hastily replied. "Get a life and get an automatic."

Before she could respond (and probably lie about having an automatic), I clicked over, only to hear a voice I'd successfully dodged for the past five months.

"Shawn," she said startled, "I'm surprised it's you. I'm so used to talking to your machine."

"I'm aware of that Jasmine," I said flatly. "How are the husband and the boyfriend?"

"What's that got to do with anything?" she asked.

"It's got everything to do with anything," I answered sarcastically. "I've got to go," I interrupted. "And would you please stop calling my machine. You're wasting your time, and my tapes."

I hung up and though the phone rang again, I hurried to the shower. I couldn't wait to talk to Dawn. I didn't know who would say what first, but I knew exactly what would be said. I couldn't wait to say it or to hear it. As the warm water rolled down my back, I realized Dawn had all but hooked me at the Four Season's on New Year's Eve. I smiled when I realized that her luring me in was anything but accidental. It was a calculated and well-conceived maneuver. Even Dawn realized that "making love to her mind," had its limits. *She knew exactly what she was doing the moment she picked that dress out,* I thought, laughing.

I quickly dressed, dashed for the door and was in my ride when it struck me that what we were about to do mandated a gift. I didn't have time to get to a store and wasn't sure if it mandated a major investment, so I figured I'd get her one of those $1.99 roses from 7-Eleven. It was weird, but I felt like one of those cartoon light bulbs popped on over my head. I remembered I still had the heart I'd bought for Troi when I went to Chicago. I hurried into my bedroom and pulled it from my top dresser drawer. *This is perfect,* I thought while buffing the heart on my sleeve. I knew that I'd bought it for Troi, but she was gone like a case of bad breath that collided with a bottle of Listerine. The heart was important to me, just as Dawn was. I had no problem presenting it to her, and I knew she'd graciously accept it.

I walked pass my answering machine and though I was in a hurry, I had to respond to the blinking red light that told me I had a message. *It's probably Dawn asking why you're not there yet,* I thought smiling.

"Hello handsome," said a familiar voice. "I'm sorry I haven't been in touch, but I've been tied up."

I couldn't believe it. She hadn't changed a bit.

"This is Troi, in case you don't recognize the voice," she continued.

Troi who? I sarcastically thought.

"Anyway, I have bad news, good news, and some even better news," she went on. "I'll start with the bad news. My father fought his way back into the business, so as you can imagine, I'm totally stressed," she stated. "Now for the better news," she continued. "The political marketing piece actually worked out," she said, excited, "so I'm moving to D.C. in about a month!"

Troi in D.C., I thought as I clutched the heart and prepared to leave. *That should be interesting.*

"Now for the good news," she calmly added. "You always save the good news for last."

Just get to it, I thought impatiently. *Dawn is waiting.*

"Here goes," she said excitedly. "I think I'm pregnant. Isn't that great!"

She thinks she's pregnant? I said as I stuffed the heart into my pocket and headed toward the door. *What's so great about that?*

This can't be happening!

Troi as a mom.
Me as a dad.
Dawn as a *stepmother?* This will never work.

I'm ready to claim the love of my life, and Troi wants to start a family. How can she do this? She can't be pregnant. I can't deal with it; not right now anyway. I *doubt* that Dawn will deal with it. I have to tell her. *Or do I?* Kelly would know what to do, but I can't call her. She and Alan went to the Poconos. I wish my mom were around. She'd know how to handle this. Why did this have to happen now? I've got to do something. Dawn is expecting me any minute now. I know she'll accept my heart. She's already accepted me. But will she accept me with a baby on the way? Will she accept me with *Troi's* baby on the way?

I know what. I'll call Donnie from my ride. He knows how to deal with this kind of stuff. He'd better know. He knew how to sell me on that stupid answering machine. If he wouldn't have sold it to me, I wouldn't have gotten the message in the first place. If I wouldn't have gotten the message, I would have been at Dawn's, and she'd have the heart right now.

I took the heart out of my pocket, and looked at it again. I thought about Troi. I thought I about Dawn. I thought I was in trouble. Until the phone rang. When my machine picked up, I *knew* I was in trouble. It was Dawn. She told me to hurry up because she had some good news. More good news? I don't think I can take any more *good* news.

I can't believe it. I just can't believe it.

Write the Next Chapter—Contest

 You've read the book . You know what's going to happen next —don't you? Now, tell us what will happen in the next chapter. Write a chapter about what Shawn, Dawn, Troi, and Donnie will do next. Make it unique! Make it fun! Make it real! Make it in 1600 words or less. The judges will select a winning chapter. Winner will **re-live** Shawn and Troi's experience at the **Congressional Black Caucus** conference a 4 day trip September 10-13, 1997.

Trip for two includes:
- 4 day/5 nights stay at the Grand Hyatt Hotel in Washington DC
- Round-trip airfare*
- Dinner at Jaspers, Houstons and Hotel Washington
- Entry to 3 major CBC events
- a $50 per diem each day
- Winning chapter may become chapter 1 in the sequel to the next **Beeperless Remote** novel

Format for Chapter: Each entrant may submit only one (1) chapter. An entrant's chapter must contain 1600 words or less and be submitted in double-spaced, typewritten form. The entrant's name, address and day/evening phone number (with area code) must be include on the essay including word count. **Mail to** "Write the Next Chapter" 3870 Crenshaw Blvd., Suite 931, Los Angeles, CA 90008 or e-mail to www.pinesone.com or www.vanwhitfield.com. **Entries must be postmarked no later than August 1, 1997.** The essay must be sent to the address or the e-mail in order to be eligible or considered. Pines One Publications assumes no responsibility for late, lost, illegible, incomplete, misdirected non-deliverable or postage due mail.

Entries become property of sponsor and will not be returned.

Official Rules: No purchase nesscessary. Contest is open to all legal residents of the United States who are at least 18 years of age. Employees and family members of Pines One Publications and Van Whitfield are not eligible. Winners will be selected by the author and publisher of *Beeperless Remote.* Judging shall be based on the quality, content, and portrayal of the characters in the story. The winner will be notified by phone, certified mail and on websites www.pinesone.com and www.vanwhitfield.com on **September 1, 1997.** Winner will be obligated to sign and return an Affidavit of Eligibility and Release of Liability within 5 days of notification. In the event of noncompliance another winner may be selected. The prize is not transferable nor redeemable for it's cash value. No substitutions allowed except at Sponsor's discretion due to unavailability. All taxes, insurance, liability and other expenses not specified herein are the responsibility of the winner. Entry and acceptance of prize constitute permission to use winner's name, likeness and hometowns for promotional purposes in print and electronic mediums without additional compensation. Do not contact publisher for information as this will disqualify your entry. Use of winning chapter in sequel will be at the sole discretion of author and publisher of sequel book. Pines One Publications assumes no rights or responsibilities in this decision. For name of winner (available after September 15, 1997) send a self-address stamped envelope to: Write the Next Chapter-Winner, 3870 Crenshaw Blvd., Suite 931, Los Angeles, CA 90008.

*Compliments of American Airline.